# the almost love birds

# THE ALMOST LOVEBIRDS

Jasmine Falls Love Stories, Book 1

## LUCY DAY

Blue Crow Books

**Publisher's Cataloging-in-Publication Data**
Day, Lucy 1978-.
The Almost Lovebirds: Jasmine Falls Love Stories/ Lucy Day.
p.____ cm.____
ISBN 978-1-947834-44-6 (Pbk) | ISBN 978-1-947834-68-2 (eBook)
1. Women—Fiction. 2. Love—Fiction. I. Title.
813'.6—dc23

Blue Crow Books

Published by Blue Crow Books
an imprint of Blue Crow Publishing, LLC
Chapel Hill, NC
www.bluecrowpublishing.com
Cover Design and Cover Illustration by Lauren Faulkenberry

# Contents

*for A., with all the love*

# Chapter One

## FIONA

EDDIE GILMORE WAS JUST A DISTRACTION. A really handsome one who was supposed to shake me out of my dry spell, but still—just a distraction. As I studied him from behind my easel, it dawned on me that this truly was my rock bottom: in the last six months I'd lost my home, my fiancé, and a commission that would have covered me for months. And now I couldn't even paint a decent portrait.

Full disclosure: I was having two major dry spells. My romantic one was pitiful enough to inspire a hit country-western song, but my creative dry spell was the killer. It was costing me a fortune and ruining my reputation as one of the hot young emerging painters in the area.

Losing my creative mojo was super annoying. Not knowing how to fix the problem? Infuriating.

Two years ago, my friend Janet had started selling my paintings in her gallery in Asheville, North Carolina. Her gallery was a funky building in the River Arts District that got a lot of attention from both the locals and the tourists. For a while, my work had sold like hotcakes—Janet was pretty amazing at selling art—but then six months ago, my fiancé Dean yanked the rug out from under me and my whole world fell apart. Turns out, these pieces of my life were connected in ways I hadn't expected. Now, at 29, my life was a pile of rubble.

Like, the-fall-of-civilization rubble.

After the Dean fiasco, Janet had taken pity on me and rented me her "tiny house"—the four-room cabin she usually rented to tourists through the summer and fall. But now, six months later, I was behind in rent for the first time ever and not at all happy to feel like a charity case. She was too nice to kick me out, but I knew what the going rate was for a weekly cabin rental in the peak summer season. There was no way I could stay.

Problem was, I had nowhere to go.

Shoving those thoughts aside, I tried to focus on Eddie instead. He sat in a leather chair just a few feet from me, lit by the warm glow of a stained glass floor lamp. I tried to concentrate on the line of his shoulders but was distracted by the way his tee shirt strained against his biceps. Eddie had great arms: tan, muscular, and tattooed with vines and birds. He also had big brown eyes with lashes I'd kill for and a gaze that was firmly set to smolder.

He was the kind of guy you write pop songs about.

Okay, I might have a little crush on Eddie. We've been friends for a while, and his family owned a winery a few miles outside of town. Whenever Janet ordered a case of wine for one of her gallery openings, he always brought me a bottle of my favorite pinot noir and did some A-plus flirting that left me wondering if a little fling wasn't such a terrible idea.

Tonight's portrait session had been Janet's idea—"You just need a muse," she'd said. "Painting a live person will get you back into your groove." Usually, she was right about these things. Eddie was certainly fun to study, so why, tonight, did each brushstroke look wrong the second it touched the canvas?

So far, this night had just made me realize how far I was from that groove—as in, completely outside it, a few counties over. Painting portraits had always been my way of loosening up and getting over an artistic block—it was fun to quickly capture light and personality in a few brushstrokes. But tonight, it wasn't working. I had a pile of horrible paintings scattered on the floor to prove it.

"You know, Fiona," Eddie said, his eyes resting on mine, "When you asked me to come over and sit for you, I thought you were trying to seduce me."

I blinked at him from around my easel, waiting for him to say more.

"And yet here you are," I said.

He gave me a hint of a smile. "Didn't say I was opposed to the idea." His eyes, brown with flecks of amber, zeroed in on me, sending a very distinct message that I was trying hard to ignore. I had rules, for heaven's sake—and fawning over men like Eddie Gilmore broke the biggest one of all. Not only was he hot as an afternoon in August, he was *nice*. Just the kind of guy I'd fall for.

Dean was a nice guy, too—and look where that got me.

I was not allowed to get attached. Getting attached just led to heartache, and I'd had enough people walk out of my life already. You'd think by now I'd be used to it, with my heart a little harder, but you'd be wrong.

Being left was still the worst kind of hurt. It never stopped hurting.

"Shhh," I told him. "I can't paint your lips when they're moving."

*Great*, I thought. *Now he knows I'm staring at his lips.*

Eddie had an interesting face—okay, it was gorgeous—striking and chiseled, just like every other part of him. But you wouldn't know that from this pitiful attempt at a portrait. It looked like I'd painted it using my feet.

Making the paint come alive used to come easy to me. But not now. The last time I'd hit a wall this hard, I'd been a junior in art school, terrified my scholarship would go *poof* when a professor looked at my portfolio and said I really couldn't draw.

Later, it occurred to me that what he meant was *I didn't draw realistically,* like he did.

My scholarship did not go *poof.* But my confidence did. I drifted away from the bright colors and exaggerated shapes, and painted in ways that earned me higher grades and fewer furrowed brows. I painted the wild colors in secret, and mostly felt like an impostor.

Now I felt like an impostor all over again. My eyes felt broken, not capable of seeing the world the way they once did. Colors weren't vibrant like before. Textures didn't come alive. I kept adding layers of paint, but the result was nothing I could get excited about.

There was something very, very wrong about that.

"Hey," he said, "Did you see that guy on TikTok that sells paintings that an elephant makes? He works at an animal sanctuary and just gave a paintbrush to the elephant one day. They sell for like ten-K each."

*Thanks, Eddie.*

"I bet Janet would loan you her cat," he said. "We could train him to hold a little brush in his teeth. Or at least do enough creative editing to fake it."

"She can't even train that cat to use the cat door," I said. "And besides, I'd prefer it if my career wasn't based on a schtick."

He raised a brow. "You'd really say no to ten-K per painting, just based on who was doing the work?"

"I will die on that hill, yes."

After a pause, he said, "You're right. Maybe we could train him to knock paint buckets off the table and onto a canvas. That's more his style."

IT HAD STARTED AS A JOKE—JANET, trying to convince me to put paintings in her gallery, told me *I can sell anything with the right story.* So after a couple glasses of wine, I whipped out an abstract mountain landscape with shades of blue and green that looked vaguely like the local terrain if you squinted hard enough. *Good luck,*

I said to her, and then she sold it the next day. When I called that a fluke, she said, "Bring me three more like that and let's see who's laughing, Miss Smarty Pants."

She sold those, too.

I'd stumbled into a style that people liked, so I kept painting them, and Janet sold them as fast as I could deliver them. Then I started getting commissions: first a state senator's wife, then a regional bank, and then a fancy hotel that wanted a show-stopping piece for their main lobby.

For the first time in my life, I had money in a savings account.

I was making a living with a paintbrush. My dream. But then after Dean left me, my creativity dried up.

Now, every time I picked up the brush and started one of those stupid landscapes, I thought about him. And us. And what we were supposed to be. These mountains, the Blue Ridge, were supposed to be our forever home, and now as I tried to paint them, I just thought of everything I'd lost.

For the first time ever, it hurt my heart to do what I loved most.

The last straw was when I wrecked my biggest commission. A real-estate mogul who lived in a house big enough to have its own zip code had commissioned three enormous paintings after seeing my work at Janet's. He'd offered me more money than I'd seen in my whole life. After Dean left, it had been absolute torture to work on those paintings. I kept asking the guy for extensions, hoping I could just soldier through the heartache and finish.

But I couldn't. No matter how many hours I spent in front of those canvases, I couldn't do it.

The real estate guy canceled the order, tired of waiting. And then he'd blabbed to all of his bazillionaire friends about how I couldn't deliver. And boy, word traveled fast in a circle that tight and a town this small.

Without that money, and with no new sales, I'd had to work for Janet in the gallery just to cover my bills. She was just trying to help because she knew I was burning through my savings, but working there made me feel hollow inside.

The winter months were slow in a tourist spot like ours—so slow that Janet didn't need me. Now it was April, and the tourists were coming back. My checking account was leaner than ever, and I had no choice but to work for Janet this season, until my work started selling again. But in order to sell paintings, I had to make paintings—and get over this block that had swallowed me whole.

I was supposed to have spent the last three months painting my heart out and getting ready for the next wave of art-loving tourists. But I didn't have a single decent painting—because stupid Dean had broken my stupid heart.

Eddie, with his angular face, his close-cropped brown hair, and arms that I'd fantasized about a million times, was supposed to shake something loose tonight. Usually it would be easy for me to concentrate on the way light revealed shapes and expressions in a face.

But not today.

This painting was a mess, just like all the others I'd started and failed to finish in the last several months. It was more evidence that something in me was broken—and made me think too hard about Eddie's suggestive stare and kissable lips.

Nope. Not happening. I'd sworn off dating ever since Dean.

"This house is pretty great," Eddie said. "How long are you staying?" He had one of those North Carolina accents that was particular to the westernmost counties—all soft edges and dark promises.

A few miles outside of Asheville, the cabin was nestled in the woods, built up on stilts so you felt like you were in a treehouse. The tin roof made rain sound romantic, and the constant birdsong put me at ease.

"Just two more weeks until the vacation season starts. Janet has it booked through August already."

Finding a long-term rental in this town was like finding a gold nugget.

"And then what?" Eddie said.

"That's a great question," I said. "I have no idea what to do next. I'm failing at everything."

"Don't be so hard on yourself," he said. "You're just going through a rough patch."

People really needed to stop saying that to me. This was way worse than just a rough patch. I was walking through ten thousand miles of post-apocalyptic doom. Why did everyone try to make it sound like my problems would just go away, like a leg cramp or a heat rash? Didn't they see that my life was an utter disaster?

Training that cat to knock paint cans over was looking better and better.

Eddie's eyes bored into mine. "What makes you happy?" he said. "Maybe you should start there, and the rest will fall into place." His voice was deep and smooth, and—good grief, I was hopeless.

"You make it sound so simple."

He smiled. "I'm a simple guy." He arched a brow and raked his eyes over me. "You seem very tense, Fiona. I think you need to relax and make time for a little self-care."

I laughed, trying to hide the blush that was surely spreading across my cheeks. "Are you going to tell me you can help me with that?"

"I have some ideas."

I bet he did.

"This is hopeless," I said, motioning toward the painting. It kind of resembled Eddie if I squinted my eyes.

Definitely a failure.

Eddie stood and moved toward me with his slow, easy walk that made it seem like he had all the time in the world. He looked at the painting, then down to the pile that I'd scattered around the floor.

"Looks like I need a haircut," he said.

I snorted.

"Actually, I like this one," he said, pointing to one on the floor. He rested one hand on his hip as he studied the painting. My eyes tracked his thumb as it slid along the smooth leather of his belt. He had big square hands that gave firm handshakes and built Adirondack-style chairs in his spare time, and more than once I'd imagined what a firm grip they might apply to certain parts of my body in very specific scenarios.

A growing part of me was thinking that kissing Eddie Gilmore wasn't such a terrible idea after all.

Brushing his finger over my cheek, he said, "You have a little paint here." His big brown eyes locked on mine, and he tucked a strand of hair behind my ear. "You're incredibly talented, Fiona. Don't let anyone convince you otherwise."

Eddie and I had been friends for a while now, but tonight there was a chemistry that hadn't been there before. Cute, charming, Eddie had been right here ever since Dean left me—but I'd been too chicken to do any A-plus flirting of my own. Ever since Dean left me, it was hard for me to take the leap. Even with a nice guy like Eddie.

Nice guys could break your heart, too.

When his gaze dropped to my lips, I thought for sure he was about to lean in and kiss me. I was still working out exactly how I felt about that when a piercing ring filled the room.

We both startled.

"Sorry," I said, striding to the kitchen island to silence my cell phone. Leaning back against the island, I said, "You were saying?"

He smiled and stepped close to me, his breath warm against my neck as he started to whisper something about what he'd been thinking of the whole time he'd been sitting in that chair. He planted his hands on the kitchen island, on either side of my hips, and my heart pounded in my chest.

My rules seemed kind of stupid right now. Eddie had some great ideas.

The landline rang, filling the cabin with an obnoxious tinny sound that made me curse Janet for being practical enough to have a phone that was not a cell.

"You need to get that?" he said, pulling away just a fraction of an inch.

"Nope. Janet's answering machine works just fine."

He grinned, sliding his hand along my arm, his thumb tracing tiny circles, and—nope, making out with Eddie Gilmore did not feel like a bad idea anymore.

And then my mother's voice pierced the air like a fog horn, and my hands fell to my sides in utter defeat.

"Yoo-hoo," my mother said, her voice obnoxiously perky. "I know you're there, dear. Your little friend Janet told me you were staying over."

Only Penelope McIntyre would refer to a thirty-four-year-old woman as her grown daughter's "little friend."

I gritted my teeth, trying to ignore the shrill voice.

"Hell-oooooo. I need you to pick up." Her voice was oddly singsong. Chipper, even. "Pick up, pick up, Fiona. I'm waiting until you do. I have nowhere to be tonight and neither do you." There was a tapping sound, like she was banging a pen against her phone just to irritate me into submission.

I glanced at Eddie. He was frozen, as if my mother had actually walked into the room.

Penelope McIntyre could ruin anything, even from two hundred miles away.

# Chapter Two

## FIONA

"I'M STILL WAITING, FIONA ELEANOR," Penelope said, her voice rising on the answering machine. Using my middle name meant she was extra annoyed.

"Um," Eddie said, peeling his hands from my waist.

I rolled my eyes so hard they hurt. "She's just going to keep chattering until I pick up."

Penelope McIntyre did not tolerate being ignored. She was already talking again, her words filling the cabin like a thousand hungry mosquitoes.

Free of Eddie's grip—and not one bit happy about it—I walked around the kitchen island and grabbed the phone, cutting my mother off mid-sentence.

"Mother," I said. "What's the emergency?"

"Oh good," Penelope said, her voice a chirp. "You're there."

"What's the matter? It's late."

"Have you not received my other messages?" she said, her tone all false sweetness. "I've left you several on your cell."

"The reception is spotty out here. I didn't see you called."

Eddie raised a brow, then walked back over toward the painting.

I sighed, wishing my mother would hang up so Eddie would come back to the island.

"Well," Penelope said. "I tried several times. The thing is, I need you to come home and look after your aunt Delia."

"What?" I felt my voice catch. "Is she all right? What's happened?"

"No need for melodrama, dear. It's just knee replacement surgery. But I have to go out of town, and she needs someone to stay with her."

"When?" I said.

"By Friday."

"As in two days from now?"

"Since you're bohemian now, I figured it would be easy enough for you to come down for a few days."

"Bohemian?" I said. "Really?" She couldn't bring herself to say *unemployed*. Instead, she made it sound like I traveled with a carnival.

"She didn't want to ask you," Penelope said, "but I convinced her. She had her surgery a couple of days ago, and she really can't do for herself right now. She can't drive, she needs someone to take her to rehab, and I have to go to Amsterdam."

She said that last part like it wasn't an unusual event. Penelope had always been good at burying the lede.

"Why didn't you tell me she was having surgery? And why do you have to go to Amsterdam?"

"The tulips, dear, and the subject just didn't come up. Simon got a last-minute deal and surprised me. There's a whole big festival—it's amazing that he got us tickets—and I think we're due for a vacation, don't you? We have to fly out Friday to get the special rate, and you know how he is, the hopeless romantic. I couldn't say no, and he already paid for everything, so you see the position I'm in."

Simon was Penelope's boyfriend, though she refused to call him that. Penelope had traveled most of her life for work, but now she traveled with Simon. A retired financial planner from a big firm down in Charleston, he'd hardly ever taken vacations and had saved every dime he ever made from what I could tell (except what he spent on his two kids' college tuition). Now that he was widowed and retired, he apparently planned to spend all of his money traveling with Penelope. At fifty-six, she was just as fit and feisty as she had ever been, and had no intention of slowing down any time soon. She was like a hummingbird, moving from one enticing spot to the next, and didn't light in any one place for very long. She'd been that way for my entire life—even the few photos I had of her were blurred, as if a camera couldn't even catch her.

I was glad that she had Simon. If a handsome man wanted to spend all of his money taking me around the world, there was no way I'd argue.

"When will you be back?" I asked her.

"Two weeks," she said. "Give or take. You know Simon. Sometimes he gets a wild hair and wants to take another adventure."

I was running out of time. In less than a month, I needed to finish a new bunch of paintings for Janet's gallery and find a new place to live. Neither was going to be easy.

But this was Aunt Delia. Aunt Delia who had practically raised me while my mother was working all those long hours, building her architectural firm from the ground up, and making a name for herself. Aunt Delia, who had made me birthday cakes from scratch, who had taught me to ride a horse, drive a stick shift, and kick a boy in the balls if he tried to pressure me to do something I didn't want. Aunt Delia, who had watched over me for two whole years while Penelope was awarded a prestigious grant that sent her literally around the globe: Switzerland, Tokyo, Christchurch—I'd kept all the postcards she'd sent, which included details about the architectural wonders she was studying, but never a word about missing me.

Aunt Delia had always made me feel loved when my mother did not.

So saying no to Delia wasn't on the table.

"Okay," I said. "I'll be there Friday."

"Wonderful," said my mother, all business. "I'm so glad you could make time for her in your busy schedule. I'll call her and tell her you're coming."

I hung up the phone and put my face in my hands.

Eddie said, "Everything okay?"

"My mother's going to put me in an early grave. The last place I want to go right now is my hometown."

"It can't be that bad." He gave me a friendly smile.

"Oh, Eddie. You have no idea." Going back there meant capital-F failure. "I worked so hard to get out of that place." And away from my mother, who made a sport out of telling me everything I did wrong. She was controlling, demanding, and threw her opinions around like stones. Once she learned I was homeless, jobless, and penniless, she'd have plenty to say about that.

He put his hand on my shoulder and said, "You'll be okay, Fiona. You're stronger than you think."

I blinked at him. It was a sweet thing to say, but it sounded like a lie.

"I should probably hit the road," he said, squeezing my shoulder.

"You don't have to go." I tried to sound nonchalant—*Stay if you like, Eddie, I'm easy-breezy.*

He smiled, but looked like he'd decided that whatever was happening over by the kitchen island had fizzled out. "It's okay. We kind of lost the mood, wouldn't you say?" He leaned over to lace up his boots and any chance of seeing those lovely tattoos in their entirety went *poof.*

I wanted to tell him that the mood could be found again. It wasn't so elusive.

Sigh.

"I'll see you later," he said, walking towards the door. "When you get back." There was that tiny smirk again, the one that was full of promises.

"Hey," I said, and he turned back. "Thanks for coming over."

"Any time," he said. "I hope you find your inspiration. But I've got a feeling you will."

That made one of us.

# Chapter Three

## FIONA

JASMINE FALLS, South Carolina was a town so small it barely made it onto the Google map. Getting there meant driving on two-lane roads for hours on end. At least the drive was pretty: rolling hills, a big blue sky, pastures full of contented-looking cows. This was the part of the state where people ate shrimp and grits, argued over the best mustard-based barbecue sauce, and spoke with warm, rounded syllables that leave the 'g' off the end of every single word.

There were no chain restaurants on this road and no Starbucks for a solid fifty miles. Desperate for lunch, I stopped at a gas station that had an old church pew out front where two white-haired men sat talking in the shade. Inside, I had to settle for a hot dog that had been rolling around under a lamp for probably a decade and a cup of coffee that would likely burn a hole through the car's upholstery.

By the time I called Janet, I was regretting both.

"How'd things go with Eddie?" she said. "Inspiring, I hope." Her voice crackled, because there weren't many cell towers out here, either.

"Not exactly." I told her about painting the lousy likeness, then how things near the kitchen island unfolded. "It's probably a good thing my mother called and interrupted us."

"Oh, for heaven's sake," Janet said. "That woman destroys all of your fun. She's like a black hole, gobbling up any particle of joy."

"I probably dodged a bullet anyway. Eddie gives me a great discount on wine, and I'd hate to lose that."

"Look," she said. "I know Dean did a number on you, and I wish I could go back in time and put Nair in his shampoo, but not every man is like him. Not everyone is going to leave you."

"I know."

"Do you?" She sighed. "Eddie's an alright guy, but he's not the sort of man you need."

"And what kind of man do I need?"

"One who adores you, and values you, and isn't going to disappear because he's not serious enough to commit to a real relationship. I mean, Eddie could be a fun fling, but I don't think you want that."

I shrugged. "Maybe I do."

"No you don't. You don't do flings."

"Maybe I should. Flings are safer."

"Unless you happen to choose someone who'll chop you up in pieces and bury you under the back porch."

"I'm a good judge of character. I can spot those true-crime types a mile away."

Janet sighed. "When you're ready for a real relationship again, you need to find yourself a grown-up man who knows how to treat you right. Not one you know you're leaving from the get-go."

"I don't want anything complicated right now," I told her. "I just want to not feel alone."

"Go enjoy your change of scenery," she said. "Your aunt sounds pretty great."

"She is. The opposite of my mom." Delia valued her independence and wouldn't want to be waited on hand and foot. Penelope had no qualms about making constant demands, but Delia wasn't like that.

"I sure hope so," Janet said. "The world could hardly stand two of Penelope McIntyre." After a pause, she said, "You're still bringing me a series at the end of the month, right?"

I cringed and chirped, "Absolutely!" Janet would give me wall space again, but only if I brought her new paintings in time for the season's big opening. If I didn't deliver, another hungry artist would, and then I could lose my spot forever.

"Go make something amazing," she said. "I know you can do it."

"Will do." I swallowed hard, thinking, *That makes one of us.*

She ended the call and I said, "You got this, Fiona."

Delia's could be my sanctuary. I'd set up my easel in her sunroom, a place with plenty of light. Maybe I'd take Eddie's advice, and do some morning yoga to clear my head, and then spend the whole day painting.

No thinking allowed.

I'd paint until I shook something loose. In two weeks, I'd have a bunch of new work for Janet, and I'd start getting commissions again. I could fix this. I could have my dream again.

Even if I had to take a detour back to Jasmine Falls.

It had been over a year since I'd been back. Jasmine Falls was a typical small southern town: everybody knew each other since they were toddlers, every person in town knew your business and made up what they didn't know, and most people would give you the shirt off their backs without you even having to ask.

Still, part of me cringed as I thought of going back. The last time I'd been there, I'd been engaged—a year ago. The announcement had been in the paper, for Pete's sake (because my mother had insisted), and then every single person in town knew when we were over.

Nothing stings like having your failures made public.

I hadn't been back since the Dean debacle, and I wasn't looking forward to everyone expressing their opinions about my broken engagement to the man who my mother thought wasn't good enough for me anyway. We'd kept the real reason secret, but

Jasmine Falls folks liked to speculate, so there was no telling what people had decided happened with me and Dean. But one thing was for certain: I didn't want to hear a single peep about it.

There were parts of our story that no one knew about, like for example the debt I'd racked up from paying all of our household bills while he finished his degree in parks management. Afterward, he'd taken the first seasonal job he'd been offered, all the way up in Kenai Fjords, Alaska. He was supposed to spend just one summer and get his foot in the door so he could get a better job closer to our home in the mountains. But then at the end of the summer, in a brief email, he told me he'd fallen in love with another ranger. He said he "knew this was the life he was meant to live"—in the wilderness, with Kodiak bears, caribou, and some woman I imagined was like an Amazon version of me.

I liked nature, but not enough for Dean. He apparently needed a woman who could live in a secluded forest without indoor plumbing and internet.

So Dean had stayed in Alaska and left me behind—with the rent, a mountain of debt, and the feeling that I was the biggest sucker alive.

No one in Jasmine Falls needed to know those things. They'd probably cooked up a juicier story, anyway. But I knew as soon as I showed my face in that town, it would start all the tongues wagging again. By the time I crossed the state line into South Carolina, a knot was forming deep in my stomach, because while Dean had humiliated me, he wasn't the first to break my heart.

No, that honor belonged to Alex Fox. And he'd lived in Jasmine Falls, too.

Every time I went back there—ever since college—I wondered if I'd bump into Alex. So far, by some miracle, I had not. Word was that he'd left town after dumping me—the reason why varied, depending on who you talked to—and I hadn't seen him since.

That suited me just fine. Some things were better left buried in the past.

"You can do this," I said, hoping that hearing the words over and over might convince me. Seeing Delia would be good for me, and my mother would be thousands of miles away. As long as we were separated by the Atlantic, everything would be fine.

I could handle small-town curiosity. I could keep my head down, help Delia, and paint until my fingers were numb. No problem. Delia had a big old farmhouse with lots of light. I could paint outside, in the fresh air and sunshine. I'd be like Monet, painting in the French countryside, and my only other task would be taking Delia to her doctor's appointments.

It would be the perfect escape.

My mother and Aunt Delia had lived in Jasmine Falls all of their lives—Delia now in their parents' house, and Penelope in one that she'd designed herself and built down the road from it. They lived just next door to the Congaree National Park, which had just been called a swamp until a few years ago. It didn't get the number of visitors like the Smokies or the Everglades—not by a long shot. But being elevated to National Park status had brought it more tourists. People went canoeing and kayaking there, and bird enthusiasts went looking for elusive species. It was like a primordial forest, full of ferns and reptiles, and cypress trees with big curtains of moss.

Since my mother was away so often for work, I'd spent most of my childhood over at Delia's house, romping around the yard with the animals she'd kept—chickens, ducks, goats, and even a couple of quarter horses—and loved every minute of it. My mother kept a house that was spotless—sleek and modern, like a museum. But Delia's house was cozy, filled with overstuffed couches and chairs, braided rugs, and stained-glass lamps. Her yard was peppered with concrete animals and metal sculptures that spun and twirled in the wind. She even had a canoe we'd take out in the pond behind her house.

Being at Delia's house always felt like an adventure. For Past Me, that was everything.

For Present Me, it would be just the place I needed to give me focus and to get myself unstuck. Everything in the mountains reminded me of Dean.

But Delia's place was mine.

---

DELIA'S big farmhouse was set way off from the road. Delia had fifteen acres, mostly flat with dense woods in the back. She'd made her home into an animal sanctuary, with all her adopted critters, but it felt like the perfect sanctuary for me, too. There was a big gray barn about fifty yards from the house and a little pasture next to it. From the driveway, I could see a few goats and a couple of big shaggy dogs that stood like sentinels. The land here was mostly flat, with lots of woods and wetlands. A million years ago, they'd grown soybeans here, but now it was just Delia and all of her adopted animals.

"Anybody home?" I called. Delia's back door was open, just like it always was, because no one around here locked their doors. The kitchen, all white tile and stainless steel, was sparkling and smelled like lemons. Real lemons—not that fake bottled smell.

"In here, kid!"

"Hey, Aunt D," I said, rushing to give her a hug. "How are you feeling?"

In the den, Delia lay propped up on her big overstuffed floral sofa, her leg atop a pile of throw pillows. She squeezed me tight.

"I'm so glad to see you, kid. I can't thank you enough for coming."

"You know I wouldn't pass up the chance to crash with my favorite aunt for a couple of weeks."

She smiled. "I'm your only aunt, but I appreciate the sentiment."

"You look good," I said. Her white hair fell in loose waves to her shoulders, and the only wrinkles on her face came from decades of laughter. Not at all like my mother, who had a permanent frown line between her eyebrows, as prominent as a crack in marble.

"Thank you," Delia said. "It's probably the pain meds giving me a youthful glow."

"How's the knee?"

She turned it just slightly, eyeing the wrapping, and said, "It looks like Dr. Frankenstein got a hold of me, and it hurts like a son of a gun. But they seem to think I'll be walking like a teenager again in a few weeks."

"Good," I said.

"It's made of titanium," she said. "I won't be running any marathons, but I can at least get out there and cut the dang crabgrass. It'll be knee-high after another rain."

"Let me handle the crabgrass," I said. "We can make a list of all the things you need to be done around the house."

"Thank you, sweetheart," she said, and smiled like it hurt a little to do so. Short and wiry, Delia had always been a dynamo—one of those women who seemed to stop aging around fifty. But this time, she looked more like her real age of sixty-six, and that tugged at my heart.

"Where's Mom? I thought she was staying until I got here."

"Good lord, I sent her home." Delia waved her hand like she was shooing a fly. "I love your mother, but she was on my last blessed nerve."

I snorted back a laugh.

"She thinks now that I'm hobbled, she can come in here and redecorate the bedroom and reorganize my pantry and terrorize Rufus with the vacuum. I told her to go put that nervous energy into packing for her tulip tour."

"Rufus?"

"My latest rescue kitty—he just showed up here one day, sitting out in the yard in the hopes of being fed. So of course I did, because he seemed like a smart animal, and he decided to stay right on. You might see him in a couple of days, when he gets over the horror of the vacuum. He's fat and orange and has a bell so he can't sneak up on the birds. He's surprisingly spry to be so enormous."

Delia had always liked to take in strays.

"No vacuuming," I said. "Got it."

"Well, she could at least have the decency to put poor Rufus upstairs. But she can't stand the idea of getting a single cat hair on her fancy clothes, so she just chased the poor thing from one hiding spot to another. He's probably only got one life left by now."

"Well then, he's lucky to live it here."

Delia's old farmhouse was a four-on-four style, complete with a tin roof and a big front porch. The downstairs had one bedroom and bath, plus a small sitting room, the den, and the kitchen. The upstairs had four additional rooms and one bath. Two had always been made up as bedrooms, for family or friends that stayed over. One had been Delia's craft room, and the last room was storage. There was a finished attic, too, that I hadn't been inside in years.

"Hey," Delia said, "your mother did do one useful thing. She made up the bedroom upstairs for you. I haven't even been up there since before Christmas, so she assured me she dusted off all the cobwebs and put fresh sheets on the bed."

"Thank you," I said.

"You can use any of those rooms up there while you're here. Use my little room as a studio if you like. Or the attic—it's nearly empty anyway."

"Sure, maybe I will. I'm supposed to get some new paintings to Janet in a few weeks."

Delia nodded. "I heard you were having to leave your friend's early. I hated to ask you do to that, kid." Before I could interrupt, she said, "But we can make this a retreat for you, too. I don't need you to sit in here and make a fuss over me all day long, so you do whatever you need to do. But I'd be lying if I said I wasn't looking forward to the company." She smiled then, but her eyes looked tired.

"Sounds perfect," I said. "I'm looking forward to it, too."

Delia leaned her head back against the pillows and winced as she moved.

"Can I get you anything?" I said. "A glass of water? Something for pain?"

"It might be time," she said. "Your mother wrote down the last time she gave the pain pills to me. Look for a sticky note on the counter."

In the kitchen, there was a note that read "meds 2:30." I located two green pill bottles on the counter, and took them out to Aunt Delia with a glass of water.

She sat up a little and said, "I know you're worn out from that drive. Why don't you go get yourself settled and we can catch up later. These usually knock me out anyway."

"I'll bring some things in and be back down in a little while."

She nodded and lay back against the pillows. "I'm glad you're here, Fiona."

"Me, too."

Outside, the grass was already ankle-high, and the first weeds were sprouting in the flower beds. It was cool for April, not humid the way it would be in another few weeks. The air was different down here—salty and heavy—not like it was in the mountains. Summer could be scorching, too hot for Delia to be out gardening.

Other houses in this area had been toppled by tornadoes or the occasional hurricane, but not Delia's. The old barn's paint was now gray like driftwood, but the weather vane with its metal rooster and glass orb still sat proudly on the eave.

Delia James was just as sturdy. She moved through the world with an ease that I'd envied my whole adult life.

. Upstairs, my mother had indeed made up the bigger bedroom for me—the one that overlooked the barn and goat pasture. Now I saw that there were in fact three little goats—one black and white one that was much smaller than the others—and two big white dogs that were positioned on either side of them, as if in a tactical formation.

The bedroom had sparse furniture—just a small desk with a chair, a double bed, and a dresser with three drawers. There was a trunk at the foot of the bed, and a brass floor lamp by the desk, but no other knick-knacks around. Down the hall, the other bedroom was made up, too, as if expecting another guest. The door to Delia's workroom was open, but it looked like it hadn't been used in a long while. A six-foot wooden table was pushed against one wall and by the window was a drawing table with a stack of books on top. With its open space and bright sunlight, it would be the perfect place to paint.

Heading back downstairs, I heard voices and thought at first that Delia had turned on the TV. But upon entering the den, I saw who my aunt was talking to, and felt my throat twist into a knot.

It was the one person I had never wanted to see again as long as I lived on this earth.

Alex Fox.

The first man who'd broken my heart.

The man I'd never get over.

# Chapter Four

FIONA

ALEX FOX LOOKED STARTLED, like someone had thrown a cooler full of ice water on him. Mouth open, he held a casserole dish covered in tin foil. He wore a button-down gray checkered shirt that was tight across the chest and biceps and jeans that fit him like a glove. He looked even more gorgeous than he had in high school—his jaw was more chiseled, his dark hair was thick and tousled, and his eyes were still that striking deep shade of green. He looked to have packed forty pounds of solid muscle on his six-foot-three frame, and life seemed very, very unfair right now.

The last time I'd seen Alex was eight years before, and I remembered it as clearly as if it had happened yesterday.

I'd come home from college and surprised him with a visit, and he acted like he couldn't get me out of his house fast enough. Instead of going out for dinner in town (where people would see us, I realized later), we sat outside on his porch. He leaned against the banister, hands shoved into his pockets as he sputtered the words so quickly, like he just wanted it all to be over—while his eyes darted past me as if I were already gone.

*This isn't going anywhere.*

*We're chasing different dreams.*

*We're not headed to the same place.*

It all sounded like a bunch of clichés smashed together, which in turn made his words feel like a lie. The whole time he was talking, it was like he was maneuvering around the truth, leaving out the parts that mattered most.

But I hadn't argued with him. I didn't want to be with a guy who didn't want to be with me—it was as simple as that. And I certainly didn't want to waste my time waiting for some guy to decide how he felt about me—even if I happened to be head over heels for the said guy. If he didn't know after three years of being together, then I was better off moving on. So I'd left him sitting on that banister rail in the dark, calmly driven out of his yard, and then cried all the way to the state line. The hurt had been like nothing else, but I'd tamped it down and put Alex Fox out of my mind. It wasn't until later that I'd heard about Lori Gifford, and that just made me despise Alex even more for the way he'd treated me. If I could have gone back in time and punched him in the cool blue moonlight of that porch, I sure as heck would have.

Later, I'd heard that he married Lori, whose sole purpose in high school had been to make me suffer. She'd been nothing but horrible as long as I'd known her, and even now I couldn't imagine what in the world had drawn him to Lori.

Well. I had a couple of ideas.

Rumor had it that he'd been seeing her while we were still together. I'd been in college only a few hours away, but at twenty-one years old it felt like Alex and I were thousands of miles apart. Alex had never admitted that he'd cheated with Lori, but I knew it had to be true. As soon as I'd heard the stories, all the pieces had come together. Lori was nearby when I was not, and sometimes proximity counts for more than it should. I thought I'd finally gotten away from my biggest bully by graduating high school, but Lori had managed to hurt me one more time—and in the worst way that she could, by turning my first love against me.

Later, they'd gotten divorced. They hadn't even made it a year together. The rumors had flown around about them, too, but I didn't pay any attention. Alex Fox had already taken up enough space in my life. I refused to give him any more.

For the last eight years, I'd managed to avoid Alex whenever I came to Jasmine Falls. I thought he'd moved away until this moment, standing in Delia's living room. Alex had become a distant memory after a while, and even my mother had the good sense not to talk about him after I'd moved away. She'd never approved of us dating anyway because she had some beef with his whole family that went back thirty years. Probably back to someone who broke her heart when *she* was in high school.

Aunt D never talked about him either, but that was because I'd basically issued a gag order. My visits to Jasmine Falls had become less and less frequent over the years, down to a few birthday gatherings and Christmas. My time there was limited, and I didn't want to spend it hearing about Alex Fox.

Looking at him now was like staring down a ghost.

A very handsome ghost with a ridiculous smirk that I wanted to knock right off his stupid gorgeous face.

My breath caught in my throat and I felt like I'd surely faint or vomit, and it was hard to say which would be worse.

"Fiona," he said. "I didn't know you were here."

Hearing my name on his lips made my ears tingle. It also made me want to gag. That feeling of being dumped, like you've been punched in the gut? Turns out that feeling doesn't go away so easily. It comes back just as quick and fierce, like passing a dead skunk on the highway.

This was the first guy who broke my heart, and the last thing I wanted was to like the way my name sounded on his lips.

"You never know what you'll find when you drop by unannounced," I said, trying to keep my voice bright. It was snarky, but I couldn't help it.

He opened his mouth like he wanted to say more, but Delia interrupted him.

"He brought us supper," she said. "Isn't he a sweetheart?" She sat up straighter on the couch, her eyes twinkling. I'd never told her the specifics about why Alex and I had broken up. As far as she and my mother knew, we'd just fizzled out when I left town for college, the way so many high school couples do.

Now, seeing Alex standing there in Delia's den, smiling his rakish smile as if he hadn't lied to my face and smashed my heart into a billion pieces, I felt heat rising in my cheeks. I wanted to take that casserole dish and dump the contents right over his head.

But it would ruin the carpet, and Delia would be mortified. And really, the contents of that dish smelled amazing. My aunt might be a little five-foot bundle of dynamite, but she hadn't raised me to be rude. As long as I was a guest in her house, I'd have to remain civilized and push aside all those fantasies of how I might get even with Alex Fox.

And there was no way I could cook her anything that smelled as enticing as what was inside that dish. I could barely make grilled cheese.

"Well, I'll leave you two to chat," I said, all fake sweetness. "I've got a little unpacking to do before bed."

"Unpacking?" Alex said, his voice chipper. "Are you staying a while?"

When I turned his way, trying to rearrange my face into something that was not a scowl, he arched a brow as if he might be able to read my mind after all.

"For two weeks!" Delia said. "Penelope insisted on calling her, even though I'm perfectly capable of doing the essential things by myself. But now that she's here I'm glad her mother badgered me into submission." She winked at me and said, "But you can never tell your mother that, because she loves to remind me of how she's always right, and she'll be insufferable for the next decade."

I smiled at that and said, "Yes ma'am."

"Why don't you stay for supper, Alex?" Delia said. "It'll give y'all a chance to catch up, too."

Aunt Delia, it seemed, most certainly could *not* read my mind.

Alex smiled and my cheeks started burning all over again. Oblivious to my glare, he said, "Well, sure, Mrs. D. I'd like that. Let me just go heat this up in the oven."

*Stay calm*, I told myself, following Alex into the kitchen. He's just a neighbor bringing over a casserole. He doesn't make my heart hurt. Doesn't remind me of one of the worst nights of my life. Doesn't have any effect on me at all.

Nope. None. Zip.

He put the casserole in the oven and I pulled three plates from the cabinet.

"How have you been, Fiona?" The way he said my name still made me shiver. He let it linger on his tongue, like a favorite wine. "It's been a while."

"It sure has," I said. "Feels like a century and you haven't changed a bit." I leaned against the counter and placed a hand on my hip. "And I'm doing really great. Just glad I could get the time off to come down here and help Aunt D." The last thing I wanted him to know was that I was homeless and unemployed. "How about you?"

I was raised by women who could shower you in niceties while wishing they could pound your face into the pavement. This was a practiced art down South, a charade that had played out in the McIntyre house a thousand times before—my mother was a master, and I'd been a fast learner. One useful thing she taught me: there's a time to let all of your emotions out, and there's a time to tamp them down. Life's a lot easier when you know the difference.

"Good," he said, and a tight smile touched his lips. "I hope it's okay that I stay for dinner. I hated to tell her no."

"Of course," I said. "Why wouldn't it be? It's just so nice of you to look after Aunt D." I knew I sounded just like my mother, but I didn't care. I'd stay cool, breezy—welcoming, even. Alex Fox would not leave this house thinking that he still could affect me—even though I was finding it difficult to breathe. Standing this close to him had made my heart hammer in my chest, and watching his lips move made me think about how he'd been such a great kisser.

I definitely did not need to think about that.

He arched a brow and leaned against the kitchen counter, leveling his deep green eyes on mine. How was it possible that he'd gotten even more handsome? There really was no justice in this world.

"It's good to see you," he said, crossing his arms over his chest. I caught the way the sleeves strained against his broad upper arms and the way his eyes slowly raked over me, but chose to focus on napkin folding instead.

"And you too, of course," I said, setting up a tray for Delia.

"I'm sorry it took so long," he said, and gave me a sheepish smile. "I kept hoping I'd run into you one day."

I poured three glasses of iced tea and took three forks from the silverware drawer, willing myself to ignore the way his gravelly voice still made my heart flutter.

My stupid, traitorous heart.

"Is that right?" I said, and my voice was suddenly entirely too chipper.

"I'm glad you'll be staying with her a while. She'd never admit it, but I think she needs more help these days."

I turned to face him, surprised by the words. "What makes you say that?"

"I don't mean to overstep," he said. "I've just been helping her around the house, and it seems like some things are harder for her now."

"What kinds of things?" Was there more my mother wasn't telling me? And why was Alex Fox helping Delia around the house? Did he know more about her health than I did? True, I didn't get to visit as much as I wanted, but that didn't mean I was completely out of touch. Did it?

He shrugged. "Just odd jobs. Fixing the washing machine, mowing the grass. Sometimes I help her with the animals." His eyes settled on mine and my skin tingled like it does when lightning strikes.

I didn't even know how many animals there were, aside from goats and dogs, but I sure as heck wasn't going to ask Alex. I was ashamed I didn't know more about how Delia was living. Earlier, she had suggested we make a list of daily tasks because I knew so little about her routines. The idea that Alex might know more about my aunt than I did made me want to scream.

"I'll be able to help her with all of that now," I said.

He nodded, but he didn't look convinced.

"What, you think I can't mow grass and feed goats?"

He laughed, shaking his head. "I didn't say that. There's lots you can help her with. I'm glad you're here."

The nerve of him, acting so protective of Delia. Like I was the outsider.

I took the casserole out of the oven, cursing to myself. It was a chicken tetrazzini with about a pound of cheese bubbling on top. It smelled amazing. Why, on top of everything else, did Alex Fox have to be a good cook?

Annoyed, I stepped past Alex (he even smelled amazing, dang it, like a cozy campfire and cedar) and took Delia a tray of food so she could stay seated on the sofa. Then I scooped myself a small portion and took my plate into the den. When Alex came in with his plate, he plopped down in the chair right beside me. He could have picked the big leather chair clear on the other side of the room, but no. He sat right next to me and had the nerve to smile at me like we were old pals.

*The nerve.*

Delia, digging into her casserole, said, "Fiona's getting ready for a new gallery show. I'm hoping this can be like a retreat for her." She went on to tell him about my paintings, beaming as she recounted the last few years of my life. Alex listened with interest, asking me about my new series.

*Fine,* I thought. *Ask your questions.* I leveled up my fake politeness. *You will not get the best of me, Alex Fox.*

I had no intention of letting him know how badly he'd hurt me. He probably never gave our breakup a second thought and considered us ancient history—and I wasn't going to give him any hint that I'd felt any differently. I should have gotten over him years ago, and part of me wondered, now that he was sitting here in front of me—why hadn't I?

"Fiona," Aunt Delia said, "Did you know that Alex is a full-time artist, too? He makes these incredible metal sculptures—you just have to see them. He's had all kinds of big time commissions all over the state." She turned to Alex and said, "By the way, how's the one for the library coming?"

For the first time that evening, Alex Fox looked rattled. *Interesting.* He chewed slowly, as if waiting for me to change the subject.

No way was I throwing him a line. Plus, I was curious—when had he turned his art hobby into a career? "What sculpture, Alex? I'd love to hear all about it."

He stumbled over his words. "It's ah—good. For the most part." He shifted in the chair and went on. "There's just one logistical piece that has me a bit stumped."

"Alex is working on a commission for the library," Aunt Delia told me. "It's part of the gala this year."

"Is that coming up soon?" I said. The gala was the biggest event of the year, hosted by the Arts Council. There was a big art auction and VIPs from all over the region came to spend a pile of money and support the arts. If Alex was creating a piece for the gala, that really *was* a big deal. That made me feel even worse about my failing career. Alex Fox had managed to build an art career here in Jasmine Falls?

"Three weeks," Delia said. "And Alex here is creating the biggest piece of the year—it's the centerpiece of the night." She turned to him and said, "Everybody's so excited. They can't wait for the next meeting. I ran into Maxine the other day and she can't stop raving about it." Maxine Bell was Jasmine Falls's biggest patron of the arts. She used to live in New York and hang out with Andy Warhol. Now she mentored young artists and started grassroots programs all over the region.

I wanted to be Maxine when I grew up.

"Wow, the centerpiece," I said to Alex. "You must be thrilled. I'd probably crack under the pressure. Is there a big unveiling?"

Alex swallowed hard. It was fun watching him squirm.

"Oh, yes," Aunt Delia said. "They'll unveil the sculpture right before the auction—it sets the tone for the whole evening—and the bidding!" She grinned at Alex. "The whole idea is to knock everyone's socks off and get them excited to write those checks. Last year the governor came and dropped a hundred thousand on a glass sculpture after seeing the centerpiece."

"Sounds like a huge honor," I said. "I can't wait to see it."

Alex looked positively green.

"Maxine raised a boat load of money for the library," Aunt Delia said. "And the Arts Council. I'll re-introduce you, dear. She hasn't seen you since you were knee-high. I'm sure she'd be interested in your work, too." Delia joined the Arts Council a few years ago— enthusiastic about the arts, she'd been one hundred percent supportive of me when I declared my art major. Unlike my mother, who thought it was a waste of time.

"Well, with all of these fans, I can't imagine anything would have you worried," I said to Alex. "What's got you stumped?" I was dying to know what had Alex Fox tied up in knots.

Alex arched a brow at me and squirmed in his chair.

I smiled my most polite Penelope McIntyre smile.

"Just a minor design element I need to sort out," he said. "No big deal."

"Maybe Fiona could help you," Aunt Delia said, and I almost choked on my tetrazzini. "If y'all are both in a funk, maybe it'd do you good to get together and trade ideas. Fiona, you'll love all this metalwork that Alex is doing. And Alex, you probably haven't seen any of Fiona's work, either."

Once I was certain I wouldn't choke to death, I said, "Aunt D, I'm sure the last thing Alex needs is me." And he'd most likely rather eat glass than ask for my help.

"Nonsense," she said. "Artists can't live in a vacuum. You two could stand to get out of your own heads for a while."

When I turned to Alex, he gave me a small shrug. No help at all.

Aunt Delia smiled and winked at me. It sure hadn't taken her long to start matchmaking.

Super.

BY THE TIME Alex and I had cleared the plates and put everything in the dishwasher, it was nearly eight-thirty.

"I should go," he said. He wrapped the casserole back in its tin foil and put it in the refrigerator.

"Thanks for bringing her dinner," I said. "That was nice of you."

"My pleasure." He looked as if he wanted to say more. His eyebrows were pulled together in—confusion? disappointment?— and he stared at me like I was a puzzle he didn't quite know how to put together. But then went back into the den to say good night to Delia. When he came back through the kitchen, he paused at the back door. "It really was good to see you, Fiona," he said, his voice low. "I guess I'll see you around."

*Not if there's one ounce of karma in this world*, I thought.

"Have a good night, Alex," I said, a fake smile firmly in place.

He set those deep green eyes on mine again, his lip curving in the smallest smile. Then he nodded once and shut the door behind him.

My nerves felt like they were tangled into knots.

Alex Fox had stood in this kitchen, smiling at me and chatting like he hadn't ripped my heart out and stomped all over it. He'd acted as if we had no history at all—or worse, as if he didn't remember any of it.

So much for this place being a sanctuary.

I let out a heavy sigh and walked into the big pantry. Somewhere in these floor-to-ceiling cabinets was a bottle of emergency Scotch that Delia kept on hand for natural disasters, family meltdowns, and other trying evenings like this one. After opening five of the lower cabinets, I found the half-empty bottle of Macallan's and one disheveled orange tabby cat with amber eyes as wide as saucers.

"You must be Rufus," I said.

Rufus blinked at me and then stepped carefully out onto the floor as if he were testing the effect of gravity. Satisfied the world was as he left it, with no vacuum in sight, he padded into the kitchen, his tail high and his nose twitching at the smell of chicken casserole.

If Delia hadn't enjoyed it so much, I'd have given all the leftover tetrazzini to the cat. Because to heck with Alex Fox, and to heck with his casseroles, too. He didn't get to waltz in here and be Mr. Sexy Friendly Neighbor and wipe the slate clean between us. When I put a handful of dry food into Rufus's bowl by the back door, he stared at it for a moment, and then looked back up at me and narrowed his eyes like he knew there was a better option, just out of reach.

I sipped the Scotch, thinking that it was time to put my past mistakes behind me and move on to my better option. Enough wallowing, already. These two weeks were a chance to dust myself off and get back on track.

After Dean left me, I'd read about fifty self-help books that made it pretty clear I was (1) woefully co-dependent and (2) had some hard-core abandonment issues (duh). I always thought I'd been raised to be thoughtful and polite, but really, I'd been raised to be a people-pleaser. And you know what people-pleasers get?

Screwed.

Life hadn't just thrown me curve balls—it had chucked full-on fireballs that nearly burned my life to the ground. But they'd taught me a few things. I could be a good person without striving to make everyone around me happy. I could put myself first sometimes. Now I knew that I needed to be a self-sufficient artist, supporting myself and no one else—and I needed to survive on my own, with no one else's help. It was dangerous to depend on people because it gave them space to disappoint you. Penelope had made me feel discarded. Dean had humiliated me. Alex had hurt me and walked away like it meant nothing.

They'd all left me, and they'd all let me down.

Depending on other people was a mistake—one I wouldn't make again.

# Chapter Five

## ALEX

WHEN I'D DROPPED by Delia's with that casserole, the last person in the world I expected to see was Fiona McIntyre. I hadn't seen her in eight years, since the night we'd broken up.

She looked even more gorgeous than I remembered—fierce eyes, wild curly hair, and curves that would haunt my dreams. She was more muscular now, her square jaw just a little fuller, her hair a richer brown, and eyes as blue as glaciers. Even in her jeans and blouse, I could see the shape of her full hips, and her narrow waist, and it took every single ounce of my concentration to keep my hands off of her. I'd reached out once to touch her elbow and had caught myself just in time, reaching past her for a spoon instead. I'd tried to play it off, but I just looked like a huge dork.

Fiona had left here the cute girl next door and come back looking like a goddess.

She also looked like she wanted to shove me out a window.

I couldn't stop staring at those bright blue eyes, even though they simmered with fury. She'd tried to hide it with politeness, but Fiona had never been able to hide anything from me.

My heart had nearly stopped when I first saw her. For a moment, I thought—or hoped—that she'd forgotten about that awful night on my porch, and the stupid things I'd said. But one look at her face confirmed that she hadn't forgotten a single thing.

Of course she hadn't.

She'd been hurt back then, but how could she not be? Rejection cuts like a knife—I've had my share—and if there was one night in my life I could take back, it would have been that one.

But really, I didn't have a choice. I had to let her go.

Or, I thought I did. Back then.

If I'd known then what I know now, that night never would have happened and the last several years would have been very different. To say I'd thought about her a lot over the years was an understatement.

Fi had been my first love. We'd known each other our whole lives, because everyone knew each other in a town this small—but it wasn't until high school that we became close. She'd been totally driven, focused on making good grades and going to college, and getting out of Jasmine Falls. She didn't have any interest in dating, and I'd watched her turn down a dozen guys who asked her out.

She was intimidating, even back then, because she was talented and she knew what she wanted. Fiona was a five-foot-eight-inch firecracker, and had no patience for the usual high school drama. She had a few close friends, but wasn't part of the popular crowd—and neither was I.

We didn't really start hanging out until junior year when I was flunking chemistry. I had plans for college, too, but one more failing grade would blow those plans to bits. It had taken all of my courage to ask Fi to tutor me, but she agreed. We'd started meeting every day after school, and soon those hour-long study sessions turned into dinners and late-night phone calls—and before I knew it, she'd stolen my heart.

Back then, she was living with Delia. Fi's mom was one of the most famous architects in the state, and she was even more driven than her daughter. Penelope had built her own firm and designed sleek buildings that were marvels made from steel and glass. They were beautiful, but cold—just like Penelope.

After winning some big-time awards and a prestigious grant, she took two years to travel all over the world. It was business, she claimed, the chance of a lifetime. But it meant that she left her sixteen-year-old daughter behind. Fiona had put on a good face at first, but the closer we grew, the more she confided in me. Her mother had made her feel abandoned, chucked aside like furniture you didn't have a use for anymore. There was really no way to make someone feel better about that.

But I tried. Because I loved her with my whole heart, and I hated to see her hurting.

Back then, I thought we'd be together forever. She was the only person I could imagine forever with, because she grounded me, too.

But then the worst had happened, and those dreams went up in smoke.

That night on my porch had been etched into my memory: Fiona in her cute blue sundress that made her legs look a mile long, her hair pulled up in a messy bun that begged me to take it down and run my fingers through it. Her face had been as bright as the moon when she'd showed up at my door, so delighted to have surprised me. And then it had crumpled when I'd said those awful, hurtful words. Her mouth had fallen open and her eyes had narrowed, and she'd gaped at me like I'd just told her I was leaving Jasmine Falls to join the circus.

I'd expected her to yell at me, curse me to pieces, or at the very least throw her shoe at me, because she'd always had a hot temper.

Really, it would have hurt less if she had.

Instead, she'd done a one-eighty and walked off my porch steps, right out of my world. Gone in a blink, like a cool breeze.

And that was the most miserable moment of my life. I knew she must have hated me for it, and after a few years I'd considered calling her, writing her, something—but then too much time went by, and too many other complicated things happened, and it seemed foolish to bring it up again.

Sleeping dogs and whatnot.

Tonight, she'd put on a good face, but it was obvious she could barely stand to be in the room with me. It had been hard not to stare at her—she'd always been stunning, but now everything about her was amplified: her face sharper, her legs more toned, her eyes more dazzling. She was even more gorgeous now, and when she smiled she drew all the focus in the room.

She smiled tonight, but none of those smiles were real. She was annoyed that I was there, but it was more than that. Something in her eyes looked a lot like pain. And that pain was because of me.

I hadn't been pining all these years, not exactly, but I'd be lying if I said I hadn't thought about how things could have been different between us. I liked Jasmine Falls, but after that breakup, it was the last place I wanted to be. So I went to a trade school in the upstate, and I trained with some well-known blacksmiths there. It felt good to keep making things with my hands, and it was comforting to be in a place that didn't remind me of what felt like the biggest mistake of my life. Because I knew it back then, too—I knew pushing Fiona away was just that. It would be something I regretted for the rest of my days.

But I had no way to fix it. I'd broken us beyond repair.

She'd moved on, so I'd tried to move on, too. I made some new friends, and then I married someone I thought I loved. I'd been wrong about that too, though.

I'd been wrong about a lot of things.

For a while, I stayed out of Jasmine Falls. Then when my parents died, I came back to handle their estate and lived in their house until I got back on my feet. That was about the time that my marriage was falling apart, but my career was taking off. It was a hard time to live in a small town, because boy, the stories that popped up about Lori and me were out of this world. But I had friends here, and my buddy Eli had moved here, too. And the two of us started working together, building our own forges, working toward that dream of having our own spaces to build that work we fantasized about. He kept me going through the really hard days, when I didn't feel like making anything anymore.

There were some days that I didn't think about Fiona at all. But being back in Jasmine Falls? It was impossible not to think of her, especially when I started seeing more of Mrs. D.

For a while now, I'd been helping Delia since she didn't get around as easily anymore. And some days when I took her groceries or went to mow the grass, a part of me hoped that I might run into Fiona.

And then it had finally happened, and it felt like my throat had swollen shut and I could barely string coherent thoughts together.

But it also felt like a miracle had happened.

Part of me had wanted to hug Delia when she'd suggested Fiona help me out with the sculpture, but the look on Fi's face made it clear she'd rather walk through fire.

I'd won her over once, though. With a little luck, I could do it again.

# Chapter Six

FIONA

THE TOWN SQUARE didn't have a single empty building anymore. Ever since Congaree had earned its national park status, the town's tourism had exploded. Now Jasmine Falls had a collection of small businesses that boasted everything from kayak tours to gourmet pies. There was even a boutique that specialized in pet clothing. There was a park-like area in the center of the square, and what folks called the "town square" was all of the shops that lined the park on the opposite side of the street. There were wide sidewalks lined with enormous oaks, and the Garden Club always kept the flowers and shrubs in immaculate condition. On any given day, the downtown looked like a double-page spread in *Southern Living*.

The best part of the square, of course, was its fabulous coffee shop. When I walked inside the Sentient Bean, the bell on the door clanging above my head, a shriek came from behind the counter. Gwen, my best friend from high school, darted around the register and barreled towards me with her arms wide.

"It's true!" she said, pulling me into a bear hug. "I heard you were back in town, but how am I, your best and oldest and most awesome friend, not the first to know?"

"How'd you know at all?" I said. "I've been here for like an hour."

"Delia's friend Hazel came in to get her usual dozen cupcakes," she said, straightening her apron. "And Hazel has all the latest updates. The other big news is that Thomas Brady left his wife for their personal chef, and Charlotte May's cow got out and ate all of the petunias at First Methodist. And now you're all caught up." She tucked a lock of hair up under her white cap, then grabbed my hand and pulled me towards the back of the coffee shop. "Now come here. I need a taste-tester."

Gwen hadn't changed a bit. She still zipped around like she was on roller skates. Her big blue eyes still sparkled, impossibly bright. She was a little shorter than me, with light blond hair and a face that was just round enough that it would likely make her look twenty-five forever.

She steered me past the tables and around the counter where a young woman with pixie-cut red hair was busy at the espresso machine. "Holler if you get busy out here, Maggie."

Maggie, who looked about twenty, nodded and gave her a thumbs-up.

Once we were past the swinging door and in the back, Gwen said, "I've been experimenting with a new scone recipe. Here."

Before I could protest, she'd shoved one into my mouth and my taste buds exploded.

"Wow," I said, chewing. "That's amazing. Is that bacon?"

"Maple bacon. With just a hint of sea salt."

Two years before, Gwen had bought this place when the previous owner was ready to retire. It had been a bakery that specialized in cakes, which is why it had a to-die-for kitchen in the back. Before Gwen, the only place to get a cup of coffee in Jasmine Falls had been the diner three blocks away. In just a few months, she'd remodeled the front part of the shop and created a cafe that was now a favorite hangout for locals and had a steady stream of tourists, too.

"You're a genius," I said, licking my fingers.

Gwen winked. "There's a little bourbon in the glaze."

"Heaven."

"How long are you in town? We have to catch up."

"A couple of weeks. Delia had knee surgery and I'm helping her for a while."

"Yay!" she squealed. "I mean, knee surgery, boo—but weeks, yay!"

She grabbed my forearms and jumped up and down, and my heart swelled.

"I missed you, Gwen."

"Me too." She grinned as she poured a cup of coffee and handed it to me. "This place is just not the same without you. Did you see Alex yet?"

I paused, mid-sip. "You really can't sneeze around here without everyone knowing it."

She piled the scones onto a platter and took them back out front. "Well, I figured since he's living at—"

Before she could tell me about Alex's living arrangements—which I found myself way too interested in, we pushed through the galley doors and into a burst of steam from the espresso machine, like fog in a retro music video.

"Everything's cool!" Maggie said, flashing a big thumbs-up toward us. "No problem!"

Gwen bit her lip to hide a smile as she slid the platter into one of the display cases. "We should definitely catch up soon, babe. There's a lot that's different around here."

"Wine date?" I said.

"Well, duh."

"Fiona?" Someone called from behind me. "Is that you?"

I turned, trying to place the voice. A tall woman in a green and gray uniform held several bags of ground coffee against her chest. Her dark hair was pulled back into a ponytail and her eyes were hidden behind amber aviator-style sunglasses.

She pushed the glasses up into her hair and grinned. I'd know those bright gray eyes anywhere.

"Sadie," I said. "It's been a while."

"Yeah, like a decade," she said, shifting the bags in her arms. "Last time I saw you was graduation."

"Give me those," Gwen said, taking the coffee bags from her. "You want your usual?"

"Yeah, thanks," Sadie said. Now that her arms were empty, I saw the badge and name tag on her shirt's front pockets.

"You're a park ranger?" I asked her.

"Can you believe they pay her to traipse around the swamp for a living?" Gwen said. "This woman, who refused to go on the senior camping trip because we were sleeping in tents and not the Holiday Inn."

Sadie snorted. "I love the outdoors," she said. "I just prefer not to sleep there. Once you have memory foam, you don't go back." She wrinkled her nose as Gwen passed her a brown paper bag and her travel cup. "I better run," she said. "Have to give a talk in an hour to a bunch of sixth-graders and gotta get myself properly caffeinated first." She quickly turned toward the door and said over her shoulder, "Good to see you, Fi!"

Gwen snapped her fingers in my direction. "Since you're here, you can save me a trip." She stepped through the swinging door and then reappeared with a small box in her arms. "I made some sandwiches for you and Delia." She grabbed a few of the maple scones from the display case and slipped them into a bag. "And take her these, too."

"Thanks," I said. "I'll try not to eat them all on the way home."

She smirked. "Don't make an injured woman cry."

The bell over the door clanged as a man entered, pushing a hand truck stacked with boxes. As he approached the counter, Gwen said, "Dang, I thought those were coming tomorrow. I still need to make room in the walk-in."

"I'll see you later," I said. "You're busy." Behind us, the espresso machine whirred and there was a clatter of plates on the counter.

"Call me," Gwen said, waving at the man with the hand truck. "You can come over for drinks and tell me all about bumping into Alex."

"Ugh," I said, and plucked two bags of coffee from the shelf. Gwen gave me a sly wink as she disappeared through the swinging doors, asking the delivery man how his day was going so far.

---

AFTER A QUICK STOP at the grocery store, I headed back to Delia's house, trying hard not to think about living in the same zip code as Alex Fox. Even though it was temporary, being near him felt like there was some massive imbalance in the universe.

I put the groceries away and then went out to the porch, where she sat reading in a rocking chair, her foot propped on an ottoman and Rufus snoozing in her lap. She'd been getting around the house without too much trouble, but I was glad to see her walking stick next to the rocker. The pain was minimal, she'd told me, and she was starting physical therapy in a few days. Delia James was not a weak woman, and I knew she'd pretend she was doing just fine so I wouldn't worry about her. That meant I'd have to watch her like a hawk.

I sat next to her and said, "Gwen sent you sandwiches and scones."

"That woman cooks with magic," she said. "Lucky for you, I share."

"Talk to me about feeding goats. And any other wildlife you have out there."

Delia grinned, waving her hand in the air. "The goats will eat anything," she said. "But there's grain in the barn that I give them every morning. They're friendly, but watch out for the littlest one. She likes to head-butt you when you turn your back, and she'll send you one end over the other. She even got Alex a time or two."

I grinned at the thought of Alex tumbling to the ground, taken down by a mischievous pygmy goat that barely reached his knees. *Atta girl*, I thought.

"What else?" I said.

"Dog food's in the barn, too. Sid and Nancy will ignore you most of the time, since they know their job is the goats."

"Sid and Nancy?"

"The big fluff balls that pass for dogs."

"You still have chickens?"

"Eight. Coop's down by the barn, and they go in it at night. You open the door and they'll go right inside."

"You should have told me last night!" I said. There were coyotes and foxes everywhere around here, and there was no way Penelope McIntyre had risked getting poop on her shoes to put chickens up the day before.

"It's okay. Alex put them up when he got here."

"He did?"

"He's been coming by to help with little things like that since the surgery. He really is a sweetheart." Delia grinned.

"Don't get any ideas," I said. "That ship sailed a million years ago."

Her brow arched. "Sometimes we just meet people at the wrong time, kid. Then the right time comes, and *bam*."

There was no right time for Alex Fox and me. There was the matter of my crushed heart. His scorching betrayal.

Well, it had been scorching at twenty-one, anyway. But still. People had patterns. If Alex had lied to me and hurt me so easily back then, I figured it wouldn't be hard for him to do it again. And I had no intention of letting him get that close. Delia only knew parts of the Alex story, and I didn't want to fill in the gaps.

The gaps were the part that hurt the most.

Delia went over the rest of the animal list, telling me to mind

Earl the Shetland pony, who was a bit ornery and prone to love bites, and to keep an eye out for the two sheep that stayed in the goat pen. The geese and ducks, she said, had taken up here and looked after themselves.

Before Delia retired, she'd run a veterinary practice with her husband. They'd never had kids, but they'd taken in countless animals to keep them out of kill shelters. After Uncle Frank died, she kept fostering cats and dogs and brought any stray that needed a home. She'd had a menagerie for as long as I could remember.

"Anything else I need to do this afternoon?" I said. "Errands?"

"Nope." She patted my arm. "Drink your coffee, and go paint something. I'll be fine. I'm fed, I'm caffeinated, and I can hobble down the hall when need be. You do your thing, and I'll call if I need you." She pulled a cell phone with a hot pink case from her back pocket. "Your mother taught me how to text," she said. "So I can text you if I need anything."

"Okay. Just for a little while. Sandwiches are in the fridge."

Delia nodded and said, "Have fun up there, kid. Don't be afraid to get messy. That's how you let the good stuff in."

---

UPSTAIRS IN DELIA'S work room, I spread my paints out on the table and set up an easel. After selecting a small wooden panel, I laid out some colors on a palette—some greens, a little gold, some shades of blue. And one bright Veridian that was just about the shade of Alex Fox's eyes.

Dang it. Closing my eyes, I shook my head to knock all thoughts of him right out of there. It was bad enough that Alex and I were in the same state again. I didn't need him taking up space in my head, too.

I put my cell phone on the far corner of the table so I wouldn't miss any texts from Delia. Loading my brush with paint, I quickly covered the small panel in a few patches of color, just so I wouldn't have to face its intimidating blankness. I took all those thoughts of Alex and imagined shoving them into a box and closing the lid. And then dropping it into a bottomless well. And then setting it on fire with gasoline.

Outside, the twittering of birds was nonstop. Delia had several feeders hanging near the porch, directly below this room. With no curtains, these windows gave me a clear view of the front yard and the copse of trees beyond it toward the main road. This land had been a farm four generations ago, but now the yard was dotted with dogwoods, maples, and a couple of pear trees. A yew was right by the house, its branches scraping against the window.

For a while I felt hypnotized, sipping my coffee and listening to the birdsong, watching the titmice as they flitted from the porch to the trees by the house. I grabbed a sheet of paper and quickly sketched their shapes. Then a different bird appeared, a gray-green color with a bright yellow face and black markings that looked like a scarf. The bird moved its head in an almost mechanical way and then swung itself upside down on the branch, peering under the leaves for insects. It was stupid cute, the way it flipped itself upside down and right-side up again, its feet twirling around the branch like a gymnast on the bars. Its call was like the buzzing of a cicada, but shorter. I snapped a couple of quick photos with my phone for reference, and then the bird gave one final chittering call and flew to a neighboring tree.

"Okay, Fiona," I said. "Enough. Quit stalling."

I quickly drew the yellow-faced bird onto my panel with a pencil, trying to capture its shape. Then with a bit of brown paint, I blocked in the lights and darks that would become the black and gold pattern on its face. I filled in some green spaces behind it with abstract leaf shapes, trying to loosen up with broad, lazy strokes. I thought about what Delia had said, about making enough of a mess that the good stuff could seep in. It seemed like I'd made a pretty good mess of things in the last several months.

My phone chirped and I lay the brush down to check on Delia. The text wasn't from her, though. It was from Penelope.

**This is your mother,** she wrote. **Made it to London.**

I snorted. **Who's this again?** She made teasing her too easy.

**Hilarious, Fiona. Should be in Amsterdam tomorrow. How is Delia?**

**She's good,** I wrote. **Pain pills are helping.**

**I put her schedule of appointments on the fridge.**

**Got it!** I wrote. **How was your flight?**

**Business class is not what it used to be,** she wrote. **Some child behind me howled all the way across the Atlantic. It was like having a Bassett hound right by my ear.**

I chuckled, thinking of my mother with her sleep mask on, martini in hand, demanding that someone turn down the volume on that child.

**Who takes a toddler to London?** she wrote.

Certainly not Penelope McIntyre. She wouldn't even take her teenage daughter back in the day.

I rolled my eyes and wrote: **Try not to cause an international incident, ok? The flight attendants might duct-tape you to the seat.**

**I have to go. Simon appears to be stuck in his ascot.**

**I don't want to know what that means,** I wrote. **Talk later.**

**K,** she wrote.

My mother was one of *those* people now, who just texted, **K.** As if thoughts could be boiled down to single letters.

But really, that was the pattern with Penelope. Every thought and feeling was abbreviated, which left me filling in the holes.

Brush in hand, I went back to the painting. The marks were too fussy, my arm too rigid. As I started another layer of leaves, I remembered what Janet had told me about using my social media channels. *You need to post more in-process shots*, she'd said. A lot of Janet's clients had found her gallery from her Instagram posts, and she'd helped me gain around five thousand followers. Before Janet, I'd have thought that was an impossible feat—why would five thousand people follow me, an unknown painter in the middle of nowhere?

Those follows hadn't translated into sales, though. Not like they had with her other artists.

Selling work by using hashtags still seemed strange to me, but Janet insisted I keep trying. The world was changing, and I had to change with it if I didn't want to be a relic at age 29. Janet was convinced I just hadn't found my online audience yet, but I wasn't so sure. She kept telling me I just hadn't crossed the threshold yet— she'd talked about conversion rates and unique clicks until I'd agreed to try social media out of sheer boredom.

I snapped a quick process photo of the panel with the gold and gray bird and posted it to my account. **Today's warm-up painting: #inprogress #birdnerd.**

*This one's for you, Janet. Prove me wrong.*

Halfway through the second panel, I realized that the chirping from below had been replaced by a loud whirring noise. Tracking the sound, I went to the window that faced the side yard, toward the barn.

Outside, Alex Fox was pushing a mower across the vast expanse of the lawn. I told myself I was mistaken. Surely this was someone Delia had hired and I just had Alex stuck in my brain. But then he turned, and there was his angled jaw and that dark brown hair, and I knew it could be no one else. He moved with that same smooth, confident swagger, even when pushing a mower through the weeds.

I sighed, trying to keep painting and ignore the loud whirring as he moved systematically around the house. Trying to ignore the image of a very buff, very sweaty Alex Fox doing a good deed. He probably rescued kittens from trees and helped old ladies across the street, too.

Frustrated with my lack of progress, I went downstairs to check on Delia. She hadn't texted me, but that was no surprise. Delia hated to ask for help.

"Busted," she said, holding up a romance novel with a glossy cover. She was stretched out on the sofa. "I could say I skip over the salacious parts, but then where's the fun in that?"

"No one's judging," I said. "I'd have brought you my pile if I'd known you were a fan."

She grinned and said, "Would you do me a favor, kid?"

"FedEx them to you?"

"It's hot as blazes outside, and Alex has been out there for ages. Would you mind taking him a big glass of iced water? That man's as big as a house, and if he faints we'll never get him back on his feet."

"Subtle," I said.

"Whatever do you mean?" She shrugged. "It looks bad to have a fella face-down in your yard. Makes people talk."

Shaking my head at her audacity, I followed the noise of the mower down toward the barn, where Alex must have been on the other side. When the noise stopped, I walked around the back side and then nearly collided with him at the back corner.

My jaw dropped open and the glass of water nearly slipped from my hand.

Alex Fox, shirtless, with his snug jeans hanging low on his hips, was a sight too good for this world. He ran a hand through his hair, making it stand on end, and every muscle in his chest rippled in slow motion. My eyes tracked the line from his bicep to his shoulder, down his ribs, to his very defined abs—mercy, you could bounce a quarter off those—and I forced myself to move my eyes back to his face before he caught me staring. Yes, I had not seen the man in eight years. Yes, he had been somewhat scrawny the last time I'd seen him shirtless. Yes, people change.

Dang it.

The years had been kind to him in a way that was completely unfair. Alex Fox now looked like he had been chiseled out of marble, and lord help me, I couldn't stop admiring the way all the pieces of him fit so well together.

"Hey," he said, his lip curving into a playful smile.

"Water," I blurted. "You look hot."

He grinned so his dimples showed, looking pleased with himself.

I felt myself blush. "I mean, it's hot out, and you should stay hydrated. Delia would never forgive herself if you had a heat stroke."

"Thanks," he said, reaching for the glass. His fingers brushed over mine, and I thought that surely my traitorous heart would explode.

He drained the glass and wiped his brow with a bandana he'd pulled from his back pocket.

"You didn't have to do this," I said, gesturing at the mower. "This is why I'm here."

He looked a little amused. "This old mower's a beast to get started. You'd kick it to pieces with that temper of yours."

"I can manage." I crossed my arms over my chest. "And I do not have a temper."

"I think a certain Volkswagen would beg to differ."

"That hunk of junk had it coming." One time. *One time*, my car died and left me stranded on the side of the road. I got so mad that I kicked in the fender until I left a size 9 dent in it. And of course, that's the precise moment when Alex had driven past on the highway.

So his memory worked just fine.

Of course, he wasn't wrong. When pushed too far, I did have a temper. The list of people who could bring it out of me was short, and my mother still held the top spot.

He shrugged. "It's no big deal. I usually come over once a week and tidy up the yard."

That made me feel about three inches tall. There was a lot I'd missed by not being here, and yard work was just the tip of the iceberg. For the longest time, I stayed away from Jasmine Falls because of my mother. She was always flagging my failures and used every opportunity to try to get me to come to my senses (her words, not mine) and work for her. She thought "art" was a hobby and not a career choice. But the idea of being some kind of assistant to her was enough to make me gag. Putting a few hundred miles between us meant I didn't have to hear that—and her other criticisms—so often.

But it also meant I didn't see much of Aunt Delia.

Aunt Delia had always been unsinkable, invincible. After Uncle Frank had died, she'd run his veterinary business on her own until she'd sold it and retired. She'd done all the yard work around here for thirty years. She'd cared for all the animals, and done repairs on the house herself—heck, she'd taught me all the repairs that I knew how to do, and it had saved my bacon more than a few times. Somehow, I'd missed that point where the balance shifted, where Delia had to get other people to help her. She'd always been so spry that it was easy to forget she was ten years older than my mom. Delia had practically raised Penelope when they were growing up, and then she'd done the same for me when Mom decided travel grants were more important than raising a daughter.

I didn't like to think of Delia as getting old and needing help. We all get to that point eventually, but it's never easy to recognize that moment when the people we love start to decline.

I needed to do better.

"Thank you," I said to Alex.

"Of course," he said. "I'm happy to help her any way I can."

And staring at his bright green eyes, it was obvious that was true.

Dang it. Why couldn't Alex have just grown up to be a big old jerk? Why'd he have to run around doing all these thoughtful things?

"Where's your truck?" I said, glancing around the yard, desperate to think about anything except Alex being kind and helpful.

"At the house," he said. "I walked."

I must have looked puzzled because he said, "I live next door now. At Foster's place. Didn't Delia tell you?"

He could have thumped me and knocked me right over.

"Must have slipped her mind," I said.

"Foster sold it to me a while back. He went to live with his daughter down in Pensacola." His dimples appeared again and the whole world shifted on its axis.

Alex Fox lived next door.

Next. Door.

Of course he did. Because the universe had a sense of humor, and boy did it like making me the butt of a joke.

That's what Gwen had been about to tell me at the coffee shop. And that's why she gave me that sly you've-got-a-fox-next-door wink. She was going to owe me a boat load of cupcakes for this one.

"I should finish up," I said, and he nodded, handing me the glass. Past Alex might have squashed my heart like a bug, but Present Alex was being pretty amazing by helping Delia so much. Maybe he'd changed more than his muscle tone. And maybe I needed to let bygones be bygones. And definitely, I needed to chat with him for a minute. I wanted to know everything I could about how Delia was doing, and he was the only person who would tell me.

"Want to stay for chicken salad sandwiches?" I said. "Gwen sent us enough to feed the whole county."

He smiled, resting his hand on his belt, and drawing my eyes down where they definitely should not be. "I like chicken salad just fine."

"Okay then," I said, and went back into the house, feeling his eyes on me with every step.

The mower didn't start again until I'd opened the back door.

# Chapter Seven

ALEX

I TOOK the chicken salad as a good sign.

After Fiona went back inside the house, and I'd regained my ability to string thoughts together, I took the push mower back around to the other side of the barn to finish the last bit of grass.

Fiona seemed slightly less bristly today—slightly—after I told her how I'd been helping her aunt. Truth was, I'd always thought a lot of Mrs. D—she reminded me of my late grandmother Mae, but I'd never tell her that because she'd take that to mean I thought she was old. Which she isn't. She's just not quite as energetic as she once was. Plus, she's always been the first in line to help her neighbors with literally anything—from cleaning up limbs after a storm to hunting for a lost dog. After Fiona moved away, I'd made more of an effort to check up on her now and then. Fiona's mom lived not too far away, but she wasn't exactly the hands-on type. She was more of the designer pantsuit and heels type, and I couldn't imagine her mucking out the barn or even pulling a weed. Miss Delia usually got along just fine, but some days she needed an extra hand, and I could tell she just hated to ask.

. . .

FIONA HAD that same fierce independence. It was easy to admire.

Delia had called me one day a few years before, all riled up because her goats had escaped from their pen and were headed towards the neighbors' vegetable gardens. Those dogs of hers weren't the herding kind, and on that rainy June day, the animals were loose and Mrs. D's arthritis was bothering her. The poor woman looked exhausted by the time I drove up. She was spry, but she had her limit, and chasing goats through the muck was past it.

By the time she called me, she'd already turned her ankle. "I'm sorry to bother you Alex," she'd said, wheezing a little, "But you're the only person I know out here anymore who can half get around."

I'd headed straight over to her house that day, and driven my truck up and down the road in the drizzling rain until I'd found two goats in the neighbors' yards and one down in the blackberry bushes by the pond. It was easy enough to bribe them with sweet feed and apple slices and get them into the back of the pickup. Once I'd tied them in the barn, I fixed the broken fence. When I was finished, Mrs. D had a pot of chili waiting on me.

She cooked amazing chili. She also had a wicked sense of humor and loved to play cards—as it turned out, she was a ringer at gin. She also couldn't help talking about Fiona—she loved that gal like she was her own daughter.

Fiona always was easy to love.

Soon, we had a routine: once a week, I went over to check the fences and play a few hands of cards. Delia cooked supper, and I fixed little things around her house that needed repair. She rarely asked me to do those repairs, but I noticed when a door was sticking in the frame, or when a burner was out on the stove. Pretty soon I started going by more often—sometimes just to being her some fresh corn from the farmers' market or make sure the latest thunderstorm hadn't brought any big limbs down in the yard. She didn't like to ask people for help, but I saw when she needed an extra set of hands, and I didn't mind helping her one bit. My grandmother had lived her last years all by herself, and she'd had a good neighbor who helped her out, too. When I heard that Delia's neighbor Foster was moving to Florida, it took me all of ten seconds to think of buying his place. I was a sucker for old farmhouses, and Foster's had a nice workshop out back big enough to make into a studio. Delia had even put in a good word for me with Foster, and he sold me the house for a fair price without even listing it on the market.

Moving into that place, it felt like fate was finally cutting me a break. I'd lost just about everything I owned in the divorce. Lori had gotten the house, the car, and nearly everything else, including my dog Merle. She didn't even like the dog that much, but she'd written it into the settlement anyway, just out of spite.

In retrospect, I should have seen that one coming. She did a lot of things out of spite, including marrying me. Apparently, that was the best way she could think of to get back at her previous boyfriend. Who, it turned out, she kept seeing well past our wedding day.

I didn't make the best choices back then.

Things had been bad for a while. Then I hired a lawyer who saved me from Lori's wrath, and I bought Foster's house and built my dream studio out back. And then there was a light at the end of the tunnel.

And now I was getting that same feeling from seeing Fiona. Yesterday I thought she still despised me, but now I wasn't so sure. I'd seen that tiny crack in her facade and felt a little chink in my own armor, too. Little cracks are how the light gets inside—that's what Leonard Cohen said. And you know, that guy had style. You don't write songs like that without learning a thing or two about the important parts of life.

---

WHEN THE YARD WAS FINISHED, I felt like a sweaty mess. But I wasn't about to leave without seeing Fiona again. As long as she was here, I'd take every minute I could get with her. I pulled my shirt back on, because I wasn't raised by wolves, but smiled a little thinking of how I'd caught her staring when she'd nearly run smack into me earlier. Yeah, working as a metalsmith had its benefits—I'd been sort of scrawny until I'd gone to trade school, and then I'd packed on the muscle. It's hard not to when you lift actual iron all day. And trade school is serious about their trial by fire—there's no rest for the weary at that place. And now, keeping my own forge going meant that I did everything myself, from moving pig irons around to swinging the big hammers. It wasn't a bad way to keep in shape.

I'd have her expression etched into my memory forever, though —some blend of surprise and delight that made me think she might not be quite as annoyed as she let on. Her eyes had widened and her cheeks had turned just a little pink, and I'd had to bite my lip to stop from grinning.

She'd somehow managed to get even more adorable in the last few years, even when she was trying to hate me. And man, I still loved making her blush. She could keep a lot of things close to the vest, but she couldn't hide the way her cheeks got all rosy and flushed when she got embarrassed.

Devising ways to make her cheeks turn rosy—I could think about that all day long.

When I went up to the house, Fiona was in the kitchen tidying up.

"Aunt D's taking a nap," she said. "Let's go outside." She handed me a plate of scones and sandwiches and grabbed two glasses of iced tea.

I followed her around the side of the house to the porch where there were two wicker chairs and a coffee table, trying not to focus on her short cutoffs and her long, muscular legs. When she plopped down in one of the chairs, I chose the one next to her and put the plate on the small table between us.

She handed me a glass and said, "Thanks for mowing the yard."

"No problem."

Fiona was quiet for a long while. She'd never been one for small talk, but today she seemed preoccupied. She sipped her tea and picked at a loose piece of wicker on the chair like she was trying to gather her nerve.

The longer I watched her, the harder my heart thumped in my chest. Being around women never made me nervous like this. But Fiona had me torn out of the frame. If this really was a second chance, I didn't want to wreck it.

"Can I ask you something?" she said at last.

"Sure." *Here it comes*, I thought. This is the part where she'll ask me why I'd been such a jerk all those years ago. Why I'd pushed her away and disappeared. I swallowed hard, trying to decide how much I should say.

She turned towards me and fixed her big blue eyes on mine, and I swear they burned like a blowtorch, so hot and bright I almost had to look away. Part of me just wanted to run and hide because there was no way I could lie to her again. Instead, I shoved a scone into my mouth, thinking that huge bite might buy me some time because my mother would roll over in her grave if I talked with my mouth full. And I had enough ghosts haunting me, thank you very much.

"Would you talk to me about Delia sometime? I just...haven't been here as much as I should have recently, and I figured you might could clue me in on some things."

She stared at me while I chewed.

"Oh," I said, trying not to choke on blueberries and relief. "Things like what?"

Her brow furrowed. "I'm just curious about how she's getting along, what you've had to help her with, that sort of thing."

She still acted like asking for help was something to be ashamed of. I wanted to tell her it was fine, that she could ask me for anything. I'd bring her the moon if she asked for it.

I swallowed hard as she leaned closer and placed her hand on my arm. "I appreciate everything you've done to help her," she said, her voice softening. "I really do. I just feel like I'm out of the loop, and my mom won't tell me these things—because they don't even register with her—and Delia won't ever tell me something's wrong because she's too proud." Her voice dropped a little, and for the first time, she looked sad.

I wanted to pull her into my lap, fold her in my arms and never let her go. Fiona was proud, too, and I knew this wasn't easy for her to ask.

"I just want to know what I can do to help," she said. "I need someone to be straight with me. You'll do that, right?"

"Of course," I told her. "Anything you need."

She nodded, looking relieved. "Thanks, Alex." It was the first time she'd called me by name since I'd seen her again. Hearing my name on her lips felt like coming home.

I wanted to hear it again. A thousand times. A million. First thing in the morning, and in the middle of the night.

For all the nights I had left on this earth.

As she leaned back in her chair and sipped her tea, she looked like she was blinking back tears.

"Hey," I said, "What about tomorrow night? Come by my house for dinner, and we'll talk. Ask me anything."

She nodded again, avoiding my gaze, and tucked a lock of her dark hair behind her ear. Cut just below her chin at an angle, it fell in loose waves that drew my eye straight to her lovely collarbones.

"Or tonight," I said. "I've got a couple of things to finish up at the house, but we could talk tonight instead."

"Tomorrow's fine." She tapped her fingers on the glass, the way she used to when she was preoccupied with a problem.

"Fiona," I said, and resisted the urge to touch her cheek. "Come tonight. I can see you're worried about something. Let's get it off your mind."

She sighed and turned towards me again. "I'm sorry about yesterday. I was rude to you."

I smiled. "It's okay." I'd been an idiot, pushing her away all those years ago. She'd never know how much I regretted that night. All I wanted was to make that up to her. "How's eight? I'll cook dinner."

"That's not necessary." She gave me a tiny smile.

"Come on, I insist. And then you can bring leftovers back for Delia."

"Really," she said. "It's okay. I didn't mean to spring this on you."

I reached over then, before I could stop myself, and placed my hand on hers. Her fingers stilled and her eyes shifted back to mine.

"Let me help," I said. "Come to dinner. We'll talk."

She arched a brow, and there was a hint of a smile. "Okay, you win. What can I bring?"

"Not a thing."

Her lip curved upward, and it was like one more brick fell out of that giant wall she'd built around herself. I hadn't expected her to ask for my help, but I was glad that she did. I owed her a good turn, and this was a decent start.

# Chapter Eight

## FIONA

IT WAS impossible to forget the vast expanse of hard muscle that had been burned into my retinas when I'd nearly collided with Alex behind the barn. Add that to the list of unforgettable things about him, right below *heartbreaker*.

Now, watching him stride across the meadow toward the farmhouse next door, I sipped the rest of my iced tea and held the cold glass against my cheek. It was just dinner. Just to talk. About Delia. Nothing more.

I didn't want to ask him for favors. I didn't want to feel indebted to anyone—especially not Alex Fox.

And yet, spending a little time with him today hadn't been completely awful.

He'd been around Aunt Delia more than I had in the last few years, and I had questions that needed answers. But why did he have to be so dang charming? And ridiculously hot half-naked? He wasn't making it easy to keep my distance from him. I might have let go of that grudge I'd held against him for ages, but if Penelope taught me one useful thing, it was that you forgive and *remember*.

Regardless of the perfect hair and sculpted abs. Remember.

"Focus," I said out loud. "You have work to do. The last thing you need to be thinking about is Alex Fox's six-pack."

When I said it the second time, I almost believed it.

---

"GO HAVE FUN," Delia said. "You're wound up tighter than a rattlesnake in a pea patch."

"It's just dinner," I said. "I want to talk to him about some repairs you need over here."

Delia waggled her hand dismissively. "I won't wait up." That twinkle in her eyes was unmistakable—it meant she'd slipped fully into matchmaker mode.

"I'm going to check in on you every hour," I said. "If you don't answer, I'm coming home."

"You worry too much," she said. "Rufus and I are going to curl up and watch a movie—something with that adorable Ryan Reynolds and some kissing in the rain. We'll be fine."

I grabbed the bottle of wine I'd bought in town and headed across the meadow toward Alex's house. First I'd thought about baking a pie for dessert and then decided not to. Wine was better. Pie was an investment in time, and it sent the wrong message—it meant love and caring, and I couldn't have Alex Fox thinking I'd spent hours baking something for him. Wine was neighborly. More aloof and mysterious.

Never mind that it had taken me twenty minutes to choose the wine in the market on Main Street.

My stomach twisted into a knot as I walked closer to the house. *It's just dinner*, I told myself. *It's just to talk about Delia. This is not a big deal.*

I didn't find myself super convincing.

Alex's yard was huge, thick with lush grass, and lined with camellias and lantana that were already blooming. The barn behind the house looked like it had been remodeled into a workspace.

Beyond it was a copse of trees where the woods gave way to the wetlands, where a chorus of chirping frogs made the air vibrate.

Taking a deep breath, I walked up onto the porch and knocked on the door.

Inside there was a crash, then the thumping of feet approaching.

When the front door opened, Alex said, "Fiona. You're right on time," and there it was again, the sound of my name lingering on his tongue, making my skin tingle the way it does in a summer storm.

Super.

"No traffic," I said, handing him the wine. "Hope you like red."

"Thank you." He smiled warmly and led me to the kitchen, where there were stainless steel appliances, a small island with bar stools, and a rustic dining table set for two. This wasn't a date, but already I was wishing I'd at least changed out of my tee shirt and paint-splattered jeans. Alex wore a green button-down shirt tucked into dark slim-cut jeans, with a tooled leather belt that kept catching my eye.

I'd wanted to make sure I sent a message that said this was casual, but now I just felt like a slob.

"You getting used to Jasmine Falls again?" he said.

"Sure." I sat at the island, trying to focus on something in the room that was not Alex's eyes, or shoulders, or hands. "It's somehow really different, but still just the same."

He smirked. "Accurate. Sometimes it feels like a time capsule."

"How long have you been in this house?" I said.

"A little over a year. After I got back on my feet. Turns out the place needed more repairs than I'd thought, though. Gave me a chance to practice my carpentry skills."

Had I really not been in this town in over a year?

"The house really is beautiful," I said, and he gave me a tender smile.

He deftly opened the bottle of wine, and I didn't miss the way the muscles of his broad forearms rippled when he popped the cork out. He poured two glasses and handed me one. When his fingers brushed mine, there was a tingle along my skin that I tried desperately to ignore.

"I didn't know you liked that sort of thing," I told him, imagining what, in this giant house, he might have remodeled. Aside from obvious updates in the kitchen, it was nearly impossible to tell—no part of it looked out of place.

"I didn't either," he said. "But it turns out, building with wood is almost as satisfying as iron." His eyes rested on mine as he sipped his wine and said, "Here, let me show you around."

He gave me a quick tour of the downstairs: there was an open floor plan kitchen and living room area with a bedroom suite off to one side, an office, and a big screened-in porch off the back. The wood paneling had been pickled so it was a pale brown, and the rafters had been left exposed. With sparse rustic furniture, the overall effect was one of comfortable open space—but somehow it also felt empty.

"When I bought this place, I needed a project to take my mind off—well, everything." He gave me a sad smile and said, "You probably heard about all of that. This town has zero secrets."

That much was true: Delia had filled me in on all the details about Alex's marriage, and divorce, back when it was the top gossip in town. Apparently, because of legal problems (or more specifically, Lori trying to grab Alex's inheritance), they'd been separated longer than they'd been married.

"I'm sorry," I said. "That must have been so hard." As angry as I'd been with Alex, I didn't wish that kind of awful divorce on anyone.

"Feels like another lifetime." He stared at me for a long moment.

"For the record, there were some wild stories about where you were for a few years." Despite my gag order, Delia couldn't help herself. She'd told me the most outrageous stories, only because there was no way they were true.

"Such as?" He gave me a good-natured smile but stiffened like he was bracing for a hurricane.

"Like you'd gotten married again and moved down to Florida to work at an animal park."

He sipped his wine. "Nah. Just the one ex-wife."

"Or that you'd gone full-on cowboy and were working on a dude ranch in New Mexico."

He smirked. "I'm terrified of horses. I'd rather have the alligators in Florida."

"Or that you'd won a ton of money on scratch-offs and had bought some mansion on an exclusive island near Charleston and were living like Pablo Escobar."

He laughed that deep laugh that filled the whole room and made my chest vibrate.

Lordy, I'd missed that sound.

"Surrounded by coked-up hippos," he said. "Great."

"Okay, I might have made that last one up," I said, laughing so hard that I snorted.

"Well, let me put all the rumors to rest." He leaned closer and set his bright green eyes on mine. "The truth is that right after college, Lori and I got married. Then we got divorced, shortly after my parents died. Then I went up near Aiken to apprentice with one of the most famous metalsmiths in the region." He took a sip of wine. "I wanted to start over. So I did. But sadly there were no private islands or winning lottery tickets."

"I was really sorry to hear about your folks. I should have gotten in touch." Delia had told me all about it—a freak car accident. By the time I'd heard about it, it was months after the fact.

"Thanks," he said, looking thoughtful. "It was a weird time. But then I got my fresh start. I came back here, settled their estate, and bought this place. Built the studio. Things are okay now."

I nodded, wishing I could think of something more supportive to say.

"I heard some wild stories about you, too," he said. His friendly smile was back, and he looked more at ease.

"Oh boy," I said. "Fair's fair, I guess."

His brow arched. "Like you were a forest ranger working in some remote part of Alaska, and the only way you could get there was by plane."

"Close, but not quite. My ex was the ranger."

"Or that you were working as a cruise director, moving from one exotic Mediterranean island to another."

"That one doesn't sound half bad. Not sure I'm perky enough for a cruise ship, though."

He grinned. "No way that one was true. Not unless you magically became a morning person."

I snorted. "Not even close."

"The fiancé, though…"

"That one was real," I said.

"I'm sorry. That he hurt you, I mean." His brows knit together in a thoughtful way. "But I'm not sorry you're here."

His gaze was intense, drawing me closer. But I wasn't ready to be quite so close. Something in my heart squeezed at the thought of Dean, and that humiliation hit me all over again. I took another drink of wine and tamped those thoughts down as far as they would go.

"I wanted to thank you again for taking care of Delia," I said, eager to change the subject. "I hadn't realized how concerned I was until today, and then it just hit me like a brick. I've just been away so long, and there are all these things I should know. It feels wrong being in the dark."

He nodded, walking over to the oven to peek inside. "It's okay, Fiona. I get it."

I felt overwhelmed again, by gratitude, by shame, by embarrassment. "I really am sorry about yesterday. I was being hard on you, and I shouldn't have." He'd no doubt seen right through my fake politeness, and yet he'd been nothing but kind.

"We should talk about that sometime." His tone was friendly but serious. "But the short answer is, bygones. I deserve a little anger—honestly, maybe a lot. There's a lot I wish I could take back. But we're older now, and I imagine we're both pretty different than those kids we were back then." He leaned against the kitchen island and said, "If it's all right with you, I'd like to start over."

This older version of Alex was straightforward, confident. He seemed guarded, but at the same time, his eyes were wide and hopeful. I considered his words for a moment, and then clinked my glass against his and downed the last bit of wine. Being here, in this house, so close to Alex in his own space gave me an unsteady feeling. I felt lost, like I didn't know how to behave in Jasmine Falls anymore—with him, or with Delia. Who was I anymore?

"I'd like that, too."

A tiny smile touched his lips as he refilled my glass.

He turned back to the oven, pulling out a covered dish of pot roast and vegetables that smelled magical, and I let out a heavy sigh. Was there anything Alex Fox couldn't do?

If he wanted to mend fences with pot roast and casseroles, that was fine by me.

"You're not a vegetarian, are you?" he said, raising a brow. "I should have asked that earlier."

"No way."

He smirked and took the dish to the table. As he brushed past me, I tried—and failed—to ignore the way his jeans fit him perfectly, drawing my attention exactly where it did not need to be.

"Sit," he said. "And let's get down to business."

And then my traitorous body felt full of electric current.

*Stop*, I thought. *Alex Fox broke your heart. Alex Fox does not get to give you butterflies. You came here for one reason. Get it together.*

But as Alex sat across from me, his deep green eyes steady on mine, that reason left my brain entirely.

Alex was confident, but not cocky. He was charming and polite, obviously trying to put me at ease. He still had that mischievous twinkle in his eye, and hair that was just unruly enough to stand up like he'd just rolled out of bed. The deep bass of his voice was soothing, and each time he spoke, he seemed to chip away a tiny piece of that wall I'd so carefully built around myself.

Still, I couldn't let myself get too close. I couldn't think of his muscular arms, his woodsy cologne, his scruffy beard stubble that made my skin tingle. That was the path that led to heartache, and I couldn't go through that again.

Alex Fox was off-limits. Full stop.

"Delia," I blurted. "How do you think she's really getting along?"

He raised a brow, the spell broken.

"She's good for the most part," he said. "A little slower getting around, but heck, so am I. A while back I started mowing her grass, trimming hedges, sawing up dead trees, anything that required moving something heavier than a bag of cat food."

"That's really good of you to do. I don't know how to thank you for that."

"You don't have to," he said, taking a bite of beef. "She's a sweet lady, and she's been kind to me over the years."

"Has she had any health problems that you know of?"

He shook his head. "She doesn't tell me everything, but the only thing she ever mentioned was a little high blood pressure. She was annoyed that she had to take a medication for it, but I've never heard her mention anything else." He sipped his water and said, "I just see her slowing down some, you know? She can't work outside in the heat anymore, or spend half a day weeding her flower beds. She's in good shape for her age, but she's just not as spry as she once was."

"I know." It made me sad to think about Delia being able to do less of the things she loved. "I should have been around more. I let Mom push me away, and that was stupid."

"What do you mean?"

I bit my lip. I hadn't intended to tell Alex these things, but here I was, singing like a canary as soon as he gave me a few warm smiles and a delicious beef roast. "She didn't like my ex, so I didn't come to visit. I could have just come without him, but that felt like giving in to her." I shook my head, still angered by the thought. "I never should have done that, because it meant I didn't see Delia, either."

"Your ex," he said. "As in the ex-fiancé?"

"He who shall not be named."

He raised a brow. "So if she didn't like him, why'd she put that half-page announcement in the paper?"

I groaned. "Tradition. She said it looked like you were trying to hide something if you didn't make a big announcement." It was completely ridiculous, but my mother put her reputation above nearly everything else, and she never did anything halfway. "She couldn't have everyone thinking I'd had a shotgun wedding or something."

He scoffed. "Doesn't she know those aren't a thing anymore?"

"You try arguing with Penelope and see how far you get."

He stared at me for a long moment, like there was more he wanted to say. Then he reached for his glass.

"The best part was when she announced the wedding was canceled," I said. "Like she just had to rub my face in a failure. Publicly."

"Yeah, there's nothing like having your mistakes broadcast to the whole world."

He was referring to Lori, of course. Now was my chance to get more of his side of the story, but when his brow furrowed, I couldn't do it. It felt like poking a wound.

"I've wondered about the day I'd bump into you again," he said. He rested his chin in his hand, his eyes wide in the soft light. His fingers traced his stubbly beard and I tried not to imagine how it would feel against my skin. "I considered a hundred things I could possibly say."

"Like what?" I said.

He smiled at that. "'I'm sorry' doesn't feel like enough. I hurt you, Fiona, and I know that. Leaving you was the biggest mistake of my life."

I didn't know what to say to that, but it felt like a sizable chunk had fallen from that wall around my heart.

"I don't expect you to tell me it's okay," he said. "I just wanted you to know that it wasn't something I just forgot about. You weren't someone I forgot about."

My phone buzzed in my pocket and I glanced down.

"Do you need to get that?" he said.

"It could be Aunt D." I pulled it from my pocket and tapped the screen.

**I'm still alive, FYI. Tell Alex hello.**

Had it been an hour already?

**I'll check on you in an hour,** I wrote.

**I won't wait up. You're old enough to have sleepovers.**

**OMG,** I wrote. **Stop.**

"Sorry," I said to Alex, shoving the phone back into my pocket. "I told her I'd check up on her every hour."

He smiled. "She's lucky to have you here." There was a softness in his gaze that made me want to simultaneously climb into his lap and run out the back door.

What on earth was happening to me? This was not a road I should venture down again. *Fool me once,* and all of that.

Off-limits. If I repeated it like a mantra, maybe my heart would get the message. So far, it was being pretty dang stubborn.

"What's in the building out back?" I said, changing the subject. "It looks like you remodeled it."

"That's part of the reason I bought this place," he said. "It was a decent workshop. Now it's a forge."

Of course: Delia had mentioned the sculpture he was working on for the library, and the numerous commissions he'd had. "Sounds like you're kind of a rock star," I said, finally feeling more relaxed from the wine.

He smiled. "Hardly. But I'm finally making a living at it."

"That makes me happy to hear," I said, thinking of my stalled career. I'd been so close to making a living, too. And now here I was, homeless and penniless. Mojo-less. I leaned back in my chair, thinking of the stack of unfinished paintings, the feeling of dread I had when I picked up my brushes, thinking that I'd never sell enough to be successful. "I'd give anything for that."

He smiled and said, "It sounds like you still put a lot of pressure on yourself. Maybe you need to do something different and get out of your head for a while."

Raising a brow, I waited to hear what Alex Fox would propose to get me out of my head.

He stroked his chin, and my eyes followed his fingers a little too closely. "What if I had a proposition for you? A project that wasn't a waste of your time?"

The mischievous glint was back in his eyes.

His words were entirely too tempting.

# Chapter Nine

## ALEX

FIONA LOOKED SKEPTICAL. "What kind of proposition?"

"Let me show you." I led her out to the barn, which I'd completely gutted and turned into a studio. When I pulled the big sliding door open, Fiona let out a little gasp that made the back of my neck tingle.

It *was* kind of amazing. Modeled after my friend Eli's studio, it had polished concrete floors, nine-foot ceilings, and three distinct works spaces including one kept clean for drafting. There was a big furnace in the back, a couple of stations with smaller coal furnaces, a power hammer, an anvil the size of a small dining table, and a wall filled with all of my hanging tools. If I was going to build a studio, I was going to do it right.

"Wow," Fiona said, picking up one of the hammers. "You're not messing around."

"It was sort of a gift to myself."

"Show me something you've made," she said, her eyes coming back to rest on mine.

My heart swelled as I watched her. She was interested in the space and she was curious about my work. That was a very good sign.

In the back, I showed her a five-foot section of iron railing I was trying to finish.

"This is for a gate," I said. "There's a resort down in Folly Beach that commissioned it. I have to install it in sections, but once it's done, it's about sixty feet of railings with a twelve-foot gate that opens for visitors."

"This is incredible," she said. "Delia said your work was beautiful, but I never imagined it being like this." She studied the curved pieces of iron, sliding her fingers over the hammered surface. It was one of my favorite designs, but a beast to complete. With its slim rails and intricate curling vines, it had taken over a hundred hours already. When it was finished, it would have copper leaves with an antique finish.

On the work table were a bunch of loose pieces that hadn't been soldered into place yet—mostly vines and leaves made from other metals. Fiona picked up a foot-long section of brass vine that had a life-sized hummingbird attached and studied it carefully.

"I sort of fell into it," I said. "I started out doing really basic handrails and functional pieces. Then after my mentorship, I picked up a few commissions from local people who wanted fancy door knockers and lamps and things, and then I made yard ornaments and sold them in the little gallery downtown." I picked up a section with copper leaves and ran my finger over a rough spot. "Then I got a couple of big commissions for a golf club in Charleston, and then the library in Columbia, and then it just sort of took off."

She turned to me and leveled those big blue eyes on mine, and all I could think was how lucky I was to have her back in the same room with me again. "You've got a ridiculous amount of talent," she said. "But I know it takes a lot of work, too."

"I got lucky. Met the right people at the right time."

She brushed a lock of hair behind her ear, her expression thoughtful.

"And the community here's been great, too," I said. "The art scene's growing. The gala's a big draw, and there's even a few pop-up galleries here."

"I never thought people in Jasmine Falls cared that much about art. It's kind of why I left." She looked off to the side. "Well, that and my mother."

*And maybe me*, I thought.

"I never expected to come back, either," I told her.

"Why did you?" she asked. "I thought you couldn't wait to get out of here."

"That was true when I was twenty. I couldn't get out of Jasmine Falls fast enough." Especially after Fiona left. Everything reminded me of her, and it felt like I was suffocating.

"Yeah, me too." She spoke so quietly that it felt like a punch to the ribs.

"It was hard being here sometimes," I said. Through all the Lori stuff, in particular. I'd been afraid that everyone would side with her and make me out to be the villain. But in the end, they hadn't. Lori hadn't been able to fool them all the way she'd fooled me. My friends here had stuck by me, and then things took a turn for the better.

"I guess after the dust settled, I realized this place had all the things I wanted," I told her. Except for one really important thing.

Fiona.

But I couldn't say that.

She smiled. "I'm really glad it's working out for you."

"It could work out for you, too. We could arrange a show in town for you with your new work, and I know some businesses in town would hang your paintings for sale—you know Gwen would."

She bit her bottom lip, like she was considering it, and my chest felt like it was full of butterflies. I knew it would take a while to earn back her trust. I just wanted enough time to get there. I had to convince her to stay.

"This county's not big enough for me and my mother," she said.

"She's like a neutron star. The closer you get, the more doomed you are."

My chest tightened. Fiona's mother had always been a bully, and I couldn't understand why Fiona didn't just tell her where she could shove all her controlling, pretentious nonsense. Penelope had always struck me as snooty and entitled and had specific ideas about how her daughter should spend her life.

Spoiler alert: it wasn't as an artist.

My parents, though, they'd supported me in all of my creative pursuits, even when they flopped. They'd taught me that failures were just stepping stones to successes, and though I'd taken some hard blows over the last few years, I still believed that—even after they'd died. It was because of them that I'd refused to give up when my first freelance business had failed, and when my marriage had crumbled. I couldn't imagine how I'd have gotten through those times with parents like Penelope.

If only I could wave a magic wand in Fiona's general direction and clear away all that self-doubt. She was brilliant, talented, and too good for me, for sure—but she could never quite seem to see it, and for that I blamed Penelope.

"You could avoid her here," I said. "All this dirt and swampland —how often does your mother set foot on actual grass?"

Fiona smiled so her dimples showed. Mercy, I loved those dimples.

"Her power increases with proximity," she said. "It's best for us both if I'm as far away from her as possible. Besides, I've got no reason to stay here. I'm just here long enough to help Delia, and then I'm out of here."

The words stung. I'd lost her once and didn't want her to slip away again. I knew what it was like to feel trapped in a small town, but I knew how supportive this community could be, too. Everyone here loved Fiona, but she didn't seem to see that, either.

"Donate a painting for the gala," I said. "That's a good way to get into the community and let people see your new work. There's a great tourist market here, and I think people would love your paintings. You said you wanted a fresh start, right?"

She shrugged, leaning against the work table. "I don't know."

"Give it a shot," I said moving next to her. "What do you have to lose?"

Her eyes rested on mine again, and I was not thinking about the gala anymore. My heart hammered in my chest as she turned toward me, her face softer, and she stared at me like she wanted to kiss me. The thought of that sent my head spinning.

I reached over and brushed a lock of hair from her eyes. "Why did you want to come here tonight?"

"I was worried about Delia." Her eyes dropped to my lips.

I slid my hand over hers. "Is that the only reason?"

She bit her lip as she looked up at me, and my heart was melting. I placed my hands on either side of her hips, gripping the edge of the table. When I leaned down so our eyes were level, her lips were almost touching mine.

My heart pounded as I imagined her kissing me with those full lips, sliding her hands down my back. She looked at me like she was imagining the same, and the thought nearly set me on fire.

"I thought I'd never see you again," I whispered. "I dreamed about this moment a thousand times, and now here you are."

Her eyes widened and her cheeks flushed, and I was a goner. When I brushed my lips against hers, she let out this tiny sigh that completely unraveled me. When I deepened the kiss, my whole body lit up.

All that stuff about how it feels like fireworks? It's completely true.

I slid my hand along her jaw, hoping this would never end, but then she gasped and pulled away.

I moved back, trying to read her expression.

"I should go," she said. She stared at me through those long lashes and put her hand on my chest, gently putting more distance between us. "It's late."

"What's wrong?" I said, but I knew full well, and I couldn't blame her. The last time we'd been alone like this, I'd pushed her away. I'd hurt her, and she'd never seen it coming.

Being struck with the power hammer would have hurt less than seeing her look at me this way—like she didn't trust me.

Before I could say anything more, she'd slipped through my arms and was hurrying towards the big bay door.

When I got to the door, she was already in the field, walking away from me as fast as she could.

Well. I screwed that up. Royally.

I opened my mouth to call after her, and then thought better of it. No need to make this more awkward by hollering across a field.

I shouldn't have kissed her.

We were supposed to just have a friendly dinner and chat about Miss Delia—that's what I'd offered, and that's what she was expecting. I'd just wanted to do something nice for her and try to put her mind at ease because I could tell she was worried about her aunt. And then here she was in her paint-splattered jeans, smiling so those tiny laugh lines at her eyes showed, and I felt like I was seeing her again for the first time. When she'd finally relaxed a little and decided I might not be the big bad wolf after all, she'd laughed that raucous laugh of hers that was completely contagious, and all I could think about was convincing her to spend the next hour with me.

And then she did, and it was like winning the lottery.

Then I got hopeful and screwed it all up.

Pacing around the studio, I stopped in front of the disaster that was my piece for the gala. I hadn't even gotten a chance to show it to Fiona and ask her what she thought. At first, I thought she was just humoring Delia by agreeing to look at it, but then she seemed so interested in the forge and the way things worked that I thought she might be into it. When Delia had first mentioned it to her, I'd been horrified. Usually, this kind of work came pretty easy to me, but this piece had me stumped. How hard could it be to make a tree?

This piece could mean lots of future commissions—or it could be my last.

I'd wanted to propose a plan that could help us both—but she'd run out of here before I could.

My fingers traced the tangle of pieces that made up the iron tree trunk. I'd gotten so wrapped up in making the texture and shape of the tree that I'd lost sight of the bigger picture they wanted it to represent.

I'd woven slender pieces together to make a trunk that looked like cypress, with undulating roots that would roll along the ground before sinking beneath it. In my head, it had been a brilliant idea, but now it seemed too literal.

Part of me wanted to melt it down and start over.

Sort of like I wanted to do with Fiona. A few days ago, she acted like she wanted to feed me to Delia's cat. Then tonight, she'd warmed up, and I felt a spark of something between us. I could have sworn she felt it, too.

But then I kissed her, and she bolted.

I slid my fingers over the tree. Maybe I'd read everything wrong.

But maybe that was the point.

Fiona had never been petty, but had she led me on just to hurt me? Make me feel rejected? It was evident she still felt hurt by what I'd done back when I was twenty-two and too much of a coward to tell her the real reason I was breaking up with her. Had she really just come over here to toy with me and then push me away out of spite? When she first saw me at Delia's, she looked like she couldn't get away from me fast enough. After all this time, I'd assumed she'd gotten over us, especially when I heard she got engaged. But maybe that wound went deeper than I'd thought.

I'd gotten ahead of myself, thinking of all the ways we could start over, and all the ways I could try to make this up to her, and show her I wasn't that dumb kid anymore. Show her that I'd fight for her this time and that nothing would make me walk away.

And I'd let myself believe that maybe, just maybe, she might feel the same way.

I leaned against the work table, in the spot she'd been just a little while earlier. There was just the faintest hint of her perfume, hanging in the air like a ghost.

After some thought, I pulled my phone from my pocket and started to text her. I should just send a message and try to clear this up. First I typed **I'm sorry**, then tried **Can we talk for a minute.**

I didn't want to believe it, but the more I thought about it, the more it made sense in a weird kind of way. Her coolness that had seemed to change in just one dinner into something that felt like a spark. It had certainly felt real to me, but maybe it really was just an act.

I deleted the text, feeling like a fool. And thinking I probably deserved it.

Message received. Loud and clear.

# Chapter Ten

FIONA

HALFWAY THROUGH THE FIELD, I was wishing it was a longer walk back to Delia's. I needed time to cool off and push all these thoughts of Alex Fox right out of my brain.

When he'd leaned in close to me, caging me in with his arms, a current had zipped along my skin. His breath was warm against my neck, stunning me like one of those rabbits hypnotized at the fair. When he'd kissed me, I'd felt my whole body light up like a Christmas tree and I'd wanted to feel those lips on every part of me.

But then I thought of that night on his porch all those years ago, and how he'd so carelessly pushed me out of his life after being with another woman, lying about all of it to my face. Dumping me out of the blue was bad enough, but cheating on me was something I'd never thought he would do. I'd trusted him completely, and had thought he was the one person who would never hurt me. He was the only one who understood how hurt I'd been when my mom left me behind with Delia, and he knew how hard it was for me to trust people and let them get close.

And when he'd betrayed that trust, it hurt worse than anything my mom had ever done. I expected her to hurt me—but never Alex.

As much as I wanted to feel his big arms around me, feel the strength of those solid hands that forged metal from fire, I couldn't shake the thought that he could hurt me all over again. And when he said those words—*I thought I'd never see you again, I dreamed about this a thousand times*—they stung like a slap across the cheek.

I'd let him get so close, making myself forget about all that hurt. But when his lips were brushing mine, I'd felt like I was about to tumble over the side of a cliff. Panic had washed over me like a wave.

He'd looked at me, so full of longing, and my heart felt like a grenade with the pin pulled.

"What's wrong?" he'd said, and I thought, *Nothing. Everything.*

---

"HOW WAS YOUR DATE?" Delia asked me the next morning.

"It wasn't a date." Disaster? Yes. Dumpster fire? Absolutely. Date? No way.

Delia's Sunday morning ritual was to sit on the porch swing with coffee and the crossword. I'd just finished feeding all the animals and was in dire need of coffee and some magical pill that would make me forget everything that had happened the night before.

"Did he show you his studio?" Delia said this with a twinkle in her eye, like *studio* was some sort of euphemism.

I sighed, thinking of that massive work table and how he'd looked at me like he wanted to lay me out on it. One intense gaze from Alex Fox, one stroke of his fingers along my cheek and I'd melted like butter in the summertime. So much for my solid resolve.

"It's quite the setup," I said, trying to think of anything except what had almost happened on that workbench. "His work is amazing." *His hands are amazing, his lips are amazing.*

*Stop it*, I thought, biting my lip. *No thinking of lips, hands, and other delightful parts.*

"Oh yes," Delia said. "He's had some high-profile clients. A couple of celebrities down on Sullivan's Island, a resort at Hilton Head. He even did a sculpture for the state art museum up in Columbia."

"Holy smokes." If only I had some clients with deep pockets. Alex had made a name for himself as an artist, and here I was with no home, no inspiration, and no savings account.

And no clue about what to do first to rectify that.

"He stays busy year-round," she said. "I heard there's a two-year-long wait list for him."

"Good for him," I said, trying not to sound crabby. "I wish I was in that position." I thought again of the precarious position we'd been in the night before, him holding me exactly where he wanted me without even touching me. I'd do better to work toward my own two-year waitlist. I did not need to be all smitten with Alex Fox.

"You will be," Delia said, matter-of-factly.

"What?" I said. Had I said that last part out loud?

"It seems to me you just haven't found your audience yet," Delia said. "You'll get there." Sipping her coffee, she said, "You two have a lot in common. I'm glad y'all bumped into each other again."

I snorted. "Bumped into each other?" Like Aunt Delia hadn't carefully scheduled a collision.

"Mmm-hmm," Delia said, as if she didn't catch my meaning. "Did he show you the piece for the library?"

"Actually, no." I'd bolted before he could show it to me and tell me what had him so perplexed. He'd also mentioned a proposition, but we hadn't made it to that, either.

Or had we?

She glanced up at me and grinned. "Too busy catching up, were you?"

Studying the floorboards of the porch, I said, "You've got some loose nails coming up. Where's your hammer?"

"Kitchen drawer, next to the oven mitts."

I went back inside and rummaged through the drawers until I found the small hammer. Fixing floorboards was better than thinking about Alex. Or thinking about how well all of his parts fit together and how they used to fit with mine.

Good grief. What on earth was the matter with me?

Back on the porch, I got down on my knees and knocked the first nail back down. There were at least a dozen that were popping up like little seedlings, just high enough to catch a shoe and trip you.

"I always liked Alex," Delia said. "He's grown into a nice young man. And handsome, too."

"Don't get your hopes up, Aunt D." I kept my tone breezy, like it was a laughable idea, and pounded the next nail down. "Nothing is happening between me and Alex."

She smiled, pushing the swing.

I asked, "How's the knee?"

"Hurts a bit, but not as bad as it was. I'll make it." She sipped her coffee, thoughtful.

"I know what you're thinking, but it won't work. We have too much history."

She arched a brow, but said nothing, as if she didn't believe that for a second.

Smacking the next nail down, I said, "He broke my heart."

*Bam*, another nail.

"Oh, honey," she said. She didn't know all the details of the breakup—I hadn't even told my mother, because even back then, I knew how much Penelope relished being right. My mother was bitter about love back then. She'd softened a bit over the decades (see Exhibit A, Simon), but even with him, she didn't appear affectionate. She was friendly with him, but that wasn't the same thing as being tender. Not by a long shot.

No, my mother had thought love was a waste of time when I was a teenager. She'd constantly warned me about the perils of dating and marriage, making both sound worse than a zombie apocalypse. So when Alex Fox crushed me into a million little pieces, the last person I wanted to know about it was my mother.

Instead, I'd told her and Delia both that Alex and I had just grown apart when I was at college, and I'd just wanted to focus on my degree. That proclamation had delighted my mother, who still managed to squeeze in a deftly placed, "I'd hoped you'd come around to that epiphany yourself without my having to help."

Now though, there was no reason to keep Delia in the dark anymore. "It's true," I said. "It was awful. I came home from college one weekend to surprise him, and he'd been cheating on me with Lori Gifford. He dumped me that night—wouldn't even let me come inside his house! For all I know, she was in his bedroom the entire time. I felt like a fool."

Delia stopped pushing the swing, her eyes widening. "What?"

"He'd been seeing her for weeks. Maybe months, even. I should have kicked him in the balls, like you taught me. If I had a time machine, I'd do it."

She frowned. "That training was only for emergencies. Like a kidnapping. It's not intended for general use."

"You going to tell me you think he didn't deserve it?"

Her eyebrow arched. "Well, hon, I think he got his fair share of comeuppance for that lousy move." When I didn't respond, she said, "He married Lori, and she treated him like a dog. She fooled around with some fella behind his back, and everybody in town knew it except Alex. I felt so bad for the boy. He was working his tail off to build a house she wanted. Then she divorced him and took almost everything."

I whacked another nail into place and felt a twinge that stung like heartburn.

"That was one messy divorce," she said. "They were separated longer than they were married because first, she said he beat her, then she claimed he cheated on her, and then she threatened to sue him for lack of affection or some such nonsense." She shook her head and twirled her fork. "She had the whole town thinking he'd done something awful to her, and if he hadn't spent his last dime on a good lawyer, he really would have lost everything—including what his parents left him."

I swallowed hard, feeling like she'd just punched me in the gut. "Well, now I feel like a jerk."

"I'm just saying, what he got was a lot worse than being kicked in the balls. I think you can let that go." She offered one of those thoughtful stares that only white-haired ladies have mastered—the kind that makes you feel about two inches tall.

"Why did you never tell me any of that?"

She shrugged. "You made it pretty clear you didn't want to talk about him. I figured there was more to your breakup, but I also knew you'd tell me when you were good and ready."

I smacked another nail down.

"I don't think he's been in a serious relationship since he's been back here," Delia said.

"Surely he has." That was three years ago if I was doing the math correctly.

She shook her head. "He's been known to date here and there, but there was never anybody else serious. I think she might have broken him."

"Well, there you go. I don't need someone who's broken. I'm broken enough myself." Dean took more than my money with him when he went to Alaska. He took my trust, too.

She gave me that thoughtful look again that could cut glass and said, "Sweetheart, we all get broken sometimes. The whole point of living is to figure out how to put your pieces back together into something better."

It wasn't hard to see that she was talking about herself. Uncle Frank had died of a heart attack ten years before and left Delia all by herself. She'd never dated anyone else after him, and I'd often wondered why she hadn't. Did she feel like she'd put herself back together? Did she still feel like part of her was broken, even after all this time?

"We don't always get a second chance," she said. "That's all I'm saying."

"Okay," I said, my tone softer. "I get it." I forced out a smile because I didn't want Delia to think I was turning hard like a rock, the way my mother was. Plus it made me sad to think about Delia losing Uncle Frank and being by herself all those years. Then I was sorry I'd made her think about it. I wanted Delia to at least feel like she proved her point, that it had been worthwhile to reach back into that memory.

On the far corner of the porch, there were two nails left. A pro now, I knocked the first one into place with one solid hit.

"You know," Delia said, "you shouldn't give up on Alex so fast. Y'all would make cute babies, and your eggs won't last forever, kid."

The hammer banged against the floorboard, missing the second nail entirely.

"Delia!"

She chuckled like she'd made the funniest joke.

But her words made me think of how close we'd been the night before, how his fingers had felt as they'd brushed my cheek. I'd wanted so badly to feel his hands, his lips, his whole body pinned against mine. There was a time when I felt like he knew me better than anyone else in the world, and there was no one else I'd felt that way about since. I shook my head to push the thought away. No matter how similar we were, I couldn't let myself fall for Alex Fox again. I wasn't ready to give him a second chance, kindred spirit or not. He'd hurt me without even trying, and it was impossible to push aside the thought that he could so easily do it again.

Not every broken thing could be fixed. Not every hurt could be forgotten.

"All done," I said, knocking the last nail into place. "Good as new."

Delia was right about one thing, though: I had put the pieces of myself back together, into something stronger. And I wasn't going to let Alex Fox—or anyone else—shatter me again.

# Chapter Eleven

FIONA

BLANK CANVASES WERE my worst enemy. They were even more annoying than Alex Fox.

For two hours, I'd been trying to paint upstairs in Aunt Delia's workroom. The light was perfect. The breeze was perfect. The room was quiet. Relaxing. Peaceful.

So why couldn't I get anything done?

I'd sketched out a few studies and did some underpaintings, just thin layers of paint to block out where the light and shadow would go when I went back in with more color. I was trying to loosen up and get myself in the groove, just focusing on step one—the composition of bird shapes on the canvas—and not the whole picture.

But it was no use. The canvases I'd started were already a mess.

Desperate to do at least one thing that felt productive, I logged into Instagram to post a few in-process shots: the beautiful studio room, my array of paints, a bird sketch. But no close-ups of the canvases that I'd definitely paint over, because no one needed to see those. When I logged in, an alert popped up with a direct message from a few hours before.

**From @birdwatcherSC:** Is this painting done from a live

specimen? Or a photo? I'd love to talk more with you about it. Please email me at ereiker@camden.edu I have an important question to ask you. Thanks!

My first thought was that this person was interested in buying the painting I'd shared in my post from a few days before. Surprising, since it was such a rough study. It had a nice energy that I liked, but it was nothing special. I'd quickly done it on my first day here, based on the gold and gray bird with the odd markings.

I quickly typed an email in response, telling @birdwatcherSC that it was indeed painted from a bird that I'd seen outside my window.

But then Janet's business-like voice piped up in my head again. "Stories sell, Fiona!" she'd told me. "People want to hear about inspiration. They want to know what drives you to paint. Give them meaningfulness that resonates with them, and they'll connect with a piece and want to take it home."

With Janet's voice in mind, I revised my response. "This was a bird I hadn't seen before, and one that seemed just as curious about me as I was about it," I wrote. "Birds always make me feel like I'm home." Then I sent it—not my best, but it would do.

As I scrolled through the rest of my page, I saw there were a few hundred likes for each painting, which was a good start. Statistically speaking, it took around three hundred likes before I sold a piece. It wasn't a great ratio, but it wasn't nothing. Janet's mantra was *post process and post often.*

When she'd first suggested that, I'd snorted with laughter because my process was about as messy as you could get.

I snapped a photo of my cluttered desk upstairs—my palette smeared with a dozen different colors, some brushes, a couple of sketches, and another small study that looked unfinished. By the time I wrote a quick caption and filled in a few hashtags, I had an email from @birdwatcherSC.

*Dear Fiona,*

*Thank you for writing back to me. I'm a graduate student in ornithology at Camden, and I've followed your Instagram for a while now (fellow #birdnerd). Your paintings are wonderful. The one you posted Friday caught my eye because I believe it could be a rare species that has been deemed extinct for over 40 years. I'm trying not to get too excited yet because there have been many false alarms over this bird. But if this is the bird I think it is, well, it's a big deal. Would you be willing to meet me one day so I could ask you a few questions? If you have photos or other sketches, I would be very interested in seeing them. I'm happy to drive down to where you are and meet you wherever you'd like.*

*Thanks so much,*
*Eric Reiker*

I read the email three times, looking for the catch. Was this a person who would kidnap me and then hack me up into little pieces that he'd leave out in the swamp for gator bait? Or could this be a legit scientific discovery? After considering my options, many of which ended in my demise and a few that ended in TV interviews and internet fame, I went to the Camden University web page and snooped in the ornithology department.

It was, predictably, a small crew.

There were three professors and two teaching assistants listed with contact information. One of them was Eric Reiker. Based on his photo, he was in his early to mid-twenties. The photo was underexposed and a little blurry, as if he'd been caught off-guard before his morning coffee. But he looked harmless enough, with a swoop of blondish hair and black-framed glasses that were a little too big for his angular face.

Reading back over the email, I considered brushing him off, or simply not replying. I was no Luddite, but I wasn't exactly the grand dame of social media, either. I usually got along fine with people in their analog form, but cyberspace was daunting because it left all kinds of room for miscommunication.

Still, I was curious. If this bird was that big a deal, what could it hurt to show the guy what I'd found? Being part of an important scientific discovery didn't happen to everyone. It could be inspiring. It could shake me out of my funk.

It could take my mind off Alex Fox.

Turning back to my laptop, I typed and deleted and typed again until I had the right combination of breezy and slightly aloof.

*Hi, Eric-*

*I don't want to get your hopes up, and I'm no bird expert. If you're up for a road trip down to Jasmine Falls, I'll meet you there. There's a coffee shop on Main Street called the Sentient Bean. I have a couple of blurry photos and one painting, but I'll bring them so you can have a look. When would you like to meet?*

*Fiona*

There. The coffee shop would be a safe place to meet, and if anything weird happened, Gwen would be there for backup. We'd just be two strangers meeting in a public place, and my private information would remain private. If he was some super weird internet dude, I'd be out an hour of my time and a latte—and Gwen could practice the self-defense tactics she'd learned at the extension. But if this did turn out to be something important, then I'd done something to help a young student out. I could probably stand a little good karma.

When I picked up my paintbrush again, my email chimed.

*Dear Fiona,*

*Thank you so much for being willing to meet me! I'm happy to come to Jasmine Falls—it looks like a cool town. Any chance we could meet tomorrow? Say around 4:00? Coffee's on me.*

*Eric*

Well, Eric was certainly eager. Hopefully, that was because he was an overzealous grad student on the trail of an important find, and not because he was a serial killer hungry to find his next victim. I'd be sure to tell Janet, too, even though she was hours away. I typed out a response and hoped this wasn't a mistake that would land me on one of those true crime TV shows.

*Hi, Eric-*

*4:00 is fine. I'll see you there tomorrow.*

*Fiona*

Done. Sent.

Hopefully, this was not something I'd regret.

When I went downstairs, I found Delia napping on the couch. Not wanting to disturb her, I went into the kitchen and searched the cupboards for something I could cook that didn't require a lot of steps.

I'd never been a good cook, despite Delia's efforts to teach me the basics—but if I had a good recipe to go by, I could get by well enough and at least make something edible.

Usually.

At the back of Delia's recipe box, I found one for chicken pot pie. I appreciated a recipe that let you toss all the ingredients into one dish, and then pop it in the oven and walk away with no fear of burning the house down. After adding all the vegetables and chicken into a saucepan to simmer, I rolled out the dough and made a top crust that the chefs on TV would call "rustic." Convinced it was passable, I plopped it on top of the pot pie just as I heard a car come up the driveway.

When I went to the window, I immediately regretted it.

Alex Fox was climbing out of his truck. From ten paces, I could see that he was wearing his snug, broken-in jeans and a slim-cut tee shirt.

My whole body froze. I was not ready to see Alex again. Not after that awkward exchange the night before, with the hands, and the lips, and the pounding heart. And then running away like a rabbit.

Did the man not own any loose-fitting clothes?

He knocked on the back door just as I shoved the pie into the oven, and part of me wished I could climb in there and hide.

"Hey," Delia called, "Is that someone outside?"

Alex peered at me through the glass, his eyebrow arched as if he were somehow not expecting me to be there.

"Hi," I said, opening the door. My voice came out cracked.

"Hi, yourself. I'm returning your goat." Next to him, on the end of a rope, was a small black and white goat with nubs for horns.

"Because you borrowed it?"

"What's that on your face?" His tone was light, teasing even.

I wiped my forehead and cheeks, realizing there must be streaks of flour there. There was a fine dusting of it all down the front of my shirt. It was probably in my hair, too.

Super.

"I was cooking," I said. "Why do you have her goat?"

He squinted, glancing at my shirt. "Domino's her escape artist. I found him a ways down the road again, so I figured the fence might need repairing."

"Oh." I waited for him to say more.

He didn't.

The goat let out a bleat of protest and shook its head as if trying to lose the rope. It was just barely taller than Alex's knees. This was the pygmy goat that Aunt Delia had warned me about—the one that liked to knock people flat so they were eye-level with him.

Delia called from the den. "Is that Alex I hear?"

He looped Domino's rope over the banister rails outside and

stepped past me into the kitchen. His arm barely brushed mine but sent a current rippling over my skin. I followed him into the den as he said, "Hi, Mrs. D." His voice was chipper. "How are you feeling?"

"Can't keep a good woman down for long," she said, sitting up a little. "But sometimes it seems the universe likes to try."

"Domino got out again," he told her. "I brought him back, but I figured I'd take a look at your fence and see if he knocked a board loose."

Delia sighed. "Don't you want to take him back to your house? A man needs a pet."

He smiled and said, "I think he'd just escape and come back over here."

She frowned. "The grass is always greener, I suppose."

His eyes landed on mine as he said, "That's a fact."

My jaw fell open with an audible pop. Did he actually say that to me?

His lingering stare was all the answer I needed.

I glared at him, my cheeks burning. How dare he? I crossed my arms over my chest and said, "Maybe something spooked him. Or maybe he had a lot of feelings and just wanted to leave."

Alex raised a brow and smiled. "Maybe he was just bored," he said, his tone breezy. "Or had something to prove."

My jaw tightened. Was he really trying to shame me over leaving him last night? Could he really not understand how hard it was for me to be there with him?

"Or maybe he knows trouble when he sees it," I said sweetly.

Delia looked from me to Alex and said, "Well, thanks for bringing him back, hon. I don't know what I'd do without you."

"I'll go on down and check the fence," he said. "Shouldn't take me long to fix it." Before I could say anything else, Alex had slipped back through the kitchen and out the back door. I watched as he walked Domino down to the barn, hoping the goat might have the good sense to knock him over along the way.

He didn't, of course. Domino trotted next to him like a puppy.

Annoyed, I went out to the barn where Alex had tied the goat by the trough and was walking the perimeter of the fence, looking for holes.

"What was that back there?" I said, trying to tamp down my anger. The last thing I wanted was for Alex to see how he could still upset me.

"Happens all the time," he said, tugging at a section of the fence. "I fix the holes, and he makes new ones. It's a little game we like to play. I think he just likes a challenge."

Surrounding the barn was a five-foot wire fence with holes that were three inches square. The section of fence that joined the barn was built with wooden slats, like a picket fence, and at the corner was a simple gate. A loop of chain with an S-hook connected the swinging gate to the post at the corner of the barn, but it was old and brittle enough that the goat had been able to push it open and slip through.

"Are you trying to tell me all of that was about a goat?" I said.

"What else would it be about?" He gave me a quick smile as he stepped past me and into the barn. Then he knelt down to rummage around in a toolbox by the door.

"Alex," I said.

"I can do a temporary fix today," he said from inside the barn, "just to keep him from getting out again. I'll come back later and put up a new one."

"A whole new gate?"

"It's not that big a deal."

He'd said he wanted to start over. Be adults about this. But now he was being cheeky and blasé and pretending like these little barbs weren't barbs at all.

Fine. I would be the adult here. I would apologize because he was obviously hurt. Or annoyed. Or something.

"Listen," I said stepping towards the doorway, "Last night was...I...well, I don't know what that was exactly."

He pulled a roll of wire and a pair of cutters from the box and slipped past me. Was he wearing cologne? He smelled woodsy and mysterious and it made me want to stand closer to him.

"I didn't mean to make things awkward between us," I said. "I was just…overwhelmed, I guess. Being back here is all kinds of weird for me."

He knelt down by the broken gate and then ran the wire through the wooden slats. His big forearms flexed as he cinched it against the post.

"Alex?" I wanted to tell him that it was too much, seeing him again. Being so close to him. I was attracted to him, sure—even more than I had been years before—and I hadn't expected that. But when he'd started to kiss me, I'd been yanked back to that night when he'd so callously pushed me aside, and the hurt and the anger had risen up like a tide. And I panicked, as one does when she sees a tsunami coming.

So I did the only thing I knew to do that would make that feeling stop.

I ran.

He slipped another loop of wire through and pulled. "I get it, Fiona," he said, his tone practically chipper. "Message received."

He was calm and collected. Mr. Cool-As-Ice. No ma'am, nothing to see here.

Confused by all this pleasantness, I waited for him to say something else. When he didn't, I said, "Alex, I don't know what you think that was, but—"

He grunted, twisting the wire to hold the gate shut, and my eyes were once again drawn to his ridiculously muscular arms. And shoulders. And *good grief*.

Satisfied with the gate, he stood up and brushed his hands off on his jeans. "Look," he said calmly, "I think you wanted to give me a little payback. And you know what? That's okay. I probably deserve it."

I felt my jaw drop open. "Are you serious right now?"

"Point taken," he said. "Well played."

My head felt hot. "That's not even close to what was happening."

He waved his hands between us, as if in surrender. "It's okay, Fi. I'm not mad."

"I can't believe you'd even suggest that," I said. "Did it ever occur to you that not all of this is about you?"

Domino let out another pointed bleat.

I pointed at Domino and said, "That goat's got more sense than you do."

Irritated with both of them, I stalked back up to the house. The nerve of him, saying ridiculous things when I was trying to apologize and spare his feelings. How dare he accuse me of being so petty, as if I just wanted to toy with him.

I had plenty of feelings about everything that had happened between us, but not once had I wanted revenge.

Well, not unless you counted wishing he'd get head-butted by a feisty goat.

If he couldn't even discuss what happened last night like a grown-up, then I wasn't going to waste my time trying to smooth things over. The last thing I needed was to be tangled up in Alex drama again. I wouldn't be here that much longer, and I had enough hurdles to get over.

I could avoid him the rest of the time I was here. No problem.

# Chapter Twelve

## ALEX

FIONA WAS PLENTY ANNOYED NOW.

But that was a good sign, too—it meant she cared more than she was letting on. And I guess she had reason to be aggravated with me. After the way she'd acted the night before, I'd been convinced she was just trying to yank me around and get a little revenge, but clearly, I was wrong.

Huh.

It was impossible to ignore the fury that simmered in her eyes, but there was something else there, too.

She'd never had a decent poker face.

Before she'd turned on her heel and stomped back up to the house, she'd glared at me with an intensity that said she simultaneously wanted to sucker punch me and kiss me stupid.

I was really hoping for the latter.

Domino pawed at the gate and I bent down to give it one more look. The little stinker was already looking for a weak spot. Guess I couldn't blame him for being persistent.

At first, I'd felt bad about last night. After she left, I'd replayed the night over and over in my head, wondering if I'd misinterpreted everything she'd said and done at dinner. She'd seemed a little cool at first, but then she'd moved closer to me and looked up at me through her big dark lashes as she talked, and it sure seemed like she wanted me to kiss her. I'd been happy to oblige—because ever since I saw her last week, I'd been thinking about what it would be like to feel her lips again.

She was the one that I never got over. I'd wondered about her so often, and hoped that I might somehow have another chance with her. I'd gone over those conversations in my head a thousand times, imagining what I might say to earn another shot, how I might tell her all the words I'd keep inside for so long.

Things had been going well at my house—so well that I got too comfortable. Too confident.

And then she'd gotten all frazzled and hurried out of there like the building was on fire.

But I was the one on fire.

She was torn, though. That much was obvious. It was like she started to have fun, and forgot she was supposed to be mad at me, and then suddenly remembered that I was supposed to be the bad guy.

I had assumed she'd gotten over the breakup all those years ago, and part of me thought maybe she'd finally learned what had really transpired—but now it was clear that she had no idea about the real reason I'd pushed her away. Part of me figured her mother would have told her by now, in that callous way of hers, but clearly, that hadn't happened. Fi would have to know the truth if we had any chance of starting over, but I didn't want to be the one to tell her. I was afraid she wouldn't believe me, and that would make everything even worse.

Domino watched me work on the gate the whole time as if reverse engineering it in his little goat brain. Mending the broken wire wasn't all that hard, and a new board would stop him from getting out again, at least until he found another escape route. Too bad not everything could be mended as easily as the fence.

But I could try.

When I finally finished, I put Domino inside the fence and went back up to Delia's house. In the kitchen, Delia and Fiona were sitting at the table, eating what looked like a chicken pot pie. Miss Delia waved me over to sit, but Fiona didn't even acknowledge that I'd walked into the room.

"Miss D," I said, "I think what I did'll hold Domino for now, but I'll come back and do a real fix in a couple of days. I think I have a plan that will outsmart him."

"Thank you so much, sweetie," Delia said.

"Something smells awfully good in here," I said, eyeing their plates. "Didn't realize it was suppertime."

Fiona narrowed her eyes at me, so I gave her my warmest smile. She could be mad at me all she wanted—I could wait her out because she was worth waiting for.

"Well, sit down and have some, honey," Miss Delia said. "You know where the plates are."

Fiona shot her a look that said she might have kicked her under the table if she hadn't had that bum knee.

"Well, thanks," I said. "I skipped lunch and whatever this is smells fantastic."

"Fiona's been cooking a pile of food for us," Delia said. "There's enough here for a small army. You know you're welcome to join us anytime."

When I sat down across from her and took a bite, Fiona looked at me like she hoped I might choke on a pea.

"Delicious," I said, and flashed her a grin.

She glanced at Delia and then gave me a tight smile. "So glad you could stay for dinner," she said sweetly. "Your timing just never fails."

Fiona McIntyre was as stubborn as all three of Delia's goats put together. She hated to be wrong, and she'd never admit defeat. Clearly, she'd built up some walls after that jerk fiancé of hers took off. Now she thought she could hide behind them and tamp her feelings down so no one could see—but the truth was, she wore everything on her sleeve. One glance into her eyes and I knew exactly what she was thinking.

Right now, for example, she was wishing little Domino had head-butted me into next week.

Last night, she'd been a little harder to read. But I could tell that she was nervous about being back and annoyed that she needed my help. I also didn't miss the way her eyes raked over me no fewer than a dozen times while we sat in my kitchen.

There had definitely been a spark. But she didn't want to admit it.

She didn't want to admit that she still had feelings for me—and there was no doubt that she did. I knew I needed to earn her trust again, and I didn't blame her for that. I'd happily spend every day earning her trust and making up for that night that I'd wrecked everything.

I just hoped I had enough time.

"Alex," Delia said, "Did you sort out that problem you were having with the sculpture?"

"Not yet," I said. "It's still got me stumped."

"He's been so secretive about it," Delia said to Fiona. "I've just heard hints from the committee, but I can't wait to see it."

"I might just need a fresh set of eyes," I said. "I was kind of hoping Fiona might help me with that." I turned towards Fi and said, "I never got to tell you about that proposition last night."

Fiona took another big bite of pie and narrowed her eyes at me.

Now for the wind-up.

"I'm in a heck of a jam and could really use your help, Fi. What do you say?"

She took another bite, ignoring me completely.

Delia beamed.

Now for the pitch.

"I've hit a roadblock, and I'm running out of time. But if you could help me, we'd have no problem finishing. I could re-introduce you to Maxine over at the Arts Council, too. She'd love your work."

*Come on, Fiona,* I thought. "And it's a great way for you to get involved with the gala and get a foot hold here in the art community."

"Oh, that would wonderful!" Delia squealed. "Fiona, you'll love the gala."

"That's thoughtful of you, Alex," Fiona said, her tone entirely too bright. "But I really don't have the time."

A swing and a miss.

I nodded, leaning forward on my elbows. "I don't expect any favors," I told her. "I'm happy to pay you for your time. I'll split the commission with you. And you'll have your name on the plaque, too." If I could get her to help me with the sculpture, it meant she'd have to stick around, at least another couple of weeks until the gala. And it meant she'd be working on a cool project that the whole town would see.

Delia grinned. "Honey, how can you say no to that? What do you have to lose?"

"Come on," I said. "It'll be fun." And it would be a way for us to spend time together. I wanted all the time with her I could get, even if it meant splitting that money with her.

Fiona arched a brow. Her eyes fixed on mine, she licked her spoon, and that long, slow teasing of her tongue nearly stopped my heart.

"Come on," I said. "I know you like a challenge."

Teasing her was too much fun. I knew she was just miffed enough to want to show me up a little. Bless her stubborn little heart.

"You said you needed a change of pace," I said. "Something outside your comfort zone to get yourself inspired. This could be the thing that shakes something loose."

She glared at me like she had a few ideas about things of mine she'd like to shake loose.

"Many hands make light work," Delia said, waving her spoon at Fiona. "Give him a hand. Don't make him beg you. And besides, he's right. You need to get out of this house some. I love you dear, but I don't need a babysitter and you're too young to be a hermit."

Bless you, Miss Delia.

"Aunt D," she said, exasperated.

"And he's right," Delia went on. "Getting into Maxine's good graces could sell you a whole lot of paintings. You could make a name for yourself here."

"Aunt D, you know this is temporary," Fiona said, her voice low.

*But what if it wasn't, Fi?*

Delia waved those words away. "Go do something fun. Get out of your head for a bit." Then she gave Fiona a look that my mom had given me plenty of times as a kid—one that meant agreement was the only option.

Delia mouthed something to Fiona that I couldn't quite make out. Fiona rolled her eyes and said, "Good grief." She leaned back in her chair and leveled her eyes on mine. "Fine, Alex. I'll look at your sculpture. But no promises."

"Great," I said.

Base hit.

# Chapter Thirteen

## FIONA

ERIC REIKER DIDN'T LOOK one bit like his picture on the website. When he walked into the Sentient Bean, it was five minutes after four, and I'd been there long enough to drink half of my large latte. I had planned to get there early so I could explain this meeting to Gwen, and so I could get a good look at him as he came into the shop. You can tell a lot about a person by the way he enters a room and orders a drink. For instance: does he hold the door for the person coming in behind him? Does he squeeze past a person coming out, too impatient to let them pass first? Does he consider the items on the menu? Does he order some silly fake coffee with whipped cream and sprinkles, or does he order something straightforward that is actually made from coffee beans? Does he tip the barista or not, or—even worse—tell her she should smile more?

When Eric Reiker opened the door, he paused for two oblivious teenage girls to walk past him, holding the door as they giggled while staring at their cell phones, nearly plowing right over him. He took a quick look around, ran a hand through his short blond hair, and scanned the menu by the counter. Then he checked his watch and surveyed the room. It took him exactly four seconds to pick me out of the dozen or so people seated at the small tables, and then he smiled and walked toward me.

"Fiona," he said, extending his hand. "Thank you so much for coming. I'm Eric." His handshake was one of those firm ones that make you remember the face that goes with that hand. Eric Reiker was at least six-foot-two, tall and svelte, with broad shoulders and hazel eyes. Dressed in khaki cargo pants and a green tee shirt, he looked more like an army ranger than an academic. His deep tan and stubbled cheek suggested he spent most of his time outdoors. Contrary to his blurry photo in the online directory, he looked closer to thirty than twenty.

Lordy, the photo had not done this man justice.

"How'd you know it was me?" I asked him. Behind him, at the counter, Gwen stared with her mouth open, fanning her face like it was suddenly twenty degrees hotter.

And really, it was.

Eric smiled a crooked smile that must have broken a dozen hearts in the last year alone and said, "You're the only one that looks like an artist." He nodded towards the empty chair, where my painting was visible under a stack of papers and Delia's field guide.

"Ah," I said. "Get yourself a drink. I'm way ahead of you."

"This was going to be my treat," he said. He had one of those low-country drawls that was as smooth as top-shelf Scotch and always put me at ease. "But maybe you'll let me get the next one." He smiled as he laid his shoulder bag down in the chair opposite mine and strode up to the counter.

He was back in a flash with a cup of black coffee. Eric Reiker was not a whipped cream kind of guy. He moved his bag and sat down across from me, and fixed me with a gaze that made my face feel hot.

*Good lord,* I thought. I should have gone to grad school.

"How was the drive?" I said.

His eyes were steady on mine, evaluating. He was definitely a science person, someone whose life goal was to observe. "Not bad," he said, stirring a bit of cream into his coffee. "Are you from here?"

"Actually, yes," I said. "I'm visiting family this week."

He nodded. "I haven't been down this way in a long time. I'm from Beaufort, but I've been in the upstate for the last several years. It's beautiful down here, like nowhere else."

It looked mostly like a swamp around here, but I didn't argue. One man's Hellhole Swamp was another man's Valhalla.

"So you're working on your master's degree?" I asked him.

He nodded, sipping his coffee. "I'm working on my thesis now, but if this turns out to be," he glanced around and lowered his voice, "what I think it is, I'll be rewriting that thesis."

"Oh," I said. "That sounds like a lot of work."

"It would be totally worth it. I'm trying not to get my hopes up just yet, but I've got a feeling about this one. This could be a huge discovery. The sort of thing that makes your career."

"I don't know the first thing about what makes an ornithologist's career," I said.

His eyes actually sparkled when he said, "This would be like George Lucas discovering Harrison Ford. This would be history. I'm just so glad you posted a picture of your painting. Otherwise, I never would have known."

"I guess you have my friend to thank for that," I said. "She's always hounding me about taking process shots. That was just a warm-up piece. Not the kind of thing that usually gets shown to people."

"That makes me one lucky guy," he said. "I stumbled on your page one day and thought your paintings were so bright and so cool. I mean, I'm a bird nerd anyway, but I just got lost looking at all of your posts—the way you see birds is just so interesting." He sipped his coffee, waving his hand between us as if to refocus. "Anyway, when I saw this one the other day, I couldn't believe what I was seeing."

His eyes darted down to the painting and the stack of books and he said, "Is that it?" He looked like a kid at a birthday party, eager to blow out the candles.

"Yeah." I laid the painting on the table between us. It looked even rougher in the bright light of the cafe.

He peered at it, then looked up at me. "And you saw this bird yourself, in the wild?"

"Yes, right outside my window."

"Did you take photos?"

I pulled my phone out and scrolled through. "I did, but they're not good. I shot through the window, just to remind myself of the coloring so I could paint it later. It was unique."

He scooted his chair closer, and I could smell just a hint of something musky, like a nice aftershave. He leaned in close and pulled a pair of glasses out of his jacket pocket, then slipped them on and peered at the tiny screen. When I zoomed in so the blurry bird filled the frame, he exhaled deeply.

"Can't tell much from the photo," he said. "The lighting is dark." He squinted at the screen and said, "Did you happen to hear its vocals?"

"It sounded sort of like a cicada," I said. "A buzzing kind of chirp."

He nodded, then pulled a folder from his bag. As he flipped through the pages, he said, "Bachman's warbler. It's very similar to a couple of extant warblers, like the hooded warbler, or the magnolia warbler. It has a bright yellow face and a distinctive black collar. Males have the brighter coloring of course." He pulled a sheet from his pile and slid it towards me. At the top of the page was an image of an Audubon print.

"That looks similar," I said. "But the head's a little goofy."

"Most of Audubon's heads were a little goofy," he said. "For a while, they all looked like doves." He pointed to a paragraph on the printout and pushed his glasses up into his hair. They were heavy tortoise-shell glasses, and they seemed just a little too hipster for him. "So Bachman's warbler was last spotted in Florida in 1977, but that was unconfirmed. There have been no documented sightings since. The common theory is that hurricanes in the 1940s and 50s destroyed their winter habitat and they died out."

I stared at the Audubon image, the male and female with slightly oblong heads. The shape was wrong, but the colors were right.

"This warbler prefers swampland," he said. "There were sightings in Charleston in the 1950s, and that's when this photo was taken." He slid another page across the table, but the photo was so grainy that I couldn't see much of the pattern I remembered from the bird in the yard. "These birds used to populate the southeastern US and then winter in Cuba," Eric said. "This area is their ideal habitat. They even had reports from around here in the late 90s and did an extensive search in Congaree in 2002. But they only found hooded warblers, and assumed people had misidentified them."

"That's an impressive amount of data," I said. He talked about this bird the way some guys recited basketball stats. It was oddly charming.

"Told you," he said, pointing at his chest. "Bird nerd."

"What makes you think this isn't another misidentification?"

"The way you painted the collar," he said. "Hooded warblers don't look like that. The ring goes all the way around the cheek. You paint birds quite accurately in terms of coloration, despite being stylized." He traced his finger along the face of the bird in the painting. "Plus, there's the call you described."

He pulled his cell phone from his pocket, swiped a few screens, and then pressed a button and held the phone between us.

A musical call filled the air, several long notes.

"Is that the sound it made?" he asked.

"No."

"Are you sure?"

"Of course. I saw its beak move."

He smiled. "That was the hooded warbler." He swiped a few

more times and tapped the screen again. Another call. Another series of notes that varied in pitch.

I shook my head. "Nope."

"That was the magnolia warbler." He swiped again and played a third recording. This one was a monotone buzzing sound. It sounded almost mechanical, like should come from a wind-up toy instead of a tiny bird.

"That's more like what I heard," I said, tapping the table. "The bird in the yard that day didn't sound like the other songbirds. It wasn't a musical sound."

He grinned and shoved the phone back into his pocket. "Fiona, the way you painted it—did you see it behaving this way?"

On the wood panel, the little bird with the yellow face was hanging upside down from a branch, like it was searching the undersides of the leaves. On that day when I'd first set up in Delia's workroom, the yew had been scraping against the window, and the bird lit on the branch. "That's what I thought was so cute about it," I told him, "It reminded me of a titmouse, you know the way they hang upside down in the branches? They twirl around like little acrobats."

"Yes," he said, and his eyes brightened.

"It seemed to be looking for bugs. I only saw it for a minute or two that day."

"Have you seen it again since then?"

"No, but I think I heard it yesterday."

He stared at me, his eyes wide. His energy was contagious, and he was absolutely buzzing with it. "Fiona," he said, his voice low and serious, "would you take me to the place you saw this bird?"

His gaze was intense, but he definitely didn't have the serial killer vibe. He seemed like a guy who was one hundred percent immersed in his passion, and it was hard to fault someone for that. I hadn't felt that kind of excitement about my work in a long time.

"First tell me this: what happens if this is the bird you think it is?"

He leaned forward on his elbows, resting his chin in his hand. "I just want to see it," he said. "To prove it's real, I'd need photos or video, and a recording of its song. That would be enough. But ultimately, it could teach us a lot about adaptation."

The thought of discovering this near-extinct species was tantalizing. This was a chance to be part of something big, something meaningful.

"Fiona, I came down here thinking I'd hear you out, and then prove you wrong, and then put this out of my mind and get back to my boring research about the declining bluebird population. But now I really think this could be the real deal. And if it is, this is a major discovery. This could be huge—like, we'd-make-history huge." He sipped his coffee and smiled his crooked smile. "What do you think?"

Finishing the last of my latte, I considered that for a moment. "Let me make a quick phone call," I said at last, and went outside the cafe. As I dialed Delia's number, I watched him through the window. He'd spread out a few of his papers on the table, and he was studying the painting again. He seemed like a nice enough guy: earnest, but not aggressive. He had this almost childlike sense of wonder about him and seemed like a guy who wanted his life to be an adventure.

What was that woo-woo thing that Delia had told me? *The universe sends us exactly what we need.*

A little adventure didn't sound so bad.

When Delia answered, I said, "How are you feeling, Aunt D?"

"Fine." Her voice was heavy, like she'd been napping. "But I ran out of crossword puzzles."

"I'll grab another book while I'm out," I said, then smiled when Eric traced his finger over the bird painting. "I have a weird question to ask you."

"It is about a handsome metalsmith?"

"No, it's about an ornithologist. Would you mind if I brought someone over to look for a bird?"

Inside, Eric was holding his old photograph of the warbler close to his nose. Gwen sidled up to the table, offering to refill his coffee. He smiled at her and nodded, and she glanced out the window at me, arching a brow in that way that meant she'd want to hear all the details about this guy later.

When I gave her a quick nod, she winked at me and then said something to Eric. He gave her a friendly smile and she sauntered back toward the counter, giving him a long look over her shoulder that he most certainly missed. His attention was back on the photograph.

When I went back inside, the bell above the door clanged and I waved to Gwen, letting her know that we'd ruled out any serial killer vibes.

Eric glanced up at me, hopeful.

"Put that in a to-go cup," I said. "And let's take a drive."

---

AFTER MAKING a quick stop in the bookstore across the street for Delia's crossword puzzles, I led Eric out to the house. He followed close behind me in his Wrangler, an older model with a soft top and plenty of mud splatters. Delia had sounded excited when I'd explained why I wanted to bring Eric over. *This could be good for her, too*, I thought. A little excitement that might take her mind off her knee and perk her up a little.

When we parked in the backyard, Eric climbed out of the Jeep and pulled a little notebook from the pocket of his cargo pants. He scribbled a few quick notes down while turning in a slow circle where he stood, surveying the yard.

"This is my aunt's house," I told him. "She'd love to meet you. She'll probably want you to stay for supper."

He looked genuinely surprised and said, "Oh, I wouldn't want to impose like that."

"She just had knee surgery and she's bored out of her mind. You'd be doing her a favor." I led him towards the front of the house, where the dogwoods and maples were. When we reached the porch, the few birds that were at the feeders flew away into the nearby trees. I pointed to the yew that was growing so close to the corner of the house. "That's the tree I saw it in. Right up by the window."

He nodded, staring up at the tree. "I wouldn't expect to see it this time of day," he said, surveying the rest of the yard. His eyes drifted over everything, taking in all the details: the mostly flat meadow, the tree line of the woods beyond the barn.

"What do you think?" I said.

"It's the right habitat. See that cane thicket down there near the pond? That's a perfect nesting area." He crossed his arms over his chest and looked up at the sky. "And this land is just beginning to turn into scrubby swamp. You're right on the edge, smack in the wetlands."

"The Congaree park's just over that way," I said, pointing toward the woods. "We're right on the boundary."

Thunder rumbled in the distance and I felt the first real rain drops plink against my cheeks. Eric blinked up at the sky, rubbing his fingers over his stubbly beard.

"We'd be more likely to see it in the morning," he said. "That's prime feeding time." His gaze had settled far in the distance, like he was thinking hard, calculating odds. After a moment, he turned to me and said, "What are the chances I could come back early tomorrow morning?"

"Come inside and say hi to Aunt Delia," I told him. "And you can ask her yourself."

---

DELIA LOVED A GOOD MYSTERY. The closer to home, the better.

By the time Eric had finished telling us about the warbler and its sudden disappearance, he'd made the bird sound as gripping as the lost colony of Roanoke.

Delia sat transfixed, sipping her tea.

"But if what you saw out there was Bachman's warbler," Eric said, "we could prove the species has survived."

"What a story that would be," Delia said, her eyes twinkling.

"It's almost breeding season," he said. "And if you had a mating pair here, that would be truly remarkable. Fiona, what you saw was the male, but the female is shyer, less likely to come out in the open. But it's entirely possible that one is here." He sounded less skeptical now, like he'd already decided that this was real, and it was happening. And it was no longer simply a dream, but a likelihood.

"So what does all of this mean for us?" I said.

"This is like the holy grail." He paused for a moment as if trying to tamp down his excitement. "I really think we'd be doing a disservice if we didn't investigate. A find like this could change the trajectory of conservation efforts around here. And you being right next door to the national park, well, that's even better."

"To think we could have that sort of magic out here in the middle of nowhere," Delia said. "It's amazing."

Leaning forward in his chair, Eric said, "That brings me to my next question, Mrs. James." He glanced at me as if silently asking for permission. "Would you consider letting me come out here for a few days and try to see it? If it is here, I'll need hard evidence to convince my colleagues. Photos, recordings, something that will prove beyond a shadow of a doubt. It might take some time, because, well, nature moves at her own speed regardless of what we want." He smiled at that, looking humbled. "But if this is what I think it is, you'd be a part of history."

Aunt Delia raised a brow and was quiet for a long moment. So long, that I thought maybe she wasn't interested after all. Finally, she set her steely eyes on him and said, "Eric, I spent the better part of my life caring for animals, and I've made my home into one for them, too. So I need you to make me one promise, young man."

"Of course," he said. "Anything."

"That the poor critter doesn't end up stuffed in a museum or caged in a zoo."

He smiled a friendly smile and said, "Absolutely, Mrs. James. I'd only be here to observe. I never want to interfere."

Aunt Delia nodded, satisfied, and turned to me. "And you said nothing ever happens in Jasmine Falls."

# Chapter Fourteen

## FIONA

ALEX FOX WAS MORE cunning than I'd given him credit for. I wasn't sure why he wanted me to help him so badly with this sculpture of his, but he'd pulled out all the stops Sunday night at Delia's when he'd dialed the charm up to fifteen and then practically begged me.

Likely because he knew I couldn't say no to her.

He'd been doing a lot for her, and yes, I felt guilty that I hadn't been around to help her more. She was excited about the gala, and I didn't want to be a storm cloud hovering over her head. So I agreed to help Alex with his stupid sculpture.

He might live to regret that, though.

Today was Tuesday, which meant physical therapy for Delia. On the drive over, she'd been talking nonstop about meeting Eric yesterday and hearing all about the mystery bird. Now, she waved at me from across the therapy room, where she was doing leg lifts with her therapist, Lavonne. The waiting area and the therapy room were separated by a long bank of windows. It was pretty state-of-the-art for a small town.

Just as I was picturing how to properly get back at Alex for setting this trap for me, my phone buzzed.

There was a text from Gwen. **Still up for that wine date?**

**OMG, the sooner the better,** I replied.

**How's tomorrow?**

**Perfect.**

**I'm done at 6. I'll text you.**

Before I could reply, my phone buzzed with an incoming call from my mother.

Sigh.

"Hi, Mom," I said.

"Oh good, you're there," she said. "How's Delia?"

"Great. We've been—"

"Wonderful," she said, interrupting me. There was honking on the other end and yelling in the distance, like the noise from a busy street. There was no telling what Penelope was doing to stop traffic. "We're thinking of extending our trip a few days. You don't mind staying a little longer do you?"

"No, that's fine." On the other side of the glass, Delia was still working with Lavonne, pedaling slowly on a miniature cycle.

"Great. We're going to stay another week and take a cruise into the fjords. They're breathtaking this time of year. Simon loves cruises."

This phone call was no surprise, really. My mother tended to extend her travel dates when she got caught up in the magic of a new place. That's how she'd ended up traveling for two years when I was in high school, leaving me in Delia's care. My mother had planned to travel until the grant money ran out, and she could be frugal when she wanted to be.

Aside from a couple of visits for holidays, I hadn't seen her again until after my eighteenth birthday. If I'd been important enough to her, I could have traveled with her, been home-schooled, and been a student of the world. That hadn't occurred to me until I was in college. When it did dawn on me, I was both heartbroken and grateful—glad it hadn't occurred to me when I was fourteen and thought the whole world hated me.

Aunt Delia had been there, though. When I was feeling

discarded and unimportant, Delia was there to make me feel like I made a difference to someone. So if Delia needed me here a few more days, then that's where I'd be.

Even if it meant a thousand awkward encounters with Alex Fox.

There was another honk and my mother said, "Okay, give Delia our love. We're on our way to dinner. Bye!"

Before I could answer, she'd hung up. Typical Penelope: get what you want, and then flitter away.

My phone buzzed again with a text.

**Want to come give me your expert opinion today?** Alex wrote.

**Are you sure you want that?** I answered. Was he serious about this?

**Yes. Absolutely.**

The last thing I needed was to be working side by side with Alex Fox, but I'd agreed to at least look at the sculpture—even though I was technically under duress.

**I never got to tell you my proposal,** he wrote. **I think you'll like it.**

**What makes you so sure?** I replied.

**I know you like a challenge.**

**Maybe I've got enough challenges on my plate.**

He sent a GIF of a cartoon dog with big sad eyes.

**Help me, Obi-wan,** he wrote. **You're my only hope.**

I sighed, thinking of all the things he'd done to help Delia. *Pay it forward,* I thought.

**OK,** I wrote. **I'll come by after lunch.**

Another GIF with a happy dog, prancing and wagging its tail.

---

WHEN HER THERAPY WAS OVER, Delia gave me a big thumbs-up and said, "Okay, kid, I'm good for another day."

"How's your knee?" I said.

"Feels like I've been kicked by a mule, but it's better."

"She's doing great," Lavonne said, patting her on the shoulder. Lavonne looked about thirty-five, with flawless brown skin and intricate braids pulled back in a ponytail. Her brown eyes twinkled when she smiled. "You got this, Miss D. A few more weeks and you won't need that walking stick anymore. You'll be going on those bird walks you were telling me about in no time."

"Well I should hope so," Delia said. "I can't miss my talks with Ranger Chris. I spotted my first white-eyed vireo on his walk last year. And he's not bad to look at himself—looks like a movie star and has nice manners, too."

"Maybe I need to go on these nature walks," Lavonne said.

"First one's in two weeks," Delia said.

Lavonne waved as we headed towards the door. "See you Thursday, Miss D."

As we drove back to the house, I said, "Mom called. She said they want to stay longer. Maybe a week."

"Well, that's nice. If you're going all that way, you might as well see all you can."

"Apparently Simon has their schedule full."

She smiled. "Does that mean you'll stay a while longer, too?"

"Of course. As long as you don't mind a houseguest."

"Not at all," she said. "That house feels big and empty these days." That was the closest Aunt Delia would ever come to saying she felt lonely. "And now you'll be here long enough to go to the gala."

"How about we stop at Gwen's and get some treats?" I said. "I've had nothing but coffee."

"Great. Then you can tell me all about what's going on with you and Alex."

I shrugged. "Nothing's going on."

"Oh please," she said. "There were more fireworks the other night than on the fourth of July."

"He needs to dial it back a notch. I don't know what he thinks he's doing, but—"

Delia patted my arm. "Maybe cut him a little slack, sweetheart."

"He can play this Mr. Charming card all he wants to, but it doesn't undo what he did." He could claim bygones all he wanted, but I was the one who'd had the heart-in-a-blender feeling for months. I was the one who'd felt like I wasn't good enough, and like the one person I could count on had thrown me away. *Again.*

He couldn't make that feeling go away with his big smile and a bottle of wine.

"Maybe he's trying to make up for all that," she said. "And he just doesn't know how."

"So far, he's just making my visit with you more complicated." I did not want to have warm fuzzy feelings for Alex Fox. I did not want to think about kissing him, and touching him, and having romantic candlelit dinners in his big gorgeous kitchen.

But my heart was very slow to get that memo.

---

ALEX'S STUDIO was like a sauna, even with a couple of fans on and the big bay door open. I called his name when I walked inside, but there was no reply.

A pounding filled my ears, and I followed the sound to the back of the building where Alex had his forge set up. He was bent over an anvil, hammering a rod-like piece of iron. He looked like one of those heroes from Norse mythology, set on tinkering with humans for a bit of fun. He wore a heavy leather apron that hung to his knees, thick gloves that covered his forearms, and welder's goggles that looked more steampunk than blacksmith. But under all that, I could still see his biceps flexing with each strike of the hammer, the red-orange of the forge glowing behind him.

If this was how he spent most of his days, it was no wonder that his arms were like solid granite.

*Stop. No thinking about big muscular arms and nice hands and all the things they can do.*

When at last he looked up and gave me a slight nod, I waved in that way that said, *Hi there, I just got here. Haven't been staring at you for the last five minutes. No sir, not me.*

He laid the tools down by the forge and sauntered towards me in that confident, lazy way of his that made it seem like he had all the time in the world. How was it fair that he could look so sexy while being so sweaty and covered in soot? The studio felt ten degrees hotter and it was already like an oven outside.

"Hey, Fi," he said. He pulled the thick gloves off and pushed the goggles up into his hair. His face was dark with beard stubble and he had a streak of charcoal across his forehead that I barely fought the urge to wipe away. Brushing his forearm across his brow, he said, "I'm glad you came. I could stand a break—it's hot as blazes back there."

Indeed. Blazes.

"How'd it go today?" he said.

I blinked, trying to remember what I'd done all day and not trace the lines of his abs through his shirt and—why was I here again? And why was it so hard to put words together right now?

"How's Delia?" he said.

"Right. Good." The text messages. Therapy. Yes. "She's doing fine," I said.

"Put your thinking cap on," he said, taking off the apron. "I'm about five seconds away from melting this thing down and starting over."

"It can't be that bad," I said, though he'd looked awfully rattled when Aunt Delia had asked him about his progress.

"Humor me. You can come tell me what's wrong with it."

Now he had me curious. Part of me was dying to know what he was making, and why on earth he thought I might be able to help.

"Okay," I said. "But I can't stay long."

He headed toward the back and I tried desperately to ignore the sway of his broad shoulders and the way his jeans clung in precisely the right places.

So very unfair. He was making it very hard to stay annoyed.

Alex led me past a work table that was littered with sketches, photos, and small models of tree-like shapes that looked like prototypes. The back side of the studio had another big sliding bay door, just like the front. It led out to a gravel area behind the shop where there were several works in progress—including the iron gate with the vines, looking much closer to finished than it had when I'd been over a few days ago.

Alex pointed to a copper sculpture off to the side, but I failed to see a disaster. It was an assemblage that looked like part of a tree, the copper and iron pieces woven together like a braid to form the trunk—like the cypress in the swamp behind Delia's house. The shape was striking, somehow rustic and elegant at the same time.

"I like it," I said. "What's the problem?"

Alex crossed his arms over his chest. "The committee mostly gave me free rein here, but we settled on a 'tree of knowledge' idea. I made all these different kinds of branches and leaves, but it's just not working. I don't like any of them." He lifted one of the branches from the ground, a similarly braided limb with small copper leaves attached. "They wanted me to work in some stained glass, but I'm just not seeing a way to make that work."

I picked up another stray copper leaf, marveling at the detail. He really had mastered his craft.

"What's the point of making a tree that just looks like a tree?" he said.

"Where's it going again?"

"At the library, on the front lawn."

It was a space that was wide open. The library itself was a Neo-Classical style building, with red brick and arched windows. It was only one story and had a big front lawn with only a few small dogwood trees.

"I need all the help I can get here. I've officially hit the wall. Totally out of ideas."

"Tell me some of these ideas," I said.

"These were the initial sketches," he said, leading me back to his work table inside. "The committee was happy with this direction, but they want to see an update in a couple of days—just in case they want to adjust anything before the unveiling at the gala."

"And that's when?"

"A week from Saturday."

Ten days wasn't much time. "You're not sleeping much between now and then, huh?"

"I'm a little behind schedule, as you can see." He gestured at the three small models of trees. One had a braided trunk like the one outside, and the others looked plainer. One looked a little like an oak, and one had no leaves at all. I glanced back at the sketches. Buried in them was a list of words I read aloud: "Creativity, inspiration, knowledge, books."

"Brainstorm," he said. "Words they associate with the point of the sculpture. It's basically about how books help us grow, make us more creative, more thoughtful. They wanted something that symbolizes knowledge. And you know how board members are sometimes. They're a literal people." He pushed one of the sketches toward me. "We settled on a stylized tree of knowledge. I thought it would be cool if it was somehow interactive."

"So how is this interactive?"

"I don't know yet. But at least I talked them out of the giant open book that you can sit on."

"Oh lord."

"Did I mention they're a literal sort?" he said.

"They're lucky to have you to save them from themselves."

He arched a brow. "Maybe don't mention luck until this thing's finished. I'm feeling massively jinxed right now."

That made two of us. The universe seemed to be conspiring to take me down a few notches.

Metal leaves lay scattered on the table between us. Most of them were solid forms, but when I picked up one that was made with a wire frame, he said, "I'd love to use light somehow, but everything I do with the stained glass looks terrible. I thought about carving the words into the trunk, but I don't like that idea, either. It seems too…"

"Obvious?"

"Exactly." He sat down next to me and raked his hands through his hair.

When I held one of the leaves under his task lamp to look at the texture, I noticed the shadow it cast on the work table. The metal had been shaped into the outline of a leaf, and he'd molded other bits of wire inside the frame—the effect was like a line drawing. When I twirled the leaf close to the light, then moved it farther away the shadows danced on the table.

On a larger scale, that could be interesting. "Put the words inside the leaves," I said. "Like your wireframe. You make the words in cursive, out of copper maybe, and then weld them to the outline of the leaf. The sunlight will cast the shadows on the ground. It's not exactly interactive, but—"

He arched a brow, watching the shape the wire-framed leaf made on the table. With a pencil, I quickly sketched my idea on the back of one of this drawings. I drew the outline of a broad leaf, then wrote the word "create" in loopy cursive lettering, inside the leaf shape, connecting the letters to the outline, then connected it to the trunk of the tree.

"You don't put a word inside every leaf," I said, drawing the trunk. "Keep some of the leaves just a wire outline, and put some wire shapes inside to give it texture. Keep some solid metal like you have already to give it some dimension. But some leaves will have a word in them, so you have to look to find them." I held the wire leaf to the light again and pointed at the shadow on the paper. "Search to discover, just like inside the stacks."

Alex stared at me with his mouth open. "That's freaking brilliant."

"Well, you don't have to sound so surprised."

"No, I mean, that's why I asked you to look at it. I knew you'd have an idea. I'm just floored that it took you all of five minutes. It's a bit humbling."

I shrugged. "Sometimes you just need a fresh pair of eyes."

"Or a genius."

Alex Fox looked genuinely grateful. And energized. He jumped up from the stool and grabbed a few pieces of florist's wire from the table. In just a few movements, he'd created the rough shape of a leaf about eight inches long, similar to the shape that I'd drawn. Then he looped some wire through the center in rough, overlapping shapes. I tried to ignore the way his big hands molded the wire into place, the way his forearms tensed. When he was concentrating hard, his thick brows furrowed and his lip turned upward in the most inviting way.

*Stop*, I thought. *Do not think about those arms. Or those lips. Off-limits.*

But as his hands shaped the wire, all I could think of was the way they'd feel if they were squeezing my hips instead.

"It's like a million degrees in here," I said. "Don't you have any AC?"

"That's not exactly practical for a forge." He raked a hand through his dark hair until it stood up in wild peaks, and why was my heart hammering in my chest?

"What do you think?" he said.

"Nothing," I blurted. *Work, brain. Make words.*

"You okay?" he said, looking puzzled.

"Me? Sure." I scrambled to put a sentence together. "I think you're just hot. I mean, I'm hot." I felt my cheeks redden and cursed my fair complexion for never *ever* being able to hide a blush. "I think the heat fried my brain."

There was a mischievous glint in his eye. "You get used to it."

I certainly could.

*Focus. This is not a road you need to go down again.*

"Would you make the cursive words?" he said. "I think you'd be way better at that part."

"Kinda have my hands full," I said.

"Come on," he said. "Please." The look in his eyes was a mix of hopeful and sad.

"Alex, I can't. Really." The room suddenly felt so small. It was hard to breathe, hard to focus on anything but him.

And I definitely did not need to be focused on him.

He stepped closer, leveling me with his stare. "Can't what?"

"This. All of it." I had my own work to do, and I did not need to be holed up with Alex Fox and his big sexy arms and his mischievous grin, and his to-die-for perfectly tousled hair. No thank you.

He leaned down on his elbows so his eyes were level with mine. "Maxine loves collaborations. She loves discovering new artists and helping get them seen. She'll flip over this."

"I don't need to be someone's pet project, Alex."

With a devilish smile, he said, "You'll have your name on a bronze plaque. You'll be famous. Or, you know, at least Jasmine Falls famous."

I tossed a balled-up sketch at him. "Nice."

He edged closer, his gaze warm. "It was your great idea. You're not going to let me take credit for this, are you?"

It was tempting, but being around him was leaving me tied up in knots. I still felt hurt and betrayed, and sometimes annoyed, and sometimes so desperate to kiss him I couldn't see straight.

"Look, let me start over." He turned around a couple of times, like a big goofball, and then leaned against the table. "I messed up. And I know I've made things awkward. And I'm really sorry."

"Okay. Noted."

He nodded. "I really need your help, and I think this would be good for both of us—professionally. You have this amazing idea, and I want you to see it through to the end. If you want to." He leaned closer and said, "I don't want any weirdness between us to stop you from making something great, and making a name for yourself here."

"I appreciate that. But I don't need to make a name for myself here, because I'm not sticking around. You have my permission to take this idea and run with it." *Atta girl. Stick to your guns.*

He raked his fingers through his hair and said, "It's a big commission. I'll split it with you, like I said."

"I'm not that broke, Alex." A lie, but I had my pride.

He frowned. "That's not what I meant." He began pacing in that way that meant he was determined to get what he wanted. "I just mean I want to compensate you for your time and expertise," he said. "This is a big project, and you'd be a collaborator. It's only fair to cut you in."

"Alex."

"I need you, Fiona."

"You do not."

"Okay, fine. I want you." He stopped pacing and stood toe to toe with me.

Something electric zipped along my spine and all the way down to my fingertips.

"I mean," he fumbled, "I want you to help me, to be a part of this." He gave me a bashful look that just about unraveled me.

"Alex," I said.

"Ten thousand."

"Excuse me?" He couldn't be serious. "Dollars?"

"That's half of what I'd net, after expenses for materials."

I laughed. "Okay, you got me. Hilarious."

He stood up straighter and fixed me with a stare. He wasn't joking.

"Ten days," he said. "For ten-K."

"You're out of your mind." Ten thousand dollars would be enough for me to start over back in Asheville. I could pay Janet the rent that I owed her and put down a deposit on a new place. I could sock money into savings *and* paint for months without working as a cashier. Alex Fox just threw me a lifeline.

And right now, Alex Fox was so close that I could smell sawdust and cedar and feel the heat of his gaze. He could still melt me with that stare and he knew it.

"But Alex, I'm not a sculptor."

"You don't have to be. You'll be the brains. I'll do the dirty work —unless you want to help with that part."

His brow lifted at the word *dirty* and there was that tingle again, running along my skin from my neck to my toes.

Have mercy.

Maybe, doing something like this that was entirely different, would end this creative block I had once and for all.

Plus, ten thousand dollars bought freedom.

"Okay, fine," I said. "Ten days. Ten thousand."

He raised a brow and gave me a sexy half-smile that made my heart beat faster. "Really?"

"I'll help you with your stupid tree."

"That's the spirit." He held out his big hand, smudged with soot, and I shook it, trying not to think of the way that hand had brushed against my cheek just a few days before. He squeezed my hand, slid his thumb along my palm, and I was a goner.

He'd totally put the whammy on me. I was supposed to be keeping my distance and now he'd managed to not only get me to solve his problem but join his team.

If everything wasn't so complicated between us, this would sound like fun.

*You can do this*, I thought. *You can work together. You can be neighborly. Friendly.*

It was just work, nothing more. A collaboration between two professionals.

No problem.

# Chapter Fifteen

### ALEX

SHE. Said. Yes.

Okay, the ten thousand might have swayed her. But I panicked. I could feel her slipping away, hiding behind those big walls of hers again. She was trying to avoid me, and that was fine—I could see she had a hurricane whipping around inside her, full of a lot of complicated feelings about me. About us.

The bell on the door of the Sentient Bean clanged as I walked inside. It had only been a few hours since we talked, but I couldn't stop thinking about Fiona. We had ten days to finish the sculpture. I had ten days to convince her to stay.

Her idea was incredible. It was way better than anything I'd come up with, and I wanted her to get some credit for it. Fiona was creative, and smart, and driven—and I knew if anyone could make the sculpture even better, it was her.

Plus, I liked the idea of working so closely with Fi. I'd take any excuse to be stuck in a room with her, but the truth was that she was a brilliant artist—even though she didn't seem to think so. She had this enormous talent, and for some reason, she was still like this hidden gem of a painter. After she left for college, she used to mail me postcards that she'd painted herself—little collages made with different papers and such. She'd acted like they were nothing special, but each of them was incredible. I'd kept them all in a cigar box that was still underneath my bed. The words she'd written had been sweet, but the paintings spoke more to her feelings for me. I knew what it meant to make something for someone—you only do that for the people you love most.

It was only a matter of time before she got seen by the right people—people with enough influence to get her the visibility she needed to have her career take off. Sometimes it's hard to get seen— I knew because I felt that way for years. People had lots of ideas about "struggling" artists. It could be hard to put yourself out there and hustle to get your work seen. Fiona had this amazing eye for color and detail—her paintings were loose and vibrant, and she had this ability to capture the feeling of a place in just a few strokes. She made it look effortless, but it wasn't easy, what she did—it was an incredible skill.

Her paintings were gorgeous, and she'd no doubt do well selling them to tourists around here. Even though she made a big to-do about just passing through here, part of me thought that she might stick around Jasmine Falls if she saw what this place had to offer.

"Hey," Gwen said, snapping her fingers. "Earth to moon unit."

"Sorry," I said. "You got a dark roast going?"

"How about a pour-over? It's fresher and I can make you the new blend I just got in today."

"Sounds great."

She reached for the travel mug I'd left sitting on the counter and started the pour-over. "What's with you, today?" she said. "You've got this big goofy grin on your face. It's unsettling."

"What, I can't be having a good day?"

"Usually you've got your grumpy pants on this time of day."

Most days, I came in here for an afternoon coffee when I was stuck and needed a jolt of caffeine to get me through to the evening. Coffee always tasted better when Gwen made it. She had some kind of superpower. Plus, it was nice to get out of the studio and get some fresh air. Too much time inside made me feel trapped.

"Fiona's going to help me with a project," I said. "She's in town for a few weeks."

She smiled, pouring the coffee. "There it is."

"What?"

"The source of the goofy grin."

"Sure, I'm glad she's back." I used my most nonchalant tone, but Gwen looked at me like she could one hundred percent read my mind.

"I'll bet you are," she said.

"It's good she's here for a while. Delia misses her."

"Uh-huh. Delia sure does."

I paid for the coffee and put a five in the tip jar.

"You talked to her already, didn't you," I said.

Gwen smirked and handed me the mug.

There were zero secrets in this town.

Generally speaking though, that wasn't a terrible thing. It usually meant that people were looking out for each other. Sick with the flu? A neighbor brought you soup. Your car was in the shop? A friend took you out to run errands. Some people found that sort of thing intrusive, but to me it was nice. It's hard to find that kind of community these days, where people look out for each other because they genuinely care.

That's why this sculpture was so important. Not only was everyone in town thrilled to death with the idea of a big flashy piece of public art, but I was excited because it meant I got to give something back to the people who had helped me so much over the years. It didn't feel like much, but it was something I could do for them that would make them happy.

When I'd been so stumped by the committee's idea, it was frustrating: not just because I couldn't seem to put the puzzle together, but because I didn't want to let everyone down. I wanted this piece to be something they were all proud of and impressed by, and it was terrifying to think that I might not be able to deliver.

And then Fiona had shown up with her brilliant idea, and the last puzzle piece fell into place. It was going to be a stunning piece, and everyone would love it.

They'd be even happier to know that Fiona was a part of it, too.

And really, the community would be good for her, too. Delia talked to me pretty often about Fiona and had told me about how embarrassed she was over her broken engagement and how her mother had treated her about it. Her mother really was a piece of work. She'd always been critical of Fi—Penelope thought she knew best, and she liked saying *I told you so.* She tried to dictate who Fi's friends were, who she dated, where she went to college—even though she was hardly around to see how Fi struggled to fit in. Fiona was smart and talented, and the other kids were always jealous of that, trying to tear her down in the stupid ways that kids do. Penelope was trying to make Fiona into a little mini-Penelope, but Fi wasn't interested. I always thought her mother resented her for it. That was why she never spend real time with her, and that was why she abandoned Fi to go travel the world. She claimed it was all for work, but it just seemed to me like Penelope didn't know how to be with someone who wouldn't cave into her every demand.

Fiona had every right to be wary of coming back here given how hard it was growing up with Penelope and her expectations, but I knew she'd fall in love with this town if she just gave it a chance. It had changed a lot since we were teenagers, and I could appreciate how close the community was now. There was a time when I couldn't wait to leave, but once I started getting commissions from folks, and once I saw the outpouring of kindness after my whole debacle with Lori, I knew there was no other place I wanted to be.

There was just one thing missing here.

And now she was back.

"So what did she tell you?" I said. "She say anything about me?"

Gwen arched a brow. "I'll tell you in homeroom."

"Funny." I sipped my coffee, biting back a smile.

"Ask her yourself, champ."

If only it were that easy.

———

WHEN I PULLED into my driveway, I heard a shout from Delia's yard. Fiona was running from the barn towards the house, yelling something I couldn't make out. I jumped out of the truck, thinking that Delia might have fallen in the yard, but then saw the black and white blur streak past Fiona toward the front of the house.

Domino had escaped the fence again. Fiona hollered an array of goofy curses, chasing him around the porch and the goat let out a string of bleats as if to taunt her. How such a small animal could be such a heap of trouble was beyond me.

With a buffer of lawn between them, Domino snatched a mouthful of leaves from one of Delia's tomato plants and Fiona crept towards him. When she got close enough to lunge, he skittered out of reach and Fiona went sprawling in the grass.

"Hey," I said, jogging over to her. "You okay?"

I reached for her hand and pulled her to her feet. Her eyes met mine and there was that spark again, like a match being struck.

"I'm fine," she said. "Aside from being outsmarted by a goat. That burns a little."

Domino sneezed, browsing the buffet that was Delia's herb garden.

"In fairness, he's had way more practice at this than you," I told her. "But I need to fix the gate for real."

"But why? Who doesn't love getting their steps in by chasing a goat?"

Slowly, I walked over to Domino. Now that he was occupied eating the mint, I could get close enough to grab him by the collar and scoop him up into my arms. He let out an annoyed bleat when his feet were off the ground, but stilled as I held him tight to my chest.

"Pro tip," I said, "he likes carrots and bananas. You bring a banana out here and he'll chase you like a puppy."

"Good to know." She followed me down to the barn, where I placed Domino back inside the fence. He'd squeezed through the gate again, but I could cinch it tighter, enough to last one more day until I could come out here with the right tools.

"Thanks for the help," she said.

"Anytime." If only I could see her anytime. She'd made it clear that her stop in Jasmine Falls was just a bump in the road for her, but I wondered how much of that was because of what happened between us before. It wasn't so long ago that my world had come crashing down like a house ripped in half by a tornado. It had been scary, but as awful as it was, it taught me who my friends were, and it showed me how caring those people were. Now I wouldn't trade this town for anything.

Well. Maybe one thing.

I just needed to reintroduce her to this place, because she didn't know what Jasmine Falls had to offer these days.

She'd like this town now, if she gave it a chance.

But more than anything, I wanted her to give me another chance.

Getting her to help me with the sculpture would buy me a little time. I just hoped it was long enough.

# Chapter Sixteen

## FIONA

GROCERY SHOPPING in Jasmine Falls felt like running a gauntlet. Between dodging tourists and people you hadn't seen in a while who wanted to tell you all about the last three years of their lives, it could be exhausting to just navigate your way through the aisles. Three days ago I had to abort shopping partway through the list just so I didn't have to spend all day there.

Today, I'd run into my sixth-grade math teacher, Mr. Hemsworth, my tenth-grade art teacher Mrs. Robinson, and Linda Maxwell, who had accidentally elbowed me in a high school volleyball tournament and given me a black eye. She was now, by the way, the mayor.

They all wanted to know how long I was staying, how Delia was, and what was I up to these days. Even though they were all as kind and friendly as could be, it still felt like that last one was a question that was just too heavy for the frozen food aisle. So I grabbed three pints of gelato and high-tailed it back to Delia's. I'd collected the most critical things: she was just going to have to live without Cheetos and ginger ale for a couple more days. Next time, I'd go earlier in the morning—clearly, midday was the time when all the locals came out and were at their chattiest.

When I got back to Delia's, the last thing I expected to see was a tent set up in the backyard. It had only been two days since I met Eric in the cafe, and now he was back from Camden University, apparently for a while. Sitting in a black folding camp chair, as still as a stone, he was barely visible in at the edge of the woods, forty yards from the house, tucked into a bramble of blackberries and dwarf palmettos.

When I shut the car door, Eric stood and held his hand up in a wave. He started walking towards me, as casual as an old friend.

"Hi, Fiona," he said.

"I didn't realize you were coming today. And, uh, setting up camp."

"Oh, that," he said, as if the tent were not unusual at all. "It's more efficient this way, time-wise."

*But also a little strange.*

"I can get an early start in the mornings if I camp out." He smiled his crooked smile and pushed his sunglasses up into his hair. It looked brighter blond in the sunlight and tangled by the wind.

"Aunt D's okay with you camping in her backyard?"

Another smile, and a nod. "I talked with her earlier today. I might only need to be here a few days, just long enough to get visual confirmation. You won't even know I'm here." He nodded towards the tent and said, "Want to come check it out?"

The green dome-shaped tent was pitched under the oak trees at the edge of the woods. It looked like one of those lightweight packable ones that could fold up like origami and fit into your back pocket—but it was tall enough that we could stand up inside it. Inside, a small folding table was set up, covered with an array of items: a notebook, a field guide, binoculars, and a camera with a telephoto lens that looked like it weighed twenty pounds.

"You sure it's okay that I'm here?" he said. As he stepped closer, I caught the scent of vanilla and citronella. He fixed his big hazel eyes on mine and said, "I just figured if I camped out here, I'd be around first thing in the morning, around prime feeding time. Then

I could watch all day, and that would give me a better shot at seeing it. Is that weird?" He shook his head before I could answer. "Of course it is. A strange dude sleeping in your yard. Kinda weird." He shuffled from one foot to the other, and for the first time looked uncomfortable.

"Well, when you put it that way," I said, acting like he hadn't voiced exactly what I'd been thinking.

He bit his lip.

I decided to give him the benefit of the doubt. "Certainly it's not the weirdest thing that's been done in the name of science," I said, though this scenario was definitely not what I'd expected.

He gave me a sheepish smile. "I just figured the more often I was here, the better my chances were." He stared past me into the trees, at some movement that had caught his eye. When he turned back to me, his eyes looked sad. "I just got excited. I didn't want to miss my chance. This is a once-in-a-lifetime deal."

He was searching for the wonder, and it was hard to fault him for that. I had that same need within myself—the one that kept me up some nights, and made me feel hollow and hungry for something that felt just out of reach. Sometimes that feeling drove me to paint all day and into the night until I was utterly exhausted. Sometimes, it filled me with such curiosity it felt like I'd surely explode. And sometimes, now that it had all but vanished, it made me afraid of what my life would be like if that thirst for wonder disappeared completely.

"It's fine," I said at last. "I didn't expect it, but it's okay. If Delia said so, that is. It's her house, and it's her call."

"Oh, of course," he said, nodding. "She said it was no problem." He grinned like a kid and blurted, "Hey, you want to see something cool?" Without waiting for an answer, he put his hand on my forearm—his hand felt solid, not like some stodgy academic's—and led me toward the tree line, closer to the pond. Curious, I waded behind him through the river cane until he stopped and held the binoculars up to scan around the pond. He put his hand on my arm again and gently steered me to his side, then handed me the binoculars and pointed. "Look in the top of that pine tree," he said, his eyes twinkling.

Trying to ignore the pleasant tingling along my skin, I instead focused the binoculars and studied the top of the pine. "What am I looking for?"

Placing his hand over mine, he gently moved my arms a few degrees toward him. Then his hip was touching mine, and he leaned in close. "There's a bald eagle nesting in the top," he whispered, his lips close to my ear.

*Is this how ornithologists flirt with you*, I wondered, and then pushed the thought aside. *Stop it, Fiona.* Alex had my brain wholly scrambled. I didn't need a sexy birdwatcher in there too. Then I took a deep breath that was supposed to clear my head and push all thoughts of cute outdoorsy guys out into the ether.

It didn't.

There was movement in the tree, heavy wingbeats, and the stark white head of the eagle popped up between the branches. "Hey," I whispered. "There it is."

"I watched her catch a fish earlier." His voice was a low rumble. His lips seemed to be moving closer to my ear, which sent a shiver all the way down to my toes.

Perched in the top of the tree, the eagle sat preening a few feet from the nest. The afternoon light bounced off the blue-black sheen of her feathers, the gold of her eye.

I handed him the binoculars and said, "That's amazing. I didn't know we even had eagles here."

"You want to stay and watch with me?" he said. His eyes were wide, golden in the bright sunlight, and there was a hint of a smile. Why did every invitation from Eric sound like an adventure?

"Maybe later," I said. "I've got some work to do, but I'll come out this afternoon when I take a break." So far I hadn't made much progress on the paintings, and without a few new ones, I'd be stuck being Janet's assistant forever.

He looked disappointed, but said, "You know where to find me." He smiled that crooked smile again and stared at me just a moment too long.

Definitely flirting.

Eric yanked a green cap from his back pocket and pulled it low over his eyes as he led me out of the brush. He looked like he was on a tactical mission, taking deliberate steps and moving with catlike grace. How on earth did he make cargo pants look so hot?

When we came out of the cane thicket, he said, "Happy painting. I'd love to see more sometime."

"Sure," I said. "Just as soon as I finish something worth showing."

"Don't be so hard on yourself," he said. "Your painting brought me clear across the state."

As he turned and walked back to the edge of the woods, I watched him a little too long. He had a slow, steady gait, moving through the world as if he knew exactly where he was going. I'd felt that way once, too, back before my whole world fell apart. These days, I felt like I'd completely forgotten how to navigate, like I'd lost track of her true north.

My inner compass was spinning again.

Jasmine Falls might have been a very, very bad idea.

---

UPSTAIRS, I tried to paint birds. But I couldn't stop thinking of the way Eric had let his eyes linger on mine, the way he'd spoken so close to my ear.

*Focus, Fiona.* I needed to get my career back on track with zero distractions.

There were nine blank wood panels that needed all of my attention. The one panel I'd nearly finished—a pair of blackbirds— might turn out to be a good painting, but it was missing something, and I couldn't put my finger on what that something was. The small study of the warbler, upside down and tumbling in a flurry of green leaves, at least had a real energy to it, though I'd muddied the colors with too much fussing. It sat propped on the other side of the room, like a muse. That one might have to stay just as it was. For a good memory, if nothing else.

Janet wanted six paintings by Memorial Day, the beginning of the tourist season. We'd agreed to leave them up for a month, like a mini-show in a small nook in the gallery. If they didn't sell, she'd give the space to someone else. She didn't say it, but I had the feeling this was my last chance. No pressure or anything.

I knew she was expecting more landscapes. But I just didn't have them in me anymore. Every time I tried to paint them, I just thought of Dean and the things I'd lost. Painting those landscapes was like trying to shove myself into a dress that didn't fit. It wasn't me anymore, and I was done pretending. Birds were better. They made me happy.

Today it felt like I just moved the paint around the panel, and it didn't land where it was supposed to. The brush didn't feel right in my hand, the colors didn't work the way they should, and the paints didn't behave the way I wanted them to.

I tried another quick painting on a small panel—two sparrows that had danced around the feeder earlier. It was a quick gestural painting, one that was supposed to loosen me up and not give my brain enough time to think the painting to death.

After a few minutes, it looked like mud.

I shoved it aside to paint over later, and tried another panel. And then another.

And then again.

When I had a whole pile that would have to be painted over later, I heard shouting from outside. Curious, I went to the side window and saw Alex hurrying across the yard. He was making a beeline for Eric, who was staring in the direction of my window through his binoculars.

*What the heck?* I was about to revoke his backyard privileges.

But it seemed like I wouldn't have to. Alex was shouting, his voice deep and threatening, like a storm. He looked like he was trying to shake the earth with every step, his fists balled at his sides.

"Crap," I said, and ran downstairs.

BY THE TIME I got outside, Alex was standing just a couple of feet from Eric, waving his arms and shouting like a hooligan.

"Just what do you think you're doing?" Alex yelled. He took a step closer to Eric, like he intended to tackle him.

"Whoa, man," Eric said. "You got the wrong idea." He held his hands out in front of him, in that universal way that means you don't want trouble.

"You're trespassing," Alex barked. "You have five seconds to get out of here."

"No need to call the cops," Eric said, his voice still calm. "I have permission to be here."

Alex sneered and said, "Forget the cops. You're going to need an ambulance," and pushed his sleeves up over his elbows.

"Hey!" I yelled, running towards them. "Alex, stop!"

Alex turned to me, his eyes wide. "I just drove up and found this guy staring in your window with binoculars." He jabbed a thumb towards Eric, his face flushed.

"Hey," Eric said, holding his hands up again. "That's *so* not what's going on here."

I grabbed Alex's arm, trying to pull him back. With his whole body rigid, it was like trying to move an oak tree.

"Alex," I said, tugging on his arm. "Look at me. It's fine." Though the two men were about the same height, Alex had at least thirty pounds of muscle on Eric, and a large percentage of that muscle was likely concentrated in his punching arm.

Alex shook his head, confused. "You know this guy?"

"I'm Eric." He started to put his hand out and then thought better of it.

"Fiona." Alex drawled my name, the same way he did all those years ago when he was irritated with me. "What's this all about?"

"Listen," I said. "Eric is a graduate student. He's here looking for a bird."

"What bird?" He glared at Eric, sizing him up.

Eric's eyebrow arched. He looked oddly amused.

Alex had never had a temper, really—I'd never seen him get into a fight, even in high school when all the guys were itching to throw some punches just to prove they could. But right now, Alex looked like he was wound as tight as he would go, and ready to spring.

"A rare one that everybody thought was extinct," I said. After giving him the condensed version of the warbler's story, Alex stared at me like I'd just told him I was going to run away to clown school.

He gave Eric a sideways glance and said, "That sounds like a wild goose chase to me." His eyes narrowed as he placed his hands on his hips.

Eric shrugged. "Not everyone appreciates the importance of conservation."

I shot Eric a warning look as Alex's jaw twitched and I thought for sure I was going to have to turn the hose on them. Instead, I stepped between them and grabbed Alex by the arm, and squeezed until he looked at me.

His forearm felt like it was made of marble. Solid, sturdy, like he could hold me exactly where he wanted me.

*Have mercy*, I thought.

"And anyway," I said, "what right do you have to come charging through our yard and attack a total stranger?" I gave Alex my hardest stare and poked him in the chest with my finger, trying to ignore how it felt like poking a brick wall. "You're acting like a caveman."

Eric smirked, shoving his hands into his pockets.

Alex glared at me, his eyes dark with disbelief. Then he stepped back. "Oh," he said. "Well, I'm sorry. The next time I see a peeping tom stalking you outside your bedroom window, I'll just let him go about his business."

"What kind of stalker leaves his car in the driveway where everyone can see, Alex?" I nodded toward the backyard, where Eric's Jeep was parked in the shade of the maple trees, hardly hidden from sight.

Alex's gaze went to the Jeep, then rested on me again. "God, Fiona," he said, breathless, as if those two words summed up his whole constellation of feelings right now. He narrowed his eyes like he wanted to say more, but then turned toward the barn, shaking his head.

"What are you doing here, anyway?" I said.

Eric backed away, moving toward the tent as he pulled his phone from his pocket. He gave me a quick wave as if to signal he'd talk to me later.

"I came to fix the gate," Alex said.

"But you fixed the gate yesterday."

"That was temporary," he said. "This isn't."

I nodded. "Okay."

He turned then and stalked back to his truck. I started to call after him, but he was trudging through the grass like he couldn't get enough distance between us. So I just let him go.

Back at his post, Eric was flipping through the pages of a small notebook with sketches. He still seemed flustered, pacing by the entrance to the tent when I approached.

"I'm sorry about that," I said. "He's just being protective."

Eric looked up and ran a hand through his hair, apparently relieved that he hadn't been clobbered. "Is that your boyfriend?"

There was a clatter across the yard as Alex hauled a stack of weathered two-by-fours from the bed of his pickup. He tucked them under his arm and walked down to the barn with his slow, confident swagger as if nothing was out of the ordinary. It had taken him all of two minutes to shed whatever cares he had about Eric. And me.

I scoffed. "Not hardly."

There was a hint of a smile as Eric said, "You sure he knows that?" He tucked the notebook into his back pocket and arched a brow as he tracked Alex's movements by the barn. "He seemed pretty upset."

"Alex and I go way back, and he helps take care of my aunt. But he most certainly is not my boyfriend."

I could think of a hundred things to call him right now, but not that.

"Good to know," Eric said, his expression a mix of relief and amusement. "I wasn't spying on you, you know. I saw a bird in the tree by your window." He gave me another lingering look as he grabbed his camera and walked back towards the thicket.

What the heck just happened?

I wasn't sure what to call anything anymore.

# Chapter Seventeen

## FIONA

"HE DID **WHAT**?" Gwen said. Her big blue eyes were wide. When I told her about how Alex had nearly tackled Eric in the backyard the day before, she strode over to the window and looked out toward the tent, as if she might see some evidence of the spectacle. "I miss all the fun."

I snorted. "If you want to babysit Alex Fox, you can come over any time. I've got enough to manage without keeping him out of trouble."

She gave me a sly smile and handed me a large to-go cup and a pastry box and said, "I brought treats. Let's discuss your more pressing problem first."

"Is that a latte?"

"It's Irish."

I took off the lid and breathed in the sweet smell of Irish creme. "I love you."

"I know," she said. "You're going to love me even more when you try those ginger carrot muffins." She sipped her coffee and leaned against the windowsill and gestured toward my work table. "Now what's all this?"

My room looked like a bomb had gone off. There were half-finished paintings scattered from one side to the other. Paint tubes littered the work table, along with sketches, small studies, and half-empty cups of tea. It was nearly four in the afternoon, and I'd been painting since nine.

"Garbage," I said, motioning to the paintings."Why do I even bother?"

"I fail to see any garbage." Gwen said, scanning the room. "I especially like that one." She pointed toward a twenty-inch painting of two goldfinches with lots of blues and greens.

"This is hopeless."

"I think you're putting too much pressure on yourself," Gwen said. "I have an idea. Let's give you a low-stakes deadline."

"Meaning?"

"Here's the deal: we both tend to overthink things. We both have a mean streak of perfectionism. I find that when my inner critic shows up with her Voldemort face on, the solution is to give myself a deadline for a task that is so insignificant that it doesn't matter if I fail." She gestured to the paintings. "So for you, let's give you a pop-up show in the cafe. You bring me six of these paintings in two days."

I nearly spit out the coffee.

"Hear me out," she said. "Don't aim for perfect. Aim for eighty percent. Just bring me six, and it doesn't matter the size. We'll hang them in the cafe, for sale. This can be a way to beta test this new direction you're trying. If they don't sell, no big deal. It's a Jasmine Falls coffee shop. Who cares?" She smiled. "But you will have finished some pieces, and you're closer to your bigger goal. And you've punched Voldemort in the face."

As she spoke, I realized it wasn't a terrible idea.

"Here's the kicker, though," she said. "You don't get to torture yourself, and you don't get to make yourself stay up all night. Spend one hour on each one and trust your gut. Do that painterly intuition thing, and don't overthink. Put on a good murder podcast so you don't think at all."

"What if they're awful?"

"They won't be."

"But what if they are?"

"Then you'll paint more. Are you really going to stand there and tell me that Frida Kahlo never made anything she didn't like? Or that Monet didn't toss a painting in the trash now and then?"

"Okay, point taken. Do I have to put my name on them?"

She laughed. "You decide."

AFTER SHE LEFT, I set a one-hour timer on my phone and put on a podcast that would distract the analytical half of my brain. Sometimes it required trickery to stop my inner critic.

Two hours later, I had two small paintings that I told myself not to touch again. They weren't perfect, but they weren't overworked, either. There was a good energy in them, some nice movement, and the birds were identifiable as actual birds. I didn't hate them, and that felt like a win.

"Eighty percent," I said. Gwen might be onto something. I'd give myself an hour on each one, and then re-evaluate. If there was anything I couldn't live with, I'd give myself just a few minutes to touch them up.

These could be studies, like the very first gestural sketches I made when I arrived in Jasmine Falls. They'd be about capturing movement, a moment in time. Not perfection. For the first time in a long while, I liked what I was looking at. My inner critic started to search for flaws, but I mentally slapped duct tape on her mouth and shoved her into a closet. This was the start of something new, and something that I desperately needed.

Finally, there was that tiny spark that made me want to do more.

Remembering Janet's advice, I pulled out my phone and snapped a photo to share on my social channels. *New work in progress,* I wrote. *New direction, maybe. What do you think? #workinprogress #birdnerd*

Satisfied with my progress, I went downstairs and found Delia out on the porch with her binoculars, Rufus curled at her feet. Next to her was a big water bottle, a dog-eared field guide, a notebook, and a bag of pretzels. It was getting close to dusk, and the frogs had already started chirping from deep in the woods.

"You look like you're on a stakeout," I said. "Any sightings?"

"No," she said. "I figured our friend has the back forty covered, so it couldn't hurt to keep an eye on this side, too." She winced, fluffing the pillow that was under her knee. She'd been on her feet too much today, though she'd never admit it.

"You going to let me handle the cooking tomorrow?" I said.

"Well, those fritters weren't going to cook themselves, as much as I'd like them to." Alex had been trying to be helpful, bringing over a basket full of squash, but it just made Aunt D think she had to hurry up and cook it.

"You know I would have helped you. I've been watching old Julia Child episodes, so I'm basically a pro."

She smiled, waving me off. "You were busy with your work. I can handle the cooking. Mostly."

I crossed my arms over my chest and arched a brow.

"Fine," she drawled, giving me a dramatic eye-roll.

"The least you could do is let me feel useful, Aunt D." I worried that when I left, she'd try to do too much and wouldn't have someone to help her when she needed it. Alex checked in on her, but she wasn't his responsibility. I needed to know she'd be okay.

Delia stroked the cat's fur. "Honey, I love having you here. But you know I can't lie around all day and let you wait on me hand and foot."

"At least let me help you while I'm here. Living rent-free and all."

"Help Alex with that sculpture of his, and we'll call it even."

I let out an exaggerated groan.

She grinned. "You'll thank me one day. Also, your mother texted me a photo," she said, pulling her phone from her pocket. "She appears to be with Vikings and I must say, I'm a wee bit jealous."

On the screen, my mother wore giant black sunglasses with a bright blue scarf wrapped around her head. A cluster of burly blond men was gathered around her, dressed in matching gray uniforms that looked nautical and entirely too flattering. Simon stood next to her, wearing a bright floral shirt. He looked out of place, but happy about it.

"She looks more interested in the Vikings than Simon," I said.

"She says she fell in love with the fjords. They're thinking of staying a couple of extra days in Norway."

"Are we quite sure she's coming back?" I said. *Are we quite sure we want her to?*

"She'll find her way home eventually. Always does."

My phone buzzed in my pocket. It was a text from Janet: **Girl, that painting is gorgeous. Keep it up.**

**Thanks**, I wrote back.

**Also, Leona Campbell called me about her daughter helping out in the gallery this summer. The job is still yours if you want it. Let me know soon, okay?**

Ugh. The more I thought about working in the gallery again, the more nauseated I felt. I was an artist. I shouldn't be working a part-time job meant for a college-aged intern.

But the alternative—stay in Jasmine Falls? Not likely. I liked to be at least a little bit anonymous, thank you very much. Here, people thought they knew everything about you—and what they didn't know, they made up.

**Can I let you know in a few days?** I wrote. But even considering the job made my stomach clench tight.

**Sure**, she wrote. **By next week, okay?**

Looking up from my phone, I told Delia, "I'm going to check on our bird man." I needed a distraction, immediately. "You need anything before I go out?"

Delia shook her head. "Take him some fritters, though. I made a pile and the poor thing's probably starving out there, living off granola bars and GORP."

"You know what they say about feeding strays," I told her, and I swear that cat gave me side-eye like he understood every word.

"Doesn't cost me anything to be nice." She smiled. "Plus, helping a nice fella out gets you good karma points." She nodded toward Alex Fox's house.

I rolled my eyes and headed to the kitchen. Mercy, she could lay it on thick.

———

OUTSIDE, Eric lay stretched out in the grass by his tent, his hands clasped behind his head—a man in his element.

"This is my favorite time of day," he said, his eyes closed. The sky was turning violet up above the treetops, the crickets just beginning to chirp in the tall grass of the meadow. "Care to join me and unwind?"

"What makes you think I need to unwind?" I said, sitting in the grass next to him. We were shaded by the tree line so the air was about ten degrees cooler. "Maybe I like being wound so tight I'm about to explode."

"You strike me as a type-A who'd rather not be." He opened one eye and glanced at the plate in my hands. "I used to be one too."

"Delia sends her regards," I said. "And zucchini fritters."

"Your aunt is an absolute delight, especially for letting me stay here like this."

"That she is. This bird thing is the most excitement she's had in a while. She's out front looking for it herself, as we speak."

"And what about you?" He arched a brow.

"I came home hoping for zero excitement. But this level is acceptable."

He smirked. "That's my goal. Acceptable."

I passed him the plate. "Here's to finding this elusive mystery bird."

"I thought I heard it early this morning," he said, staring up into the trees. "It's hard to say for sure, though. With no visuals to confirm, I'd just be guessing. I tried to record it on my phone, but I wasn't fast enough. Shy little devil."

"Can you lure him out with a recording of a female?"

"I've tried that," he said. "I found an old recording and put it on my phone, and played it through a bigger speaker. Didn't fool our guy though."

"Any other tricks?"

"Actually, yes." He went into the tent and came back out with a small model bird.

"Did you make this?" I said. It looked like it had been quickly hand-painted, as if to just give a general idea of color patterns, like duck decoys used in hunting.

"My 3-D printer did," he said. "It's supposed to mimic the female. I'm going to put a few around the yard and see if I draw him out."

"I can't believe this came from a printer." The bird looked surprisingly lifelike, despite the rough paint job. It was painted mottled brown and gray and had spindly legs attached to a small base that would allow it to be positioned almost anywhere. The shape, though, was pretty convincing.

"It's worked with other species," he said, turning the bird over in his hands. "So maybe we'll get lucky."

"Not to be a pessimist, but how long do you look before you give up?"

"It's only been a couple of days. I didn't expect it to fly out of the swamp and eat out of my hand." He smiled a rakish smile. "I mean, that would have been incredible, but that's not how these things work. Steve Winter tracked a snow leopard for ten months just to get photographs. Everybody thought it was impossible, but he did it."

"But your thesis is due when again?"

He laughed. "December. But don't worry. I don't plan to camp in your aunt's yard until then."

"I should hope not."

"Winter tracked the snow leopard through the most rugged parts of the Himalayas. Birds can be elusive, but this is hardly the most rugged terrain on earth. We just have to entice him to be less shy."

When the fritters were gone, I stretched out in the grass next to him. "So what do you do out here all day?" I said. "How does one lure a bird from the bushes?"

He laughed. "I walk around all day doing this." He brought his fist to his lips and kissed the back of his hand so he made a light smacking sound.

"What on earth for?"

"I walk the woods, making this sound that tends to make birds curious. They can't help themselves. They have to investigate." He glanced into the woods. "Finding birds is about being patient, but you also have to find their territory. The upside is that this is prime habitat—but over twenty thousand acres of it. I'm hoping that your bird considers this area his territory, but he could just be passing through."

"So you walk around blowing kisses from sunup to sundown and hope to get lucky?"

"You'd be surprised how often that works."

His lips curved into a tiny smile, and I found myself staring at his lips bit too long. How could he be so playful and laid-back about a find that could be so important to his career? If it were me, I'd be tied up in knots, doing all I could to find this bird so I wasn't wasting my time. But here was Eric, as calm as if he were on vacation, delighted to be camping in a stranger's backyard in the middle of nowhere.

"You think I'm full of it," he said.

"It sounds a little bit like the snipe hunts from sixth-grade summer camp."

He stood and reached out for my hand. "Come on. Follow me."

In the woods, the air felt cooler. The moon hung low and full already, casting the yard in dim blue light. Eric led me past the stand of hardwoods and into the fringe of the swamp where the light barely cut through the thick branches of the trees.

"I feel like bait for the Lizard Man," I said. "Wandering around in a swamp fit for a horror movie."

He snorted. "That was a few counties over. And it was totally a dude in a suit." Our local folk monster had made a few appearances over the years, usually making headlines in the summer, when school was out. Coincidence? Not likely.

"How dare you!" I teased. "He's as beloved as Nessie. There's even a festival named after him."

"I'll protect you from the Lizard Man," he said, and gave me a wink.

"I mean, they made tee shirts and everything, so it has to be real."

While I walked, I made a lot of noise, crunching on leaves and twigs, but somehow Eric hardly made a sound.

He glanced back at me, then at my feet. "If the first rule is patience, the second rule is quiet," he said playfully.

"Rude."

He paused, and I nearly crashed into his shoulder. When he reached out and held one finger against my lips, I felt a bolt of electricity sweep straight down to my toes and thought way too hard about how his lips would feel there instead.

Eric arched a brow, then brought the back of his hand to his lips and made the kissing sound again as he walked slowly, deeper into the woods.

He paused and said, "Did you hear that?"

It was hard to hear anything over the chorus of singing frogs. And my hammering heart.

He kissed the back of his hand.

A chirp came from the brush and I tracked the sound off to my left.

Eric made the sound again, and a few moments later, the chirp repeated.

I stood still as a cypress as the back-and-forth continued, the bird moving closer to us. I squinted, scanning the bushes off to my right, but saw no movement. Wherever the bird was, it was low to the ground.

Eric made another sound, almost like the cooing of a dove, and a dark melody pierced the air.

A whippoorwill—I'd heard them when I was a girl, on warm summer nights like this one. It was nearly impossible to see them since they camouflaged themselves so well in the leaves.

Eric made the noise again, and the bird repeated the call.

"That's kind of amazing," I whispered, leaning close to his ear.

"Told you it worked," he whispered back. "I never tease about birds." He stared at me hard, and my eyes dropped down to his lips. I wondered if he could hear my heart banging against my ribs. Kissing would be bad, I thought. I was supposed to be painting, and avoiding complicated things like feelings—and kissing Eric would definitely complicate matters.

Wouldn't it?

It could be fun, no doubt about that. Eric was cute, and kissable, and had this contagious energy. He seemed so content and sure of his path, and he took everything in stride. He was passing through this place just like I was, and that meant no expectations. Just two adults enjoying each other's company without worrying that the world would fall apart when one of them left.

But no. I was here to get my life in order. I didn't need any more distractions.

I should go back inside, and pick up my paintbrush, and get back to work. I should not linger in the woods with a guy who looked like he walked right off the pages of a mountain-man clothing catalog, who was getting me all worked up on nature walks and was camping right here in the backyard like some sexy woodsman from one of Delia's romance novels.

That was the very definition of trouble. Wasn't it?

He took a step closer and my breath caught in my throat. His eyes were wide in the dim light, and when his lip turned upward into a hint of a smile, I suddenly didn't want to be anywhere else.

He brushed a lock of hair from my face and I tried to tamp down that tangle of fears and enjoy that tingly tension that comes when you connect with someone and suddenly feel more alive inside.

The air rippled between us as something whooshed past my face without making a sound. I felt a few strands of hair whisk across my cheek and caught a glimpse of a dark shape with giant spotted wings.

"Omigosh," I said, the air rushing out of my lungs. My heart pounded against my ribs. I felt breathless and dizzy.

Eric laughed. "We just got buzzed by a barred owl. They're sneaky like that."

"Are you going to tell me you called him up, too?"

"Oh no," he said, smirking. "He just wants a snack. You know, like the Lizard Man." He turned then, and fixed his big hazel eyes on me again, and said, "How about you, Fiona? What do you want?"

Standing there in the darkness, dwarfed by hardwoods that blocked the light from the moon, I realized that if I'd closed my eyes and spun around a few times, I would have felt utterly lost. The path to what I wanted wasn't easy to see.

Some things were clear, though: I wanted a career as a painter. I wanted a roof over my head that was mine. I wanted to feel successful, to have a steady income, to feel like I was doing something that had meaning. I wanted to be close by when Delia needed me, and I wanted to not feel like I was doing all of these things alone. Most of all, I wanted to feel like I could do what I wanted, free of everyone's expectations of me.

But could I have that here in Jasmine Falls?

# Chapter Eighteen

## FIONA

"NO WAY," I said, glaring at the pie. "That is apology pie, and I have nothing to apologize for. Alex is the one who made things weird between us. Not me."

It had been two days since Alex nearly pounded Eric to a pulp. Alex hadn't called to ask for my help again with the sculpture, which likely meant he didn't want my help anymore.

Just as well.

*But you'll miss that ten thousand dollars.* I thought of the deadline I had with Janet and gritted my teeth. Not only I was supposed to deliver paintings, but in a few days, I had to tell her if I wanted to come back as her assistant.

Delia leaned against the kitchen counter, her hand on her hip. "I had so many apples I had to make two pies. No use having them go to waste." Her voice was a chirp. "Now are you going to help me, or are you going to make me hobble over to his house myself?"

This was her super-subtle way of making me concede and go talk to Alex again. I might as well get it over with, or she'd just call him over for some other reason and shove us in a room together until we made up.

"Go on," Delia said, practically shoving the pie into my arms. "The man needs your help, and you need to get out of your head."

"He doesn't need my help now," I groaned. "I already gave him the idea."

"More importantly, I already told Maxine you were collaborating. And she's absolutely thrilled."

"Aunt Delia!"

"Go! Collaborate! This is a great way for you to launch yourself into the art community here. And to do something fun, for heaven's sake."

She was just trying to help me, but I didn't want to launch myself into the art scene in Jasmine Falls. I didn't need yet another project with a ticking clock or another public failure here on my resume. And I certainly didn't need to be shoved into a room with Alex Fox.

"Trust me on this one," she said. "Just take the dang pie." She wrapped it in one of her fancy fabric pie carriers and handed it to me with a big smile.

"You really are relentless."

"I just believe in expressing your gratitude. Now, shoo."

I took the pie out to my car and, for a minute, considered walking over—would it be so bad if I tripped in the meadow and dropped it?—but then thought better of it and drove over to Alex's. I parked in the driveway by the front porch and suddenly felt nervous. Like I'd been caught doing something wrong, and owed Alex some kind of apology.

Nonsense.

If Alex wanted to be an overprotective caveman, that was his problem. Now he was ghosting me and backing out of our agreement, behaving as if it were my fault that he'd embarrassed himself with Eric? Like it was on me that he made rash decisions before he saw the full picture.

The more I thought about it, the angrier I got. I'd nearly decided to take the pie and drive back to Delia's when Alex walked out of the studio building and stopped in front of me, holding one hand halfway up in a wave.

Great. Now leaving would just make me look like a big, fat chicken.

With a heavy sigh, I grabbed the pie and got out of the car.

Of course, he looked hotter than Hades, standing there in his snug jeans and his thin tee shirt that strained across his chest. His forearms were streaked with soot—as was his shirt—and his hair was sweaty, standing up in wild tufts. Surely I'd melt into the ground if I stood too close to him. How was it, that after everything he'd done to me, he could still make my knees weak?

Life was so unfair.

"Hi," he said.

"You look surprised to see me."

"This is sort of surprising, considering you don't bake." His brow arched, and he had the nerve to smile his ridiculous devilish smile as if he was enjoying this.

"Aunt Delia sent pie," I said, thrusting the pie towards him. As he caught it in his hands, I said, "To be clear, that is not apology pie. That is thank-you pie. From Aunt D."

"Got it," he said, his dimples showing.

"She says thank you for fixing Domino's fence."

He nodded as if expecting me to say more.

"Okay," I said, turning to go. "Bye."

He reached for my arm, chuckling. "Fiona, wait."

"What is it?" The nerve of him, acting amused by all of this, like he hadn't left me mortified when he charged into the backyard like a bull. And then completely ignored me afterward.

"I'm sorry."

"For what, exactly?" He wasn't going to get off easy this time.

His brow arched. "For, as you say, acting like a caveman. I saw that guy and thought he was some creepy stalker, and I just kind of lost it. I can't help it if I have a little caveman in me where you're concerned."

He smiled a crooked smile that nearly unraveled me. Suddenly it didn't seem so awful that he was being protective.

"Now would you please come look at the new models I made? I really could use your expert eye."

I crossed my arms. "You still want to do this together?"

"Of course I do. Would you still like ten thousand dollars?" His tone was as casual as if he were asking what I'd like for dinner.

"I suppose."

"Great," he said. "Come have a look."

I followed him through the kitchen, where he paused to grab two forks and two plates from the cabinet before leading me out the back door and into the studio. I was about to protest but then thought if I had to suffer through another awkward conversation with Alex, I might as well enjoy a piece of Delia's blue-ribbon pie.

He set the pie on the worktable and said, "Check these out. I tried a couple of shapes for us to play with."

On the table were more outlines of leaf forms made from copper rods, scale models made about twelve inches long. This design left the whole inside empty, like a cookie cutter. The real leaves would be three to four feet long, welded into the top of the tree as if they were bursting from the top.

"I was thinking we could make leaves out of both iron and copper," he said. "I like the idea of blending two metals together, like in the trunk. It might be better to make the words out of copper, though. You think?"

"In my head, the words would be smooth, like neon. Then we could do some wire-wrapping to cover the spots where the words attach to the frame."

"Sounds great," he said, twirling the small model in his hands.

"Then you could make the blank leaf shapes out of iron, and maybe weld some pieces inside to be like the veins." I quickly sketched it out, drawing the lights and darks. It would be an interesting contrast, to have the big stylized leaf shapes made of dark iron and shiny copper.

"More visual interest and depth," he said. "I like it."

I picked up a piece of thin florist's wire from the table to bend into a letterform, but I couldn't create a precise curve. "Can you shape copper this way? Bend the rods into letters and attach them to the frame?" Shaping copper was easy enough, but making it into cursive words would be much harder because of things like crossbars in a *t*.

"Casting the copper might work better." He twirled one of my mangled attempts in his fingers and said, "I should have thought of it before. I don't have the setup for it, but my friend Eli does. You ever do wax casting?"

"Only if you count the pendant that I made in a class about a million years ago."

"You're all set, then. It's like riding a bike."

"Sure." I snorted. "If the bike is on fire and melting as you ride it." The process itself was simple, but there were a lot of steps, and those steps involved metal that was heated to the approximate temperature of molten lava. There wasn't much room for error.

"I think it'll work," he said, picking up one of the bigger leaf shapes. "We weld the word to a few contact points on the frame, and then you could still do some extra wire wrapping with the fine copper, like at the welding points. And you could fill in some other spaces in the leaf shape to give it some texture. It'll look fantastic."

Seeing him get all excited was making me more excited about it, too. I couldn't remember the last time I'd worked on a project with someone, and it felt good to be working on something bigger than just one of my own ideas. Plus, this sculpture would stay in the community for decades, if not longer. Alex had pulled me into something amazing.

He said, "The only question is how to make the cursive blanks for the mold." The critical part of this process was to make a precise blank that looked exactly the way we wanted the finished word to look. That blank would then be used to make a mold, and then wax would be poured into that mold, taking on the shape of our blank and then used for the final metal casting. If the blank wasn't right, the other steps wouldn't fix it. We had to get it right from the start. "Modeling clay, maybe?" he said. "Something flexible enough to get that elegant shape of the cursive."

I turned the leaf over in my hands, thinking of Eric's model bird. "What about 3-D printing?"

His brow arched as he considered it. "Wow, yeah. An extra step in making molds, but they'd be precise."

"We can make the cursive as fancy as you want it if we use a printer. I can do hand-lettering and make it look however you like."

He nodded. "We can print them out, and then I'll make silicone molds of them. Then we use those molds to make the wax version."

"And then cast the wax."

He grinned. "I knew you were the best person for this."

"Know anyone with a printer?"

He grinned. "Yeah, the library."

"Perfect. Let's get started."

Alex sketched out some leaf shapes and I drew the lettering so it could fit inside one of the shapes when it was cast. It was easy to work with him, and an hour later we had a file ready to take to the library. We'd print one word first, then test the silicone-wax process. If we could get a clean wax replica of the 3-D print, we'd be all set to make the other words and get them ready to cast at his friend's forge. We could do it in a couple of days if there were no hiccups, and still be able to finish the sculpture in time for the gala. We'd be down to the wire, but we could do it.

"You want to come with me?" he said. "We can probably get this done before they close."

"Actually, I have plans." My phone buzzed with another text from Gwen. I was already late and she'd threatened to finish the first bottle of wine without me.

His brow furrowed. "Oh."

"Drinks with Gwen," I said, typing a quick reply.

He nodded, looking oddly relieved, like he'd expected me to say someone else's name.

"Let me know how it goes," I said, heading towards the door. "With the printing."

"Sure. Can you come by tomorrow? We can try making a mold and prep the other files."

"How about one-thirty?" If I kept to Gwen's one-hour per painting, I'd be able to finish at least three by lunchtime and make it over here afterward.

"Great," he said. "See you then." Alex Fox actually looked sad to see me go. And seeing that expression on his face made my heart flutter in a way I was not prepared for.

---

"SO LET ME GET THIS STRAIGHT," Gwen said. "You have a hot graduate student hanging out at your house all day, sleeping in your yard, totally digging on you. And you've got Alex so hot and bothered he rode to the rescue on his big white horse? You've been here less than a week and you've already got them both chasing after you." She grinned, catlike, and poured us both more wine. "I salute you, ma'am."

"Eric's obsessed with a bird. Not with me," I said.

"Right. That's why he's walking around making kissing noises with you." Gwen leaned back in her chair, propping her feet up on the porch rail. We'd been sitting on the screen porch for nearly an hour, watching as the sun dipped toward the horizon. By our second glass, she had all the details about Alex, Eric, and the mystery bird. My secrets were safe with her, though.

"Alex is making a sport out of driving me bonkers," I said, sipping my wine. "First he acts all sweet and charming, and then he acts like a caveman with Eric, and acts like he's jealous or something. Then I don't hear from him for two days, and then he's begging me to work on this sculpture with him, despite having the most awkward dinner on earth."

She grinned, sipping her wine. "Sounds like he's hot for you and he doesn't know how to handle that. The question is, how do you feel?"

"I can't go down that road again," I said. "I thought I was over it, but clearly I'm not. At his house that night, all that hurt came rushing back like a tidal wave. I felt like I was going to faint. Or hurl. Or maybe both." I left out the part about how my whole body had tingled when Alex had stood close enough that his hips touched mine. I also didn't mention how my heart had hammered in my chest when he'd leaned close to kiss me and how I'd been a wreck ever since, thinking about all of his parts and how they used to fit so nicely with all of my parts. "From here on out, we're friends," I said. "Colleagues. Nothing more."

"Did you tell him that?"

I sipped my wine. "Not in so many words. It was implied."

"Was that before or after you got it on in the tool shed?"

"It was his studio. Not a tool shed. And we did not *get it on*."

"Distinction without a difference."

"Whose side are you on?"

She laughed. "Honey, I'm always on your side. I just think you need to use your words with him and make it clear what you want. You know I like Alex, but he's man, babe. And most men have the inference skills of a chipmunk."

"I just want to get my life back on track. I don't need to be derailed by Alex Fox. No matter how hot and charming he is."

"Okay, then." Although Gwen agreed, she sounded doubtful.

"But I don't want to make things more awkward, either. He does all this stuff to help Aunt Delia, and I'm grateful for that. I don't want him to start avoiding her because of me. She loves having him over there, even though she'd never admit she's lonely."

"Just talk to him," Gwen said. "Remember he has no idea how

you feel and how badly he hurt you back then. Tell him what you told me. Maybe that'll clear the air."

"And if it doesn't?"

"Then you won't wonder what might have happened if you'd just had the guts to speak up. And I'll serve him lukewarm coffee full of grounds for the rest of his life."

# Chapter Nineteen

## FIONA

"SO WE'RE TEMPTING him with worm cakes?" I said.

"Warblers love mealworms," Eric said. "That buffet out there is like a dream come true."

This was not how I'd expected to spend my Saturday morning, but here we were, hunkered down shoulder to shoulder in the brush, right where the yard turned swampy. Even in the bright morning light, Eric blended into the bushes, wearing an olive green tee shirt and camouflage cargo pants. Next to him, my blue tank top and jean shorts seemed bright as a flare. The ground felt squishy and damp against my knees and I already regretted leaving so much skin exposed to the briars and the scrubby brush. When I'd agreed to this outing, I hadn't asked about the dress code.

"So what now?" I said.

"Now we wait."

He peered through his binoculars, watching the feeders he'd set up in the trees at the edge of the property. There were already a few birds gathered there, and when there was movement at the other feeder, he said, "Oh, hello."

I grabbed his binoculars and stole a peek, pulling him closer to me. He grunted when his head thunked against mine, the strap around his neck pulled taut. His hair was soft against my cheek.

"Just a sparrow," I said. "False alarm."

He pulled another pair of smaller binoculars from his backpack and handed them to me. "I brought you your own pair," he said, but he didn't move away.

"What, you don't like to share?"

He raised a brow and his lip curved into a mischievous smile. "There are plenty of things I like to share. But not instruments that are calibrated just the way I like them."

"Ice cream?" I said, teasing.

"If conditions are right."

"Pie?"

"Any kind but key lime. That one's all mine."

"Noted." I smiled, thinking of what other things Eric might share. I focused the smaller binoculars and turned back to the feeders, trying to ignore the way his arm was touching mine. Maybe this sort of distraction wasn't so bad after all: a mysterious bird and a flirty outdoorsy guy with zero expectations. Both would fill up my brain till there was no more room for Alex Fox.

So far there were quite a few birds around—titmice mostly, with a few chickadees and the occasional catbird. No mystery bird yet.

"I mounted motion-sensitive cameras to each feeder," he said, his voice low. "So if our bird shows up, it'll be like he's popping into a photo booth. That way we don't have to stay out here all day watching."

"So does this mean you don't need to camp in the backyard anymore?" My heart sank at the thought, surprising me.

"Do you want me to not be in the backyard anymore?" He looked at me as if he were asking a different question entirely.

"No," I said. "I like that you're here."

He looked at me for a moment and then said, "There's plenty of other things to do." His lip curved into a teasing smile and I wasn't so sure we were talking about birds anymore. A tingle zipped straight down my spine from my neck to my toes.

"Such as?"

He stood and pulled me to my feet. "Come with me."

Moving deeper into the woods, I tried not to stumble through the brush. I wondered if we were actually going to make out in the woods like a couple of teenagers and—dear lord, could he hear my heart hammering in my chest right now?

The ground was softer now, and my feet had gone from making a soft squishing noise to one that sounded like it needed to be followed by a *pardon me*. Once again, Eric seemed to glide right through the muck without making any noise at all, whereas I left deep footprints that quickly filled with water. We were close to the boundary with the national park land, where the swamps became thicker and darker, the mud more like the pluff mud on the coast and the barrier islands.

When he stopped, I nearly bumped into him.

"What's out here?" I said. It wasn't exactly a comfortable spot to canoodle.

"Mist nets." He walked over to a little pine tree and tugged on a fine mesh net that stretched from that tree to one about fifteen feet away. It was barely visible, but when Eric reached into the bottom of it, I saw its dark threads ripple in the breeze.

*Of course*, I thought. Nets. Bird things. Not making out in the woods like teenagers.

It was a little disappointing, like being taken to the fair only to learn that there were no funnel cakes or pony rides.

"The threads are soft and fine," he said, "and when a bird flies into the net, it slips down into this mesh pocket at the bottom. Sort of like a foul ball." He reached inside and, almost like a magic trick, plucked a bird out of the net. He held it carefully in his hand, his fingers stabilizing its wings.

"Nuthatch." He held it close for me to see, and the bird let out a nasal chirp as if to confirm.

"Does this hurt them?" I said.

"Not at all." He looked at the bird and stroked the top of its head with his index finger. Then he opened his hand and the nuthatch flew up into a nearby tree. "Sometimes their feet get tangled in the pocket, and I'm sure they're not thrilled about that, but it's easy to get them out." He slid his finger along the mesh pocket. "I only leave these up in the daytime, though. You have to check them every hour for any birds that might be caught."

Eric checked the rest of the net, where I could see at least two more birds resting. Each time he found one, he held it carefully as he moved the tiny threads from around its feet and then released it.

"I was hoping, of course, that your warbler might end up here," he said. "But no luck so far."

"It seems he doesn't want to be found," I said.

He pulled a small black and white striped bird from the net and I leaned over for a closer look.

"Black and white warbler," he said. "Getting warmer." He stroked its head with his finger and said, "Do us a favor, bud. Tell your cousin to pop over for a visit."

The bird let out a low chirp as if to protest and Eric released it into the sky. "You up for a stroll?" he asked me. "I usually take a few walks while I'm waiting to check the nets."

"Sure," I said. "I like watching you." *Ack. No, Fiona.* "I mean, you're clearly doing what you love. It's cool to watch."

He smiled. "Aren't you doing what you love?"

I considered that for a moment. "It feels like maybe I am. I wouldn't have said that a week ago."

He looked puzzled. "What changed?"

I snorted. "What hasn't?" Even though I'd only been back here a week, it felt like I was finally doing what I wanted to do. "I spent too long trying to do what other people expected of me—making work that other people liked, painting what my art dealer wanted, going where my ex wanted to live. I felt like I had to do those things to be successful, and it was exhausting." Being here, though

—I liked being close to Delia, hanging out with Gwen, and painting what made me happy. It made me think I really could start over and leave all of my past failures where they belonged— in the past.

"Sounds like you keep the bar pretty high for yourself," he said.

"Yeah, I got that from Penelope I guess."

He arched a brow. "Is that your mom?"

My eyes rolled at the mere sound of her name. A pitiful reflex that I'd yet to shake. "How did you guess?"

He gave me a sympathetic smile—the kind you give someone when you realize you share the same kind of damage. "My dad's like that. He wanted me to be a doctor, and absolutely lost it when I veered off track into ornithology. Wrote me out of the will and everything."

"Yikes. Hates nature, huh?"

He ducked under a low limb. "He quit paying for college, so I had to make my own way."

"Same here. Penelope wanted me to be an architect like she is."

"What is it with parents wanting little carbon copies of themselves? Is it a mortality thing? They think they'll live forever this way?"

I laughed. "Penelope's a control freak. She'd never be satisfied with the way I ran her business anyway. She'd haunt me from the grave over the bookkeeping and the waiting room decor. And my casual attire, of course."

"Well, I think you're incredibly talented and doing just what you should be doing. If I could paint the way you do, I'd never do anything else."

It felt like time froze, like in one of those superhero movies. People had complimented me on my work before, but no *stranger* had ever said words like that. Delia did, but she was family. Janet did, but it was literally her job to. Alex did, but he had his own motives.

Some days I was afraid I'd be in fake-it-till-you-make-it mode until I died. But maybe the real problem was that I was afraid to take a leap and see what might happen if I did things differently.

"That might be the nicest thing anyone ever said to me," I said.

"Well, here's to forging our own path," he said. "I'll take the birds over most people any day."

"Present company excluded, right?" Most people I met weren't as interesting as Eric, either. Plus, I liked having him around.

He stopped and gave me a warm smile. "I like you just fine. Almost as much as the nuthatches."

"Good, because I'd hate to have to evict you from the backyard." He'd become a kind of fixture now, one that made me feel like there was still adventure to be found in my tiny corner of the world.

"That would be tragic." His eyes drifted to my lips like he was thinking about kissing me, and we were finally at that line—and crossing it would change everything. He leaned in closer—and this was definitely happening—but the next thought that popped into my head was of Alex.

Specifically, kissing Alex.

Dang it.

I couldn't be that person—kissing one guy while thinking of another. Nope. Not my style.

"Hey," I said, taking a step back. "Want to check that last net?" I tried to keep my tone breezy, like I hadn't been thinking of kissing anyone. I liked Eric, and this didn't need to be another awkward moment.

He gave me a tender smile, like he knew the score. "Sure," he said, nodding his head toward a thicket. "This way."

I followed him through the dense foliage until we came to a space that opened up. As Eric checked the mist net, I saw a flash of yellow in a nearby shrub.

"Eric!" I whisper-shouted. "Over here!"

I hurried toward the spot where I'd seen the flash of yellow, afraid if I took my eyes off it, I'd never find it again. The leaves moved and the yellow flashed again, a little further up in the treetops. Rushing toward it, I ignored the way my sneakers sank in the mud, the way the briars tore at my arms. I scrambled to get the binoculars in position and my foot caught on a root.

In that moment, three things happened simultaneously:

The bird let out a raucous, buzzing call.

My body was airborne, and my arms instinctively reached out like wings as Eric called my name.

I flew head-first into the mud with a graceless thunk-squish, my arms barely stopping me from face-planting.

As I peeled myself from the mud and clambered to my knees, I was horrified to see that my entire front was caked in mud.

"Are you okay?" Eric said, rushing to my side.

"I think so." Water was already filling my Fiona-shaped imprint in the mud. As I struggled to stand, Eric grabbed me under the armpits and hoisted me to my feet. Unfortunately, my feet were completely submerged in the muck. When Eric had me standing, I moved to take a step toward dry land and, when my foot didn't budge, I windmilled my arms to keep myself upright. He grabbed me around the waist, which startled me—because *Wow, Eric, what a grip you have*—and I overcorrected and pulled us both off-balance.

We toppled into the mud in a heap.

"Omigosh," I said. "I'm so sorry."

Eric lay on his back, mud splattered in his hair. I'd landed half on top of him, pushing him deeper into the muck. As I pushed myself up onto my knees, my hands sank into the mud. There was no graceful way to get out of this now. We both looked like we'd rolled down a muddy hillside.

"Are you okay?" I said.

He burst out laughing and wiped the mud from his face. "I've only seen that happen in cartoons," he said.

"There's a reason I shouldn't be out in the wilderness."

He stared at me for a long moment, and my eyes drifted to his lips.

In one fluid motion, he pulled himself up to standing and then reached his hand toward me.

"I think you should just leave me here to die of embarrassment," I said. "We'll consider it Darwinism."

"Come on," he said. "I'm ready for you this time."

When I took his hand, he pulled me to my feet and caught me in his arms.

"Pull your feet out of your shoes," he said, holding me steady.

I did as he said, struggling to get both of my feet free while not pulling him to the ground again. *Shouldn't have quit that yoga class*, I thought. Now my balance was non-existent, and couldn't the swamp just swallow me now?

When my feet were free, Eric knelt down to retrieve my sneakers. Then he took my hand and led me through the mud toward solid earth. I held on to his shoulder for balance as I slipped my shoes back on. They were ruined, of course, but there was no way I was walking back to the house barefoot.

"Good grief," I said. Mud oozed out of my shoes with each step.

"That was impressive," he said with a grin. "I don't think I've been taken down that way since my rugby days."

"Grace is my middle name."

When we got to the house, I peeled off my sneakers and used the garden hose to spray the mud off my bare feet. "Try to get the worst off our shoes," I told Eric, handing him the hose. "I'll be back in a minute."

Inside, I grabbed my bathrobe and a couple of towels from upstairs, careful not to brush up against anything in my filthy clothes. Delia wouldn't be back for another hour or so at least— she'd gone to brunch with her friend Hazel and that was always a half-day outing. We'd have time to get cleaned up and throw our clothes in the wash before she got home.

Back outside, I tossed Eric my bathrobe and said, "Put this on. You can use the shower downstairs, but I don't want to track mud all through the house."

He smiled. "Thanks. I thought you were just going to hose me down in the yard."

Before I could even turn around to give him some privacy, he yanked his shirt over his head and dropped it to the ground. I quickly turned my back, but not before I'd clocked an impressive set of biceps and some seriously chiseled abs. Like, the kind celebrities pay buckets of money to trainers to give them.

I took a deep breath as I heard a belt buckle come undone and tried desperately to ignore the sound of his zipper and banish the thought of how well-muscled his thighs would be.

*No, Fiona. Stop. No more thinking of Eric's chiseled parts.*

"Okay," he said. "Decent now." He'd cinched my silk robe around himself tightly. It didn't even reach his knees. He gave me a bashful smile that sent that tingly feeling all along my skin again.

Sigh.

"I'll toss our clothes in to wash while you shower," I said, and motioned for him to hand me his muddy pants and shirt. "My aunt's still out, so there's no chance of awkward interactions."

He smiled. "Copy that."

The screen door banged as we went inside and I led him through the kitchen and down the hall to the bathroom. "Next door on your right," I said. "I'll be upstairs."

"Thanks," he said, slipping down the hallway, and dang if he didn't have beautifully sculpted calves, too.

After tossing our muddy clothes in the wash, I went to shower upstairs. Once the hot water hit me, it felt like heaven. I scrubbed mud out of places I didn't even realize it could reach, and all the while tried not to picture Eric all naked and chiseled in the shower right below me.

I didn't think about his perfect biceps, strong enough to hoist me out of the mud. I didn't think about his mischievous smile and the way he'd so quickly stripped off his shirt to reveal those incredibly defined abs and the big swirling tattoo on his shoulder that definitely deserved a closer look, because I could appreciate art after all—in each of its many forms. And I certainly didn't spend one second thinking about all the parts I hadn't seen.

Once I felt human again, I quickly toweled off and threw on the first clean tee shirt and shorts I could find. As I headed downstairs, I heard the back door close, then footsteps in the kitchen. Eric no doubt had a change of clothes outside in his tent—of course, he wouldn't sit around in my bathrobe waiting on our clothes to wash.

"I'm just going to check on our clothes," I called. "We've got plenty of snacks if you're hungry." My stomach was growling, reminding me I'd skipped breakfast. Eric or no Eric, I was about to murder the leftovers in the fridge in a very unladylike way.

After tossing the clothes in to dry, I hurried into the kitchen, and then nearly jumped out of my skin.

Alex Fox was standing by the sink, a giant box of tomatoes and zucchini by his side.

"What are you doing here?" I said. "Don't you knock?"

He looked as startled as I felt. "Sorry, Fi," he said. "I did knock, but there was no answer. I figured you and Miss D were out."

"So you just let yourself in?"

He frowned. "I'm sorry. She gave me a key and I've gotten in the habit of dropping things off when she's not here. I called and texted you, but you never responded. I figured you were out somewhere."

"Well, you can't do that anymore," I said. "Or at least, don't do it while I'm here. I could be walking around naked, for heaven's sake." It wasn't unusual for me to forget all of my clothes were in the laundry room and come down in the morning to get them in nothing but a towel and bed hair.

Hearing those words, Alex Fox turned redder than the tomatoes. Why did I blurt out every thought in my head when I was around him?

Alex cleared his throat and averted his gaze. "I brought some vegetables—and even better, I got the first mold finished and made the wax model. I wanted to bring it over so you could—"

"Hey, are you all right?" Eric spoke from behind me, and I jumped.

Alex's jaw tightened as he stared past me toward the den. And just like that, friendly, happy, vegetable-toting Alex was gone.

When I turned to follow his gaze, there was Eric, leaning against the doorframe, holding a towel wrapped around his waist.

Lord have mercy. He looked like one of those guys who walks out of the ocean in a TV cologne ad. He was slimmer than Alex but lean and fit. Suddenly that towel seemed awfully small.

"I thought I heard voices," Eric said, his tone wary. He glanced at Alex and turned back to me. "Everything okay?" He inclined his head just the slightest bit as if to ask if I needed help.

Alex's stare had turned stony. He looked like he wanted to smash those zucchini to smithereens.

"Yes," I said, my voice sounding all breathy and weird. I swallowed hard and said, "Alex just surprised me, that's all. He brought Aunt D some vegetables."

"Oh," Eric said, raising a brow. He gave Alex another long look, sizing him up. "Okay."

The two men stared at each other like a couple of rams preparing to head-butt each other. Alex stiffened, crossing his arms over his chest, still leaning against the counter as if this were his kitchen. Eric placed one hand on his hip, the other still gripping the towel.

Good grief.

Alex glared at him. If looks could start a fire, that whole house would have been cinders.

I wanted the floor to open up and swallow me, right that second. There was entirely too much testosterone in the room right now, and really, I just couldn't get out of this town fast enough.

"I'm just going to go out and get a change of clothes," Eric said, turning back to me. "Be right back." He squeezed past me, his arm brushing mine as he walked between me and Alex, toward the back door.

"You bet," I said brightly, unable to ignore his perfect shoulders, his muscular arms, and the tattoo that curled along his left pectoral and down to his ribs.

Once Eric was out the back door, I looked back at Alex and—oh crap. He had definitely caught me staring at Eric. Alex was gripping the counter so hard that his knuckles were white.

"Alex," I said. "Listen."

He opened his mouth to say something and then shook his head. After gritting his teeth for what felt like five minutes, he muttered, "Tell Delia I hope she's feeling better."

As he turned toward the door, I said, "Hang on. That wasn't what it looked like."

Alex opened the back door and glanced at me."Fiona," he ground out, "Who you...*spend time with*...is none of my business." He made the word *time* sound positively filthy.

I was furious.

I followed him outside onto the lawn, the door banging behind me. "Alex Fox, you stop right there." I got so close to him that our toes were touching. He towered over me, but I didn't care. "You don't get to sneak into my house, then make assumptions about me, and then insult me on top of it all!"

Hearing those words, he looked almost sad. "I'm not trying to insult you, Fi. We're both adults here. I just don't want to see you taken advantage of."

"Seriously?" I blinked at him, but he said nothing. "Why don't you tell me what's really bothering you here?" I wanted to hear him say the words, to tell me what he'd been feeling since I came back— even if it would be scary to hear him say it.

He shoved his hands into his pockets, staring across the yard toward Eric's tent. "Just be careful, will you? You don't even know this guy, and I don't have a good feeling about him."

I snorted. He was impossible. "Alex, he's harmless. He's a good guy looking for a break. Just like the rest of us."

He turned to me then, his eyes dark. "No. Not like the rest of us. He's just here because he wants something from you."

Heat rose in my cheeks. "You have no business telling me who to hang around with, and you know it." I wanted to take those tomatoes and squish them into his perfectly tousled hair until the juice ran down his perfectly angled jaw.

"Just be careful, Fi. Some people are very good at showing you exactly what they want you to see."

"Yeah. You taught me that already."

He flinched. "What'll it take to get you to forgive me, Fiona?"

"I don't know," I spat out. "The truth, maybe?"

He stared at me, shocked, as if I'd slapped him. "If I thought you'd listen, I'd tell you anything you wanted to hear." He climbed inside his truck without another word.

He had a lot of nerve to make assumptions about hurt. The way he'd stomped all over my heart had taught me plenty. (As it turns out, time heals nothing.) But I wanted to tell him this was not about forgiveness. This was about trust. Here he was, again locking himself down tight when I needed to know what was buried deep in his heart. He was holding something back, just as he had eight years before.

As he headed down the driveway, I had another thought: why did I care what Alex thought of me? And why did I care what he thought was happening with Eric?

And why was I just a little bit pleased by the fact that Alex Fox had looked completely jealous?

# Chapter Twenty

FIONA

"I HAVE A PROBLEM," I told Gwen.

She sipped her cappuccino and smirked. "Does it involve a certain metalsmith?"

It was seven-thirty in the morning, the day after Towel-Gate, and I was not awake enough to be thinking about complex things like hanging art and determining what was happening between me and Alex. Especially because I'd been up until three in the morning painting. Yes, I'd broken my promise—I'd spent a little more than one hour on each of these paintings, but I couldn't help myself, and the perfectionist in me takes over when I'm weak with anger.

Baby steps.

Hanging art for a show meant attention to detail and math (ugh), but Gwen was doing the heavy lifting this morning. She wasn't as precise as I'd be in a gallery, but then she didn't need to be. The Bean had a funky vibe—the kind that was relaxed enough not to worry too much about perfect spacing and alignment. She'd moved her other art into the back of the cafe, proclaiming that the front was now the Fiona Gallery.

I'd groaned with embarrassment.

At the moment, Maggie was filling the pastry case and brewing the last carafe of house coffee. It smelled like heaven.

"I'm so glad you brought these," Gwen said. She hammered a nail into the wall with three precise hits, then hung my small painting of a chickadee. "They're so colorful and playful." She stepped back and adjusted the painting, then hammered another nail into the wall several inches away. "So what's the problem with Alex?"

I handed her the next painting. "He's acting all over-protective and judgmental, like we're in some Victorian novel and he's my big brother, trying to guard my virtue." I scoffed. "And, well, he might have walked in and seen Eric in a towel."

Gwen's hammer struck the wall, missing the nail entirely. "Whoa," she said. "Way to bury the lede."

"Nothing happened," I said. "We got all muddy in the swamp and—"

She laughed, pointing the hammer at me. "Busted."

"Okay, I know how that sounds. But really. It was totally innocent. I mean, I thought about it, because he's seriously hot. And he doesn't have a complicated history, and he doesn't live here, and maybe I could use a fun, little fling—but Alex got the wrong idea, and now everything's super awkward because he kissed me the other night and I might have freaked out and run away, and I can't stop thinking about him." I dropped my face in my hands. "Now I want to quit working on our sculpture but I feel like I can't because it could get me in with the Arts Council and if I quit it will make Aunt D look bad, too. And Alex offered to pay me a stupid amount of money to help him with it, like too much for me to turn down in my current situation, and even though it sounded like some weirdo devil's bargain, I said yes." I looked up at her for help.

Gwen just stared at me, her mouth in a tiny O.

"Wow," she said finally. "How long have you been holding all that in?"

I took a deep breath and a gulp of coffee. "I really shouldn't be in the same room with him. Half the time I want to punch him, and the rest of the time I want to kiss him stupid."

"Ah." She knocked the nail into place and hung the next painting.

"It's complicated between us."

"It always has been."

"I can't stop thinking about him—but it's not always good thoughts, you know? I have lots of thoughts, in varying degrees of intensity. But I know I can't go down this road again."

"You don't want to get hurt again," she said. "I get that."

"I just came here to help Delia and take some time to turn my career around. This trip was supposed to be an escape. I wanted to get away from complicated, and now I'm up to my ears in it."

"Breathe," she said, putting her hands on my shoulders. "You're a grown woman. You do what makes you happy."

Behind us, the bell over the door clanged as Maggie unlocked the door and switched the sign around to read "open."

I said, "Eric's funny. Sweet. Not complicated."

"Okay."

"He doesn't know everything about me, like the rest of this town does. He doesn't have all these expectations about me."

"If that's what you want," Gwen said, "then I don't see the problem." She pounded another nail into the wall with three clean hits, then hung the last painting and adjusted it so it was straight. "And if you don't want to work with Alex, then don't. You don't owe him anything." She brushed her bangs out of her eyes and said, "Forget everybody else. What do *you* want to do?"

"I don't know what I want anymore. That's the problem."

Before she could reply, someone behind us said, "Hey, cool art."

Sadie stood holding a large to-go cup, staring at the painting we'd just hung. Her hair was pulled back in a neat ponytail, her aviator sunglasses pushed up onto her head. As usual, her green and gray park service uniform looked perfectly crisp, her shoes shined with a mirror polish. The park service apparently didn't tolerate untidiness in a uniform. Never had I seen such perfect creases in a shirt and pants.

"These are Fiona's," Gwen said. "Aren't they gorgeous?"

"Lovely," Sadie said, her eyes widening. "I want one."

Gwen smiled at me and arched a brow that said, *Told you so.*

"Thank you, Sadie," I said.

Sadie checked her watch. "I'm running late, but seriously. That one over there with the goldfinches. They're my favorite. Can I come back and pay you tonight?"

"Of course," Gwen said. She pulled a pack of stickers from her front apron pocket. Little blue stars.

"Thanks," Sadie said, heading for the door. "Awesome work, Fiona. I'd love for you to tell me more about it. Right now I have to go entertain a group of sixth-graders and explain why you shouldn't take home alligators from the park and make them into pets."

"Try not to lose any this time," Gwen said.

Sadie rolled her eyes. "It was just that once. And he wasn't technically lost—he just split off from our group so he could follow the girl scouts instead. And the teacher would have noticed if she hadn't been so busy flirting with Ranger Chris."

"To be fair, it's very easy to be distracted by Ranger Chris," Gwen said. "Why doesn't he come in for coffee runs anymore?"

"I'll tell him you asked," she said with a smirk.

"Please do. Tell him I've got tasty treats with his name on them." She smiled and wiggled her eyebrows. "And blueberry walnut scones, too."

"You're trouble," Sadie said, shoving the door open with her hip. "See you tonight."

Gwen stuck a blue sticker on the label next to the goldfinch painting. "You'd better get started on some more of these, Fi." Across the room, a lady was standing in front of the largest of the paintings, examining it closely.

"I love these," Gwen said. "I'd buy them myself, but then that defeats the purpose of our experiment. How about I commission a few from you when these sell?"

"You got it," I said.

I felt something inside my chest flutter, something I hadn't felt in a very long time. It was that spark again, that feeling that I was headed in the right direction.

"Now," she said. "Let's sort out this Alex business so you can get on with your business."

# Chapter Twenty-One

## ALEX

THAT BIRD GUY WAS TROUBLE. Camping out in Delia's backyard? Getting all cozy like he lived there? He may have charmed Fiona and Miss Delia, but I knew he was interested in more than just a bird, and I didn't trust him as far as I could throw him.

And I kinda wanted to just throw him.

Convincing Fi that he wasn't what he seemed might be a little difficult, though. I didn't miss the way she clocked him in that towel yesterday. Seeing that look on her face had just about split me in two. She always did want to see the good in people, just like her Aunt Delia. But sometimes that meant people took advantage of her good nature—people like her mother, and people like that scoundrel fiancé of hers.

She deserved better.

Fiona would do anything to help a friend, but too often she put herself last. She didn't deserve to be put last, ever. And she certainly didn't deserve to be underestimated because of her kindness.

A little before one o'clock, I went to the Sentient Bean and ordered my usual black coffee. The cafe was crowded, as per usual in the tourist season. Most people who visited the national park came to check out Jasmine Falls, too—so almost everywhere I went in the summer had a crowd of tourists and a few locals mixed in. Maxine and Dale from the Arts Council waved from a booth in the back, motioning me over. They were early for our meeting because they were always early. To them, on time was late.

"Hey, y'all," I said, sitting across from them. "Good to see you."

"We're so excited for an update," Dale said. In his sixties, Dale always dressed like he was going for a hike—but none of his vests or hiking boots ever looked like they'd spent a minute on a trail. Today he wore a checkered shirt and khaki pants with zip pockets that made him look like a river guide.

Maxine smiled. "Everyone's excited." By contrast, Maxine almost always wore black pants and a black top, punctuated by the most brightly-colored scarf she could find. Her long braids often had different colors threading through them: today they were a bright burgundy that brought out the warm tones in her dark skin. She had glasses in every color, and today she wore bright purple ones that matched the scarf. She was like a rainbow that lit up the whole town.

Fiona was like that, too. She just didn't see it.

"So here's where I'm at," I said, opening my notebook. I'd taken some photos of the test pieces that Fiona and I had made, and I'd sketched out a new rendering of what the finished sculpture would look like. "I brought another artist friend of mine into the project— she's incredibly talented and I know you'll love her."

"Yes!" Maxine said, clapping her hands together. "Delia told us all about it. I'm so excited to see Fiona again."

"She said the same about you," I told her.

Maxine and Dale looked down at the drawings as I explained our plan, and then shared a look I couldn't decipher—intrigued or skeptical? It was hard to tell.

At that moment, a guy brushed past us, talking on his cell phone, and sat in the adjoining booth, his back to Dale and Maxine.

Eric, the birdwatcher.

My head felt hot. I took a deep breath and tried to focus on the sketch of the sculpture.

Maxine and Dale studied the drawings as I told them all about Fiona's experience and our new idea for the leaves in the tree. Maxine had her poker face on, which was always a little unsettling. I could never tell if she hated an idea or loved it until she opened her mouth.

Maxine would love Fiona—that was for sure. Fiona was just the kind of artist that Maxine liked to take under her wing and introduce to her inner circle—and once you were in Maxine's inner circle, the whole world opened up. With Maxine on her side, Fiona could have exhibits any time she wanted, charge whatever she wanted—she could make a name for herself here. Fiona didn't believe me, because she was in some kind of slump. We all get those, though—she just needed to have some faith in herself. If only I could convince her of that.

They were quiet for a moment, and I watched as another man joined Eric in the booth behind them. Several years older and many pounds heavier, he wore khakis and a button-down shirt, and one of those floppy fisherman hats that don't flatter anyone. He shook Eric's hand excitedly and sat across from him.

"I love it," Dale said, snapping me back to our meeting.

"It's brilliant," Maxine said, cracking a big smile. "And you can finish all these details by Friday?"

"Definitely," I said, but my attention was on Eric, as he handed his phone to the guy in the floppy hat. The man pushed his glasses up onto his forehead and held the phone a few inches from his nose. They were talking in low voices, in a conspiratorial way. I strained to hear them over the noise of the cafe.

"Don't you think so?" Dale said.

"Oh," I said, looking back at Dale, "of course." I cringed, having no idea what I'd agreed to, but hoping it wasn't anything too embarrassing or expensive.

"Let's set something up," Maxine said, adjusting her scarf. "I'm afraid we've got to run to another appointment, but I'll call you and we can all have dinner together soon and discuss the details."

"Perfect," I told her. I'd have to get the details about this dinner out of Dale later.

Dale shook my hand and the two of them slipped out of the booth. As soon as they were gone, I grabbed a menu and held it up to my face, pretending to read as I watched Eric and the older man. It was nearly impossible to hear what Eric was saying, but the man in the floppy hat looked intrigued. Tired of straining my ears, I eased over to the opposite side of my booth, careful to not rouse Eric's attention.

Once I was just a few inches away, back to back with Eric, I could hear him more easily.

"This changes everything," Eric said, his voice low. "This could be the find of our lifetimes."

"You don't have much to go on," the other man said.

"I just need some time," Eric said. "I know it's the real deal. Look at the coloration."

"If you're wrong, you'll graduate late. You'll kiss that internship goodbye."

"But if I'm right, we'll make history. I won't need a lousy internship."

The older man muttered something I couldn't quite make out.

"I've got it under control," Eric said, sounding way too cocky. "I can stay as long as I need to. This is going to be the best thing that ever happened to me—and the department."

Had he told Fiona these things?

At the table next to me, two teenage girls broke out into laughter. Behind me, I heard something about *grants* and *funding* and *keep it quiet*.

Bristling at their words, I sipped my coffee and closed my eyes, trying to block out all the noise from the other tables and focus on their conversation. The Bean was busy today, packed with tourists, but I wanted to catch every word they said. Whatever crooked thing was going down, Fiona wouldn't be easily convinced. Apparently, my feelings about this guy meant I was an unreliable source.

When Gwen collapsed into my booth, I nearly jumped out of my skin.

"Holy bananas," she said, a little too loudly. "Who opened the floodgate this morning?" Her blonde hair was pulled up into a loose ponytail and she had streaks of what looked like flour across her usually pristine apron. "I'm glad I ran into you. Granted this is the only spot in the whole place left to sit for a minute, but I needed to talk to you anyway."

Turning one ear toward Eric, I caught a few words that had to be about Fiona and Miss Delia. I didn't like where the conversation was headed.

I held one finger up and gave a slight nod toward the booth behind us, hoping that Gwen would take the hint—most people recognize the universal sign for *Quiet, I'm eavesdropping*, but not Gwen.

"We need to talk about Fi," she said.

I pulled my cap down further on my head and leaned forward, hoping Eric was too enthralled to pay us any attention. "Shhh," I said, holding my finger to my lips. Behind me, Eric was still talking, his tone more conspiratorial.

"Alex Fox!" she said. "Don't you dare shush me in my own cafe." Her voice seemed to fill this entire side of the room. "I don't know what you think you're doing, but she's in a rough place right now, and she doesn't need you messing with her head and making it worse."

"Gwen, I—" A few heads had turned our way and I was sure now that Eric and his friend had heard the outburst. So much for being stealthy.

"If you care about her at all, you'll leave her alone until she gets a few things sorted out."

"Gwen, I do care about her. More than you know." I kept my voice low, hoping she'd do the same.

She didn't.

"Good. Then stop yanking her around." Before I could answer, she said, "This you being hot one minute and cold the next is ridiculous. Figure out what you want, and talk to her. Like a grown-up."

I frowned, thinking I knew exactly what I wanted. I just didn't quite know how to tell Fiona yet. And having this Eric guy around wasn't helping. I just didn't want him taking advantage of Fiona or her aunt, and somehow that was making me the bad guy.

There was a rustling behind me, and I felt the unmistakable punch to the kidney that comes when someone in the booth adjoining yours propels himself out with a purpose. I tugged on the bill of my cap as Eric and the other man walked past our table and headed for the door. Staring at Gwen, I pretended not to notice them, but she smiled and gave them a little wave.

"Thanks, y'all," she chirped. "Come back and see us."

"I don't trust that guy," I said.

She laughed. "Omigod, you are such a lug nut."

"I'm serious. There's something off here."

"Yeah. You."

"I can't figure out what he's up to, but I think he's taking advantage." I didn't miss the way he looked at Fi, either—like she was another rare bird he wanted to take home.

Gwen crossed her arms over her chest and leveled her big blue eyes on me. "Not so keen on a hot guy sleeping over at Fiona's, huh?"

"He's staying in a tent. That's not exactly sleeping over."

She arched a brow.

"And he's not hot," I grumbled.

"Right," she said. "Tall, blond, carved out of marble. The opposite of hot." There was a clatter behind the counter and Gwen glanced over my shoulder. "Sounds like someone's jealous."

I finished my coffee. The last bit was bitter.

"Hardly," I said.

Across the room, there was a hiss of steam and the clang of metal, followed by a yelp of surprise.

"Don't worry," she said. "He's just passing through. He's not a long-haul kind of crush."

"Who said anything about a crush?"

"Break's over," she said, standing. "Remember what I said, though. I know there's a lot of history between you two, and I love you both to bits. But you need to quit with the mixed signals and communicate like an adult and not a moody tween." She smoothed her apron down and said more softly, "Imagine what it's like for her to be back here right now. She feels like all her dirty laundry got aired, and you know how it is here—people talk a lot and their memories are long."

A whine pierced the air and there was a clatter by the espresso machine, followed by a crash of dishes.

Gwen shook her head and said, "I've got to stop hiring teenagers."

Before I could say anything else, she'd darted behind the counter, where steam was pouring out of the espresso machine and one bored-looking barista was scrolling on her phone.

No more mixed signals. Fair point.

But telling Fiona how I really felt about her meant telling her what really happened all those years ago, and that was not a conversation I wanted to have.

Ever.

# Chapter Twenty-Two

## FIONA

"WOW," Eric said. "These are awesome." He leaned closer to examine my most recent painting of a couple of nuthatches, and I couldn't ignore the way his snug cargo pants and thin tee shirt drew my eyes to every well-defined muscle. His hair was rumpled, his jaw dark with two days' beard stubble, but his eyes were bright—despite the fact that it was eight a.m. All of the painting I'd been doing had made me zero in on details, and that in turn made being close to Eric harder because, well...he had a lot of details worth appreciating.

Eric was like a vacation: he was fun to be around and made it feel easy to live in the moment. Pro: he was passing through this town, too—just like me. He was the definition of "no strings." Con: I wasn't sure "no strings" was what I wanted anymore.

Maybe I'd cut too many strings already. Maybe strings were exactly what I needed.

"Awesome is a stretch," I said, "but I like this new one-hour rule." It had loosened me up, and I'd already started on my big painting for the gala. Not every piece was great, but it felt good to get over a hurdle. Small victories, and all of that.

Eric grinned so his dimples showed, and my heart did this weird fluttery thing that it really needed to just stop doing.

"I can't wait to see more," he said. "It's like portraits. I can tell exactly which birds you've been painting."

"Come on."

"No really. The more you watch them, the more you see they have their own little personalities."

I'd noticed that, too, but didn't believe for a minute he could pick them out of my paintings—these were almost abstractions, with big dabs of paint that gave a quick impression of color and movement.

He raised a brow as if he could read my mind. "The nuthatches you painted were Bert and Ernie."

I laughed. "Stop."

He grinned. "It's true. Bert's the one missing a couple of his tail feathers, and he always hangs upside down to eat." He pointed at the bird in the painting, whose tail was shorter than usual. "Ernie has a little ruddy patch on his belly and follows Bert around, making a sound like a little old man muttering to himself."

"You're such a dork." I swatted his arm.

He pulled a field journal from his pocket and flipped it open. "See for yourself."

The pages were filled with sketches and notes about the different birds he'd spotted. Some were detailed drawings of heads and wing shapes, and others were gestural, like they were capturing the bird's movements. Eric's small, neat handwriting flowed between the drawings.

"Okay, fine. I painted Bert and Ernie. Maybe they brought my mojo back because, for the first time in ages, I don't feel paralyzed when I sit down to paint."

He smiled. "These have a good energy. I'm no artist, but I can tell you're having fun."

It was fun. Painting for shoppers in Janet's gallery had too often felt like I'd just been forcing myself to paint things I didn't care about.

But this was different.

I was different.

Being around Eric had created this spark of curiosity that I hadn't felt in forever. His enthusiasm was contagious, and I felt like being with him made me see things differently—even things as simple as birds. Working with Alex in his forge was a similar feeling —but it made me excited about my own work. I left his studio feeling energized and excited to try something new. Both of them seemed to have no hangups about chasing what they wanted. Nothing held them back.

"I think you're a good influence on me," I said.

He grinned. "So you're saying I'm like, your muse?"

"There are no such things as muses. But you're inspiring, yes."

Also charming and handsome and kissable, but I kept those thoughts to myself.

"I've been called a lot of things, but never that." His eyes met mine and I felt a zap of electric current go straight down to my toes.

"You look at the world like it's a giant wonderland," I said.

"It is." He leaned closer and my breath hitched as he placed his hand on my forearm and squeezed.

My eyes dropped to his lips and he whispered, "Don't move."

Okay, I thought. Here goes.

There was a quizzical chirp from behind me, and Eric's gaze shifted just past my face.

"It's him," Eric whispered, and his eyes widened. His grip on my arm tightened.

I turned my head slowly and heard the chirp again outside the window, the scrape of the yew's branches against the siding.

And there, in the dense dark green of the yew tree, was a tiny bird with a bright yellow face. It cocked its head to the side as if it were studying us, too.

All I could feel was the warmth of Eric's hand on my arm and the pounding of my heart.

When the bird hopped a few inches toward the trunk of the tree,

Eric moved in slow motion, carefully pulling his cell phone from his pocket, moving his thumb along the screen. I stayed rooted in place, not even daring to breathe as Eric held his phone up towards the bird.

The warbler cocked his head from one side to the other as it hopped along the branches like a tiny hungry dinosaur. He had brilliant yellow feathers that were like a bib over his chest, with striking black bands like a collar and a cummerbund. His throat moved each time he made the strange buzzing chirp and for one instant, I could have sworn that he'd fixed his round black eye right on me.

Eric still leaned against me, his eyes darting from the screen to the bird. He didn't dare move any closer to the window, but he slowly extended his arm, holding the phone as close to the bird as he could get.

Time seemed to restart, and then the warbler took off in a blur. We were left leaning against the table with a fourteen-second video, and I had an eerie feeling that everything was about to change.

***

ERIC BOLTED DOWN the stairs and out the back door of the house, running straight to his tent. By the time I got outside, he'd already shoved his camera, binoculars, and a handful of other items into his backpack and blew past me again, back towards the house. "I need to set up in your studio," he said, his breath ragged. "Is that okay?"

"I guess," I said, hurrying after him up the stairs, which he took two at a time.

"I'll put bait on the window sill, and I'll set up a camera," he said. He opened the window and took off the screen, then pulled a small pouch from his pocket and sprinkled mealworms along the ledge. I cringed, realizing he had worms in his pockets the entire time he'd been staring at me like he was deciding where to kiss me.

Ugh.

Eric worked quickly to set up his tiny automatic camera on the window ledge, aimed towards the area where he'd just sprinkled the bait. He carefully attached the camera with duct tape, then draped the cord inside and lowered the window so it was open just enough to not crush the cord. "Do you have a towel?" he said.

I handed him one of my spare painting rags, which he stuffed into the crack in the window.

"Wouldn't want to let the mosquitoes in," he said, grinning. He plugged the camera in and then set about checking the app on his phone to make sure that everything worked.

When he glanced at me, the spark of wonder had left his eyes. Now he was a man on a mission.

"Here," he said, showing me the screen. On it, the window ledge looked like a stage. Eric held two fingers up and hopped his hand along the outside ledge of the window. On the screen, it looked like bunny ears moving along the sill. It was surprisingly high-quality video for a little camera that he'd secured to the window ledge with duct tape and a twist-tie.

"Now what?" I said.

"Now we wait." His body was practically buzzing with excitement.

He swiped at his screen and moved closer so I could see the video he'd shot a few minutes before. There was the small yellow and black bird, albeit a little blurry from the window screen. The buzzing sound that it made was clear as a bell—no doubt the bird I'd seen before.

"I can't believe it," Eric said. "I was beginning to think we'd never see it." His eyes widened as if he'd watched a pegasus fly through the window and nudge him on the shoulder. I couldn't remember the last time I'd seen someone look that flabbergasted.

"You think that's our bird?" I said. But I already knew the answer.

"Without a doubt," Eric said. "Now we just need to get good

enough photos and video to pass peer review." The wheels were turning in his mind, and now this all felt a lot more serious.

"Are you commandeering my studio?" I said, only half-joking.

"It's for science," he said, and his dimples were back. "This is the biggest find in a century."

"Haven't you heard of a room of one's own?"

He leaned against the table next to me, close enough that I could smell cedar and citronella again. "I can be quiet," he said. "You won't even know I'm here."

"I have a ton of work to do, and I can't focus if you're in here," I said. "You're terribly distracting."

"I am?" He smiled a rakish smile.

"Yes. You can't tell me you don't know that."

"This is a huge day. Let me take you out to dinner to celebrate." He raised a brow as his gaze dropped to my lips and I thought, *Why not? I deserve some fun, too.*

But I'd told Alex I'd help him with the casting tonight. With only a few days until the gala, we had to hurry and get the leaves assembled. We'd made plans to work on them tonight, and there was no way I was backing out now. I wasn't going to miss out on ten thousand dollars because Alex didn't like the idea of another man being half-naked in my kitchen.

Plus, I liked the idea of my name on that plaque. I might not be staying in Jasmine Falls much longer, but I could at least leave a positive mark on the place. Maybe it'd make up for the big mark I'd left last year: the humiliating wedding-that-never-happened.

Eric nudged my shoulder and said, "Come on, my treat. We have to celebrate wins." He was all charm, and I *did* want to celebrate a win.

"Okay," I said. "How's eight or so? There's something I have to do first."

"Any time you want," he said, his voice low and gravelly. "I'm all yours."

Oh my.

# Chapter Twenty-Three

## ALEX

I COULDN'T GET Gwen's voice out of my head.

*Stop this hot and cold. Tell her how you feel.*

She wasn't wrong.

I knew I had to tell Fiona how I felt about her, but that would inevitably mean I'd have to tell her why I'd pushed her away all those years ago. I couldn't do one without the other.

And the other scared me the most.

There was about a twenty percent chance she'd understand my reasons, and an eighty percent chance she'd tell me where to shove those reasons.

I didn't like those odds.

We were only a few days away from the gala, though, and then Fiona would take off. I couldn't let her leave me again—not like I had before.

She deserved more.

As I poured the last of the silicone into a box mold, the studio door slid open. Fiona walked inside, her face hard to read.

"Hey," I said, "I wasn't sure you'd come today." Based on the last few words we said to each other, I was afraid she'd never come back here.

She pushed her big dark sunglasses up onto her head and said, "Of coure I'm here. We have a deal."

Of course. Our deal. For Fiona, her word meant everything. She believed that you did not break promises with people you cared about.

So she still cared about me.

"Okay, then," I said. "Great."

"I'm still irked at you," she said coolly. "But lucky for you, I can separate my personal feelings from my contract work. We're adults, as you said. Professionals."

"I'm sorry about the other day," I said. "I thought no one was home, but that's no excuse. I shouldn't have come inside." Even though I'd been shattered to find that Eric person standing in her kitchen wearing nothing but a towel and smirk, I shouldn't have fussed at her the way I did.

She raised a brow in that adorable way that meant she was still annoyed at me but didn't really want to be.

"And I shouldn't have said those things about...you know. It's none of my business." Even now, just the thought of the bird guy putting one finger on her made my whole head feel hot—but I knew I didn't get a say in who she spent time with. The thought of her slipping away from me was like a knife in the chest.

Her face softened, just a little. "Correct on both counts."

"I'm just concerned about you, Fi," I said. "But I shouldn't have handled it that way. It won't happen again."

"Good," she said, her voice lightening. "Now what are we doing today?"

I stared at her for a moment, surprised she was letting this go so easily.

"You're just in time to help with the last few molds," I said. "I printed all the casts at the library and made silicone molds of all but three. We can finish those today, and then pour in the wax to make the casts. Then we're ready to do the copper casting over at Eli's."

She plucked one of the 3-D printed words from the table, a big *inspire* in looping script. She'd hand-lettered each one of these and then sent me the files. The printed models had come out great—if the casting worked, they'd be perfect.

If it didn't work, I'd need another Hail Mary.

Fiona stepped outside the studio door and held the three-foot model up above her head. On the pavement, the letters looped by her feet. I smiled then, thinking of how this would be installed on the library's lawn. They'd light it specially for the gala of course, but this would take everyone's breath away. The committee was going to love it.

"This is great," she said, smiling.

"Better than great," I said. "Genius."

Her lip quirked in a tiny smile. "Come on, then. Let's make some magic happen."

Together, we poured silicone into the last two molds—big trays about eight inches deep—and when it had set, almost like gelatin, we took the last two words and placed them on top, pushing them down deep enough to leave an impression—sort of the way you push your thumb into clay. When the tray of silicone hardened, we removed the words and a perfect impression of them was left.

"So Eric and I found the bird," she said at last. "Or rather, it found us. When I left, Delia was set up on the front porch with her binoculars and a pile of snacks."

"That's good, right? Now he can head back to the lab." Mission accomplished. No need for him to stay. *See ya, Eric.*

She arched a brow. "Not exactly. Now Eric's trying to catch it, and he set up inside my studio where it came to the window."

I felt myself bristle. It was one thing for this guy to be camping out in the yard, but now he was in the house? In her studio? *Not your call, Alex.* I swallowed all the words I wanted to say and instead said, "How's Delia feel about that?"

"She said it was fine," Fiona said. Her brows pulled together in concern. "She's excited about this bird—you know how she gets."

"You don't seem fine about it." Her voice had an edge to it, her jaw tense.

She sighed like she had the weight of the whole world on her. "I'm just struggling with this painting for the gala. I feel like I don't have enough hours in the day."

There was something else bothering her, though. I could tell by the way she was tugging the ends of her hair. She was acting like this was the last place she wanted to be, and for the first time, I thought maybe I'd had this all wrong. Maybe there was nothing I could do to make things right between us. Maybe there was no second chance.

I swallowed hard. "Are you saying you can't help with the sculpture anymore?"

"No, that's not what I'm saying." She stopped pouring and said, "Wait, do you not want me to help you anymore?"

"No," I said quickly. "I mean, of course, I want you to help me finish. That was the deal, right?"

She arched a brow and turned back to the mold. "Yes. The deal."

I wanted her to understand how much I valued her help. There were so many things I needed to tell her, but I kept messing up. The last thing I wanted to do was hurt her again.

"Look, this breakthrough idea was all yours, Fi. I'd like you to see it through to the end. If you want to."

She looked at me then, her eyes softer. "Okay," she said. "I'd like that, too."

---

WHEN THE LAST of the molds had set, we went into the kitchen to melt down the wax we'd use to make the final castings. The last thing we could do here was to melt the wax and pour it into the stiffened silicone molds, where it would harden and take on the shape of the 3-D printed words. The next step was to take those wax molds over to Eli's, where the real magic would happen and we'd be left with copper versions of these words.

Okay, it wasn't magic. It was chemistry. But sometimes it felt like magic.

In the kitchen, I put the blocks of wax into a pouring pitcher and propped it up in a pot of water on the stove in a double-boiler. As soon as the water came to a boil and melted the wax, we'd be ready to pour.

"So on a scale of one to ten," I said, "How much better is Jasmine Falls than when you left it?"

She smiled. "It's not bad. Easily a six."

"Ouch," I said. "I was hoping for at least eight."

"It's weird being back here," she said. "Honestly, I feel like everyone's watching me to see what will happen next. If I can top the whole Dean thing."

"What do you mean?"

She rolled her eyes. "I can only imagine the stories that flew around about that. Mom gave the gossip mill enough fodder for a year with her need to announce everything in the paper."

"Fiona," I said gently. "I didn't hear any mean gossip about you."

"Well, you are a man."

I snorted. "Believe me, if there's gossip, I can't avoid it just because I'm a guy. But I'm telling you, it wasn't like you think it was. Everyone was on your side."

She looked at me, genuinely puzzled.

"If any choice words were floating around, they were directed at that idiot who took advantage of you."

"Really?" She looked surprised.

"People here think the world of you, Fi. Don't you know that?"

She sat quietly for a moment, sipping her drink.

"Why did you come back?" she said, finally. "You always talked about leaving, like you never wanted to settle down here." It was a simple question, but so hard to answer.

"I guess after a while it just felt like this place had everything I wanted."

She nodded, and her thoughtful gaze pinned me down. I was a mouse under a cat's paw. Something broke loose and the words were out of my mouth before I could think twice.

"Except you."

Her eyes widened. "Alex," she started.

"I never wanted you to go," I said.

She stared at me for a long moment. "Then why did you push me away?"

I'd imagined this conversation a thousand times, but now the words were caught in my throat.

"I had to," I said at last.

"What does that mean, exactly?" Her eyes were laser-focused on mine. Her question was so direct that it knocked me off balance. I didn't know how to explain without sounding like a coward, and I was afraid that if I told her, she'd never give me another chance.

"Why can't you just be honest with me?" she said, her voice almost a whisper.

It was agony, thinking of that night, the way I'd said those words that were all lies. I hadn't believed any of it back then—and neither had she. And then she'd spent all these years thinking I'd cheated on her with Lori, that I'd left Fiona because I wanted someone else, or that I'd wanted something that Fi couldn't give me.

But nothing was further from the truth. So why was it so hard to say the words?

I had just wanted more time with her before I told her. I'd hoped that if we spent enough time together, if I showed her how much I loved her, that when I told her why I'd left, the reasons wouldn't matter anymore.

But that was foolish. Of course, it would matter to her. It had hurt her more than I realized.

Her brow furrowed. "I have to go." She slid off the stool and was at the door in a blink.

"Fi," I said, "Hang on. Please stay."

"No, Alex," she said, anger in her voice. "I have dinner plans with Eric. I don't have time for your games." And then she was gone.

Again.

# Chapter Twenty-Four

FIONA

I PROBABLY SHOULDN'T HAVE DROPPED a bomb like that, but Alex Fox had the world's worst timing. A half-hour later, I was still reeling from what he'd said when I walked up the sidewalk toward the Spare Time Grill.

Thanks, Alex.

Eric was waiting by the door, right on time. "You look great," he said. He was wearing a pair of slim-cut jeans and a button-down shirt with his sleeves rolled to the elbows. With his hair tousled just so, and with the slightest beard stubble, he'd totally nailed the sexy outdoorsy look.

"You clean up nice," I said, trying not to stare too long. Luckily I'd found my navy wrap dress buried in my suitcase—it was nothing fancy, but it was the one thing I owned that didn't have paint on it.

He smiled. "I decided to treat myself to a room at the inn. I've been dying to have a hot shower and sleep in a bed."

"Nice," I said. "Sabrina's place is pretty snazzy."

"I got the last room," he said, and his eyes lingered on mine. "It's got one of those tubs with jets, and my towels were folded into swans."

I felt my face flush as my brain was overwhelmed by thoughts of Eric in a swanky room at the bed and breakfast, all by himself, enjoying a long hot bath and—

*Get a grip, Fiona.* I pinched my hand, trying to send my thoughts anywhere else but there.

"Come on," he said, opening the door of the Spare Time. "We have celebrating to do."

Jasmine Falls had only a handful of good restaurants: a pizza place that was usually packed, a diner that had a killer breakfast and not much else, a Greek cafe that served the best gyros I'd ever tasted, and the Spare Time, which had once been the town's only bowling alley. A few years back, when bowling enthusiasm had all but vanished, Max Ekhart had bought the place and renovated it. Max had been a couple of years ahead of me in high school and had trained with a big-deal chef down in New Orleans for a few years. He'd come back to Jasmine Falls, gotten the bowling alley for a song, and made it into a farm-to-table restaurant that had since been written up in several Best-of-the-South type articles. Delia said it had been featured on a cable foodie show sometime last year, and Max had seen a huge uptick in diners ever since. Now it was a favorite spot for tourists, and tonight it was packed.

"Good thing I made a reservation," Eric said, eyeing the crowd. "Looks like everybody and their brother's here."

"Indeed," I said, already spotting several familiar faces.

Once we were seated, our waitress left two menus and Eric ordered a bottle of pinot noir.

"Max kept some lanes open in the back," I said. "Now you can enjoy a nice grass-fed steak and then go bowl a few games and get your nostalgia on."

"Sounds good to me," he said. "Can I convince you to bowl later?"

"Only if you like losing."

He gave me a wolfish grin. "You're on."

When our waitress returned to take our order, she filled our wine glasses and left the bottle. Eric held his up in an exaggerated ceremonious way. His big hazel eyes met mine as he said, "Here's to you, Fiona, the bird whisperer. I don't know how I can ever repay you."

I clinked my glass against his. "It all seems a little surreal."

He sipped the wine and smiled. "It's like a dream. Here I was, stuck in a master's project that had me bored to tears, thinking my career was headed nowhere. Then, out of the blue, you show up with that painting, and now it's like the whole world opened up." He was talking faster now, in that way I'd learned meant he was not just excited, but already thinking ten steps ahead.

"My thesis director's already talking about travel grants, big research positions, even applying for a MacArthur Genius grant. I never dreamed something like this could happen. And it's because you brought me here."

This feeling of excitement and wonder that Eric seemed to have —I wanted to feel that way about my own work, my own path.

"I might graduate much later than expected, but this is a game-changing project. It'll make the university look good and set me up for any job I want in academic research." He was talking fast, his eyes bright. "The only thing more exciting than discovering a new species is learning that one everyone thought had vanished still exists. Everyone loves a resurrection story. Nothing gives you a rush quite like a second chance at life."

"Sounds like you'll be a celebrity."

He smiled. "Well, as much as one can be as an ornithologist."

Now he could be set for life, all because of one tiny bird that could fit inside a teacup.

"I just need enough proof," he said. "Right now, we might as well be chasing Bigfoot."

Behind him, Sadie waved from a couple of tables away.

"Maybe that's just as good," I said. "People love trying to solve a mystery."

His lip lifted into a tiny smile. "That they do."

Sadie reached our table and said, "Hey, Fiona! I just wanted to tell you that I hung your painting in my office. Everyone's jealous and asking where I got it. Obviously, I told them it was from you. I hope you're ready for some commissions."

"Seriously?" I said.

"Oh, yeah. The district ranger wants one for her office. So you need to like, triple your prices. Because when the superintendent sees it, he's going to want one, too. He's an absolute bird nut, and he can't be shown up by the district ranger."

Eric smiled at me and I felt my heart swell.

"For real," she said. She glanced at Eric and then back at me.

"Sadie, this is Eric," I said. "Eric, Sadie's a ranger at Congaree."

"I'm also a bird nut," he said, shaking her hand.

"He's finishing his master's in ornithology," I told her.

"Are you doing research here?" she said.

"Yeah," he said. "I can't say much about it yet, but it's pretty exciting."

When his eyes drifted back to mine, Sadie said, "I'm sure it is." She glanced back to her table, where a handsome guy with a deep tan and carefully sculpted hair sat finishing a beer. "I should get back," she said. "Hey, look, Alex is here, too. Man, everybody's here tonight."

When I followed her gaze, I saw that indeed Alex Fox was standing just a few yards away at the register. Sadie waved at him and I thought briefly of crawling under the table. But I had no reason to hide—Alex Fox had already clocked me.

He was staring right at us, and even from this distance, I could see his tight jaw and furrowed brow.

And then he was walking toward us, because Sadie was still waving, and it was like the whole massive room shrunk to the size of a shoebox and Alex was already halfway to us and—why was there suddenly a clear path from the front desk to us? I glanced behind me, but there was no clear path anywhere else.

Again I was stuck, just like I had been in the gross swamp mud.

"Hi, Alex!" Sadie chirped. "I haven't seen you in weeks. What are you doing here?"

"Take out," he said. His eyes shifted from Sadie to Eric, and then to me.

"Can't wait to see your sculpture at the gala," Sadie said. "Everybody's so excited about it."

"Thanks," he said, turning back to her. "It's been a real roller coaster, but I think we're in the home stretch." Now he was all smile-with-dimples, nothing-to-see-here Alex.

"And I heard you wrangled Fiona into helping, too." Sadie glanced at me and then gave Alex a sly smile. "You trying to make her fall in love and get her to stay?"

Alex Fox blushed all the way down to his collar. "Um," he said, and coughed out a laugh.

"Because if so, you're not the only one," she said.

Eric raised a brow and gave me a quizzical look as he reached for his wine glass.

"I mean, who couldn't fall head over heels for the new and improved Jasmine Falls?" Sadie said, holding her hands up like she was revealing the grand prize on a game show. "Now we have everything you could want in a small town. Fiona, you're just going to have to stay. We won't let you leave again."

I nodded, sipping my wine, wishing a meteor could just go ahead and strike right now and vaporize me.

"Isn't that right, Alex?" Sadie nudged his arm and his gaze shifted to me. He looked like he was hoping for that meteor strike, too.

"I should let you all get back to your dates," he said. "Good to see you, Sadie." He gave her a warm smile and then turned and strode back toward the register.

"One minute," I said to Eric. "I'm so sorry." I rushed past Sadie and squeezed my way through the tables, hurrying toward the front of the restaurant, which now felt like it was a country mile away. Alex grabbed his takeout and shoved the door open just as two teenagers stepped in my path, their eyeballs glued to their phones.

In approximately three seconds, the following happened:

Teen #1, a tall girl with a ponytail and hot dog, full-on body checked me.

Hot dog, with everything, smashed into my chest, leaving a trail of ketchup and relish.

Teen #2, a guy who looked like he should be surfing instead of bowling, yelled "Dude!" and stared way too hard at my cleavage, which now held a huge smear of mustard and a few stray onions.

The bell on the door clanged as Alex turned his head to follow the noise, his face illuminated by the neon sign in the window.

Super.

Ignoring the gasps and snorts of laughter, I shoved my way out the door and into the neon glow. Alex stood a few feet away, his expression stony.

"Hang on a minute," I said.

"You have a little something here," he said, touching a spot on his chest.

"Look, I'm sorry," I said, brushing the worst of the onions away.

"For what?" His tone was cool as he sipped his drink.

"Alex, come on. Talk to me. You obviously have some feelings about this."

He stared at me, his eyes wide in the dim light. They were always so impossibly green, always drawing me closer. Now they seemed full of disappointment. "Good night, Fi."

"Alex, wait. I'm not trying to hurt you. Stop acting like I kicked your puppy."

"I just came for a burger," he grumbled.

When he stepped away, I followed after him, teetering in my heels. "Alex Fox, you stop right there!"

He paused and then slowly turned, his eyebrow arched. How

was it fair that this man looked so dang hot every minute of the day? In neon light, even?

"Do you have a napkin in that bag? I have relish in some places where it shouldn't be."

His eyes drifted along the neckline of my dress, which was now stained with relish and mustard and several things that really shouldn't be on a hot dog to begin with. He dug through his bag and handed me a paper napkin.

I wiped at the stain and said, "Look, it's just dinner. Two people out for a meal."

"I don't care who you date, Fiona." His tone was cool and even, but I could tell those words were an absolute lie.

"You sure about that?"

He raised a brow, sucking his iced tea through the straw. Mister Cool-as-Ice. "I just don't want to see you taken advantage of. But, as we established earlier, this is not my decision. So I'm going to go have my burger, and you go back and enjoy your evening."

"Alex, not everyone has an agenda."

His jaw tightened. "In my experience, they usually do."

"So then what's yours?"

He sipped his drink and stared at me as if weighing the question. "To get you in a room that you don't storm out of."

My mouth fell open. That was not the answer I was expecting.

When he turned away again, I realized that we were still standing by the huge plate glass window, lit by bright colored lights like two dancers on a stage. When I turned toward the dining room, I saw at least twenty faces staring back at me, their forks suspended in the air.

*Great, now we're dinner theater.*

I grabbed Alex's arm and pulled him around the corner so we were away from the window. He followed me, even though he was solid as an oak and could've stayed rooted right there if he wanted.

"Was there something else, Fi?"

"If you really cared about me," I said, my voice low, "you'd stop hiding things from me."

His brow furrowed, and I knew I'd hit a nerve.

"I'm going to go now," he said calmly, "because my burger's getting cold. See you tomorrow, Fi."

And then he did the same thing he did all those years before.

He walked away.

# Chapter Twenty-Five

## ALEX

DON'T LOOK BACK. *Don't look.* I told myself that with each step I took away from her. *Deep breaths, Fox.* One foot in front of the other.

It was only when I climbed into my truck that I looked in the rearview.

Fiona still stood by the big windows, her hands on her hips like she was wishing she could set my truck on fire with only a look.

Of course I had feelings about all of this. I had lots of feelings: most of which involved some swearing. Seeing Fiona there with that other guy made me want to yank him up by the collar and drive him out to the middle of the swamp and leave him there. Seeing her in that dark blue dress that hugged all of her curves made me want to scoop her up in my arms and kiss her until she forgot her name—even though she was covered in condiments. Neither of those was an option, though, because I would create a huge scene, bigger than the one we already made—the kind that Fiona wanted to avoid. She hated to be the center of attention—she'd always thought that was a bad thing, but that was just because she'd spent her whole life being judged by her mom, thinking that everyone else who gave her a close look would judge her that way, too.

Although to be fair, arguing outside of a crowded restaurant didn't get you the good kind of attention. I didn't want to embarrass her, but I can't say I wasn't relieved that she'd followed me out there onto the street.

No, not relieved: overjoyed.

It meant that she did care what I thought. And she did care what we meant, together. She'd always hated it when she got all worked up about something and I stayed calm. She always interpreted that as me not caring like she did. Really, though, I'd just learned that getting all worked up didn't help me out of difficult situations. Usually, if I let a wound-up person keep on winding themselves into a frenzy, I'd learn a whole lot more about them and whatever problem was at hand by keeping calm. Usually, that ended in a truth explosion.

Fiona, though, had her truths locked down tight.

She didn't like me seeing her there with the bird guy. She knew I didn't trust him, but it was more than that. I could see it in her eyes. Her expression had been pained, like she'd been caught in a lie.

There was something else in those gorgeous blue eyes, too, though: hurt.

She still had feelings for me, though she was trying everything she could to cover them up and lock them away. She still wouldn't let herself trust me yet, and that felt like a knife in my heart.

She was right, though. I was keeping something from her. If we had even the slightest chance together, I had to tell her what happened all those years before. She thought I'd just carelessly pushed her away, but that wasn't it at all. I just didn't want to tell her tonight, on the sidewalk, because that truth would definitely create a spectacle.

The truth was much harder to tell her, and I didn't look forward to it one bit. I'd wanted to tell her earlier when she was standing in my kitchen, but she ran out before I could. There was a good chance that if she knew the real reason, she'd never speak to me again.

I had to tell her, though. Because as soon as I told her that ugly part, I could tell her the part that might be enough to make her stay.

# Chapter Twenty-Six

## FIONA

ALEX FOX WAS THE ICEMAN. Cool as a cucumber.

I couldn't believe he'd stood there slurping his tea and didn't get riled up for a single second. As if he wasn't one bit bothered by me being out to dinner with Eric.

It only meant one thing: he *didn't* care that I was there with Eric. And that bothered me more than I thought it would.

When I went back into the Spare Time, every face turned toward me as I walked back to my table. Some people were polite enough to pretend to stare at their food; the tourists just glanced at me as if I were a minor interruption; but the few faces I recognized had likely stared slack-jawed at the whole scene in the window, taking notes so they could tell their friends over coffee tomorrow.

This would be more humiliating than Dean cheating on me. More humiliating than the wedding cancellation that Penelope had insisted on putting in the paper so that "everyone would be properly notified." To everyone here, our little tiff in the parking lot had likely looked like the kind of lovers' spat they'd see on daytime TV shows.

So much for keeping a low profile here.

Really, I couldn't get out of this town fast enough. At least when the gala was over, I'd leave ten grand richer. But right now, even the money didn't seem like enough. Jasmine Falls might have had a facelift, but deep down it hadn't changed at all. No one could keep secrets here. Tonight was just one more reminder that this was not the place for me. Staying here would mean constant reminders of my past mistakes, my failures, and the hurt that came with them.

"Everything okay?" Eric said. He topped off my wine glass as I sat.

"Super," I said. "Still want to knock some pins down?" I was dying to throw something. The heavier, the better.

"Sure," he said. "We don't have to stay, though, if you'd rather—"

"I didn't mean to spoil the evening. And I don't want to go home yet. But honestly, there's nowhere in this town where you can escape. Everybody here's a busybody."

He nodded. "You didn't spoil anything. And I might know a place." He took my hand and led me toward the door.

---

THE JASMINE INN was only a few blocks away, but I drove us there anyway because I was wearing heels. And I do not walk more than two blocks in heels—that's a hard and fast rule.

We parked on the back side of the house—a huge Victorian with a wrap-around porch and wooden fish-scale shingles. A garden out back was filled with high hedges and about a dozen blooming flowers that I couldn't name.

I thought Eric would lead me up the porch steps and inside to his room, but instead, he walked towards the garden, past the hedges where a bench was hidden in the middle.

"Well, this is cozy," I said.

"I wish I had a travel stipend," he said. "I could get used to this."

"I'm sorry about dinner. That didn't feel like much of a celebration, and I didn't mean to pull you into the drama that is Jasmine Falls."

"It's okay." He leaned back on the bench, staring up at the sky. "It's hard living in a place where you run into your exes all the time."

"Just the one," I said. "I couldn't stand it if there was a whole army of them."

I moved closer to him, my knee brushing against his. "You know, when you suggested we come here, I assumed we'd be inside."

He turned towards me and gave me a sad smile. "A couple of hours ago, I would have thought that, too."

"You wanted to bring me back to your room tonight?"

He nodded. "I did."

"And you don't anymore?"

He leaned closer, and there was that hint of cedar again. His gaze dropped to my lips, and my heart pounded against my ribs.

"Fiona, I think you're incredible. You're all kinds of gorgeous, and I've been thinking about kissing you since the minute we met—and believe me, that big fluffy bed up there gave me a head full of ideas—but I can't be with someone who's so obviously into someone else. Not even for one night."

"You mean Alex?" I snorted. "I know that must have looked weird back there, but it's not like that. We go way back, and...it's complicated."

He smiled. "Fiona, come on. That's not fair to either of us."

So much for easy and no strings.

"We dated a million years ago," I said. "And then he decided I wasn't good enough, and then he left. End of story." No matter how many times I'd told myself I was over this, the words still stung.

"Then he was an idiot," Eric said, brushing a lock of hair behind my ear. "Seems to me that he knows that, too, though. It also seems like y'all have some unfinished business."

"Oh, no. We're definitely finished."

He smiled like he didn't believe that for one second. "I'm sorry," he said, "But I can't be with a woman who's thinking of another guy—even if it's in an unfinished business kind of way." He gave me a mischievous look and said, "I'd try really hard to make you forget him, and we'd have a killer time—but that's just not the kind of thing I do anymore. And I don't think it's what you want, either."

"A killer time, huh?"

He smiled. "I really wish things were different. You have no idea."

I shrugged playfully. "I should go, then. Being squashed twice in one evening is my limit." When I stood, he reached for my arm.

"I hope he knows how lucky he is."

"See you at the house tomorrow?"

"Of course."

I walked back to my car, hating how right Eric sounded despite my protests.

---

WHEN I GOT BACK to Delia's, there was a small sparkly pink gift bag hanging on the handle of the back door. Inside, buried in the tissue paper, was one of those tiny spot-remover pens that looks like a magic marker. There was also a postcard inside, a vintage-looking one that made Congaree look like a paradise and said *Wish You Were Here*. On the back, there was a note.

*Fi—*
*I'm sorry I was a jackass (again). Please do all you can to save that dress. Tossing it would be a crime.*
*—A.*

I fought back a smile, taking the bag inside the house with me. How was it that Alex Fox could get me so tangled up in knots and then completely disarm me? Knowing that he was keeping secrets from me was frustrating, but it was hard to stay angry at him when he was so clearly trying to mend what lay broken between us—even as he fumbled his way through it.

And he was one hundred percent right about that dress.

# Chapter Twenty-Seven

## ALEX

IT WAS hot as blazes in the forge, but with three days left until the gala, I had no more time to waste. When I'd left Fiona last night at the Spare Time, she'd been madder than a wet hen. I figured there was about a four percent chance she'd show up again to help me finish.

I'd finally blown it. I deserved it.

I was up on a ladder, welding one of the big iron leaves into place when the studio door slid open. Fiona stood in the bright light with her big sunglasses and a giant mug of coffee.

She strode towards me, her boot heels clacking on the concrete. Today she wore a fitted tee shirt and cutoff jean shorts that made her toned legs look a mile long, even in those beat-up boots. I turned off the torch as she approached and felt something like an electric current drive straight through my chest—just like every other time I saw her.

"Hi," I said.

"Hi, yourself."

"I didn't think you were coming."

She sipped from the mug. "Why wouldn't I?"

Because I left her with a hot dog smeared on her chest in front of half the town? Because I was an idiot? Because every time she was near me she short-circuited my brain?

"I'm still mad at you, but we have a job to do," she said, her tone even. "I told you, I don't walk away from commitments." She spoke as if this were just another work arrangement with a colleague. Nothing more.

"Are we going to talk about last night?" I was hopeful, and a little terrified.

"Nope." She sipped her coffee.

"It seems like maybe we should because you seem upset."

"Nope. Not upset, Fox. I should probably thank you for putting me on everyone's radar again." Her tone was breezy, exaggerated enough that I knew she wasn't *too* mad. "Maybe it'll sell some paintings. Everyone loves dinner theater." She put one hand on her hip and cocked her head to the side. "And just so you can rest easy, my dress was salvaged."

I turned so she wouldn't see my grin. This was Aloof Fiona, pretending that she wasn't ruffled by what happened last night, and pretending that she didn't feel the sparks between us.

But there were sparks, all right. She could deny it all she wanted to, but they were definitely there—every time she set her big blue eyes on mine, and every time she let her guard down and laughed that raucous laugh at some silly thing I said. And every time she stepped within two feet of me and I caught the faint scent of her, lord help me.

I might still have a chance after all.

Because she was here, wasn't she? Giving me a hard time meant she wasn't a hundred percent angry. Fiona never teased anyone she didn't like.

"Fair enough," I said. "I'm glad you're here."

"Well, let's get on it. We've got three days left and I don't do all-nighters anymore."

"Yes ma'am. Let's get the truck loaded up."

She followed me to the back of the studio, where I'd boxed up our wax casts safely in their silicone molds. Together we carried them out to my pickup and packed them in the bed. We'd made eight, just in case we lost one in the casting process.

When Fiona climbed inside the cab and shut the door, there was the faint scent of lavender and vanilla, and I fought the urge to lean in close to her. It was driving me crazy being in the house next door to her, but being stuck just a few inches away was almost too much to bear. Couldn't we just start over now, as the adults we were today, and forget about those old mistakes?

"So how far is Eli's?" she said. "And how do you know him?"

"Half an hour," I said, trying to ignore her long tan legs. "And we went to college together. He's an incredible metalsmith. Maxine's his grandmother. He grew up down in Orangeburg, but he moved here after college."

"Can't wait to meet him," she said, her tone even.

"We'll have these done by tonight, and we can attach them tomorrow."

"Great," she said. "How's it going to be installed?"

"A flatbed and a forklift."

She turned to me and blinked.

"Or something like that. The library handles that part. I just show up and make sure they don't drop it."

---

BY THE TIME we got to Eli's, she'd said exactly twelve words to me. All in the form of one-word answers to my questions. She was not going to make things easy on me. But after leaving her on the sidewalk in full view of everyone in the Spare Time, I might have deserved a little aloofness.

Being around her really did short-circuit my brain.

Eli lived in a renovated farmhouse that looked like the kind pictured on ice cream packages. His place sat on ten acres of what once had been cow pastures and still had a pond full of ducks and an old tobacco barn that he'd made into his forge.

"Alex," he said, stepping out of the barn. "How's it going?"

"Hey, Eli," I said. "Not bad."

Next to me, Fiona sucked in a breath and her mouth formed a tiny O.

When Eli reached out to clasp his giant hand around hers, she broke out her million-dollar smile and I suddenly had the urge to put my entire body between them.

"And you must be Fiona," he said, smiling. "I'm Elijah Bell. But my friends call me Eli." His voice dropped an octave in that way that it always did when he caught a lovely woman's eye, and now my head was on fire.

I knew what Fiona saw: six feet of charming with arms like a bodybuilder and a megawatt smile.

Eli had this effect on lots of women, which is why I hated to be his wingman. Every time we went out for beers, at least one woman would come up and ask him if she could she take a selfie with him because she was absolutely certain he was Michael B. Jordan—as in the super hot villain from *Black Panther*.

He ate that up.

To be fair though, it was a striking resemblance. It made hanging out with him in the tourist season both hilarious and humbling.

"So Maxine's your grandmother?" Fiona asked him.

"Yep," he said, fixing his eyes on hers.

"Wow," she said. "What's that like?"

Eli shrugged. "She casts a pretty big shadow."

Fiona nodded. "Sounds like my mom."

"I like a challenge," he said, giving her a wink. "It keeps life interesting."

I felt my eyes roll so hard my head hurt.

"We have the wax molds," I said, breaking the spell. "You all fired up?"

He grinned at Fiona and said, "Always." As he came to the back of the truck, he said, "Let me help you carry those," and proceeded to take the fifty-pound molds in two at a time.

"Showoff," I muttered.

"What a gorgeous place you have here," Fiona said, following behind him. "Is all that pasture yours, too, with the horses?"

Now, apparently, she felt like talking.

ELI SHOWED us how to pack the sand molds around our wax casts —Fiona hadn't done sand molds before, and he took a little too much delight in helping her, placing his big hands over hers as they carefully packed the sand around the first word: *create*.

"Have you done casting before?" Eli asked her.

"Only some jewelry about a million years ago," she said. "Earrings."

"It's a similar process," he said. "Just a bigger scale."

I packed my own mold as I listened to him explain the process to her, which she likely already knew. She was eating up his attention, and I wanted to throw something.

When I glanced over, she flashed me a catlike smile. If flirting with Eli was her way of getting me back for the other night, it was…well…

Working.

"So once this hardens," Eli said, "we'll heat these up, and the wax will melt. Then we'll pour in the copper."

"Sweet," Fiona said. "Are you coming to the gala?"

"Sure," he said. "I donate a piece every year."

"That's so kind of you," she said, fluttering her big lush lashes.

"Fiona's donating a piece, too," I said, determined not to show the slightest sign of annoyance. "She's a painter, and she's working on a new series."

"I'll look forward to seeing it," Eli said, giving her a big smile. "I think y'all have this down. I'm going to go start the fire."

With Eli gone, Fiona moved on to the next mold. She brushed a lock of hair behind her ear and said, "Your friend's kinda flirty."

"That's how he rolls."

She leaned against the table and crossed her arms over her chest. "You look a little green."

I snorted. "Please."

"Why are you so annoyed by some harmless flirting, Alex?"

Hearing my name on her lips made the blood rush to my head. I wanted to hear her say it over and over—in the darkness, close to my ear, when she was thinking of nothing but me. "I'm not," I said.

"Just like you weren't annoyed by my dinner date?"

"I thought it wasn't a date." I stepped closer. "And I thought you didn't want to talk about it."

She stared at me, her eyes as bright as the sky behind her, that Carolina shade of blue that always feels like home.

I took another step toward her. "I think you don't want to admit how you're feeling about us because it doesn't fit neatly into a box. It's scary, and maybe a little confusing, and you think what you want can't possibly be right." Now we were so close that the toes of my boots were touching hers, and I could see the tiny flecks of dark blue in her eyes, like little storm clouds.

She raised a brow, and her lips parted. "And what is it you think I want?"

It was scary for me, too. It was downright terrifying to think that if she left this town again, I might never have another chance with her.

I couldn't let that happen.

"I'm trying to be the good guy here, Fiona." I rested my hands on the table, one on either side of her hips, and her eyes scanned my face. "Trying to give you time. But the truth is, it makes me crazy to think of you on dates with anyone who's not me." She pursed her lips the tiniest bit, and it was all I could do not to kiss her right there —but I knew that once I did, I wouldn't want to stop. I leaned so close my lips brushed her ear and she let out this little sigh that just about knocked me to my knees.

Mercy, I'd worship every inch of this woman if she'd let me.

"I think you want to give us another chance, too," I whispered. "But I think you don't want to admit it."

She sucked in a quick breath, and I fought to keep my hands on the table and off of her hips. I was on fire everywhere we touched: my cheek against her jaw, my chest against her shoulder.

"Tell me you don't still have feelings for me," I said. "Tell me you don't feel what I feel."

After a pause that felt like an eternity, she said, "Alex, of course, I have feelings for you." She took a deep breath and her whole body tensed. "But what's happening between us—I don't know what it means for me. I don't know how to do this."

"I have some ideas." My lips brushed against her neck and then she let out a little gasp—and my whole body was about to combust.

"Hey guys," Eli called. "You all set here?"

Fiona startled, and I quickly stepped away, sweeping up some loose pieces of wax on the table.

"You bet," I said. "Just putting the finishing touches on these."

Eli raised a brow and said. "Great. Fire's ready when you are."

Fiona sat still as a stone, her eyes steady on mine, a blush in her cheeks that was unmistakable. Another chunk had fallen from that wall of hers, and she'd finally said the words that I'd been hoping were true.

Her words had given me plenty of ideas—and judging by the heat in her gaze, she had a few ideas, too.

# Chapter Twenty-Eight

FIONA

I FELT like I'd been zapped with a live wire.

Alex's lips moving next to my ear had made me weak in the knees. Feeling them move to my neck had nearly set me on fire. I'd one hundred percent expected to feel those lips move down to my collarbone, and I was dying to feel them there.

And everywhere else, if we're being honest.

As he and Eli grabbed the heavy resin molds, I tried to give myself the talk I'd given myself a thousand times since coming back here—the talk that told me I needed to keep my distance from Alex. The talk that warned he'd hurt me again.

But it wasn't working. Because I did have feelings for Alex. I couldn't tamp them down anymore.

And I didn't want to.

My phone buzzed in my pocket. I stepped away to answer the call, leaving Alex and Eli to prep the molds. As soon as the resin and sand mixture hardened, we'd be on to the pour.

"Hi, Gwen," I said. "What's up?"

"I'm going to need more paintings," she said. She sounded out of breath, and it was hard to hear her over the noise in the cafe.

"You sold them all?"

"Yep. Right after I tripled your prices."

"What?"

"You were selling yourself short. Those people didn't even bat an eye, so obviously you can raise them even higher."

I couldn't believe what I was hearing. I'd taken her six paintings. I couldn't even do that math in my head right now.

"We've been absolutely slammed," she said. There was a familiar clatter as she moved through the squeaky swinging doors into the kitchen. "Apparently the bird enthusiasts have landed. And let me tell you, they are a noisy crowd."

"Am I supposed to know what that means?"

"Well, there's something else you should know," she said. "I sold your last three paintings today in the span of an hour—all to these people who were birdwatchers. I overheard a few things, and your bird guy has spilled some tea."

"What are you saying?"

"I'm sending you some links now," she said, and my phone pinged with a text message. I put her on speaker and opened the links.

*Rare Bird Spotted in Jasmine Falls, S.C.*

*Nessie of the Bird World Appears in Congaree.*

*Extinct Species Found in Tiny Southern Town.*

How had this happened? I skimmed the first article as Gwen told me about the rush of people. "The park was packed today," she said. "Sadie came in and said it was like the eclipse watchers in the Smokies. I didn't even know there were this many people on the entire east coast who cared about birds. As soon as this news broke, they hopped in their cars and started driving."

"Holy cow," I said, still reading a local news article that had been picked up by the Associated Press. Eric wasn't named in the article, but it mentioned a "grad student who had rediscovered a species thought to be long extinct." My heart pounded in my ribs as I kept reading further—there was no mention of Delia's house, thank goodness—but Jasmine Falls and Congaree were mentioned by name, and there was a quote from a park biologist. There was a grainy old photo of the warbler, one that hardly showed anything besides wings and a beak, but there was enough in the article to make people curious.

The other articles were dated two and three days ago. Had Eric spoken to the press? He'd made it sound like he wanted to keep this secret until the bird had been verified. It hadn't occurred to me that this could draw a crowd.

"Social media's blowing up, too," Gwen said. "You're going to sell paintings as fast as you can make them, because these people just became your biggest fans. I've taken names and numbers from twenty people who want one of your pieces and asked to be put on your waiting list."

"I don't have a waiting list."

"You do now, babe."

On the far side of the yard, Alex and Eli were standing next to a small fire. "Did you just become my agent?"

She laughed. "Get ready to get famous," she said. "I gotta go bake more scones."

---

WHEN THE MOLDS WERE DRY, it was time to do the pour. Alex and Eli insisted on doing that part since it involved pouring molten copper into the small holes left in the molds. Since the metal was approximately ten thousand degrees, I was happy to sit a few yards away and watch the pros do it from the shade of a tree.

The two of them worked well together, like they'd done this a hundred times before. They melted the copper down in a crucible, over a fire—sort of like you'd boil water over a campfire—only this was a much larger scale. Once it was ready, it took both of them to lift and tilt the crucible to pour the red-hot metal into our sand molds. They'd both suited up in heavy leather aprons and pants, leather gloves that reached above their elbows, and welders' helmets with face shields. They looked like figures out of some dystopian adventure, especially with the red of the fire reflected in their visors.

When they'd poured the last mold, Alex removed the helmet and walked over to me. He stripped off the apron, the heavy shirt, and the gloves, and then grabbed a bottled water from the cooler. I sipped my water and tried to ignore the way his tee shirt, now soaked through, clung to every contour of his chest and shoulders. I couldn't help staring at that very tight shirt or those perfectly defined abs and imagining how firm all the rest of his muscles were under those slim-cut jeans. I imagined how the tight grip of his hands would feel against my skin while he whispered into my ear like he'd done an hour earlier.

Three more days until the gala, and I could leave.

But now, a large part of me didn't want to. I was officially torn.

He raked a hand through his damp hair and then poured the water over his head, and was he reading my mind right now? His face and neck were flushed from the heat, and now somehow his shirt clung tighter, and my lungs didn't seem to be working properly anymore and I could no longer see straight.

"How is there not a single cloud in the sky?" he said, and I was the one who was burning up.

"I offered to help."

He stared at my bare legs and said, "Not like that, you won't."

"No one told me there was a dress code."

He pulled the heavy shirt from the ground and stuck his finger through a small hole in the sleeve. "That's from a tiny splash," he said, his eyes resting on mine. "You don't want to see the skin that was underneath."

"Point taken." Though I did wonder if he was talking about his own skin, and where precisely that scar might be.

"Don't worry, there's plenty of work left to do that doesn't risk melting your hide."

"Good, because I feel a little guilty about being paid to drink iced tea and watch." Only a little, though, and it was taking an awful lot of effort not to burst into flames.

He gave me a mischievous grin, and there he was—the good-natured Alex who had just a hint of naughty hiding behind those sparkling eyes of his—and I was a sinking ship. "You can make up for it later," he said, and he held my gaze just long enough to make me think those words were one hundred percent meant to send an electric current along my skin—mission accomplished, sir—and then grabbed two more bottles of water from the cooler. He gave me one last look and then sauntered back over to where Eli was examining the molds, as if daring me not to enjoy every second of that slow, easy walk of his and imagine all of the other things that he'd enjoy doing very, very slowly.

With me.


ELI HANDED me a mallet that was roughly the size of Thor's hammer. "Want to do the honors?" he said. Alex stood a few feet away, a sledgehammer resting on his shoulder. It was ninety degrees and beads of sweat were trickling down my back.

At our feet, the eight molds were lined up, several inches apart, resting on a thick layer of sand. They looked like enormous concrete blocks.

"Sure thing," I said. "Just show me what to do."

Eli grabbed his mallet, and I did not miss the way the muscles in his arms rippled as he swung a few firm practice strokes. "Hit it like you mean business, but not like you're picturing your ex." He swung like he was lining up a perfect putt and then smashed the mallet into the mold. A chunk of it fell away, and he swung again, firm but controlled. Alex swung and chipped at the opposite side. The mold cracked as more pieces fell away, and they pounded it with the mallets until the mold broke open.

"This part's like Christmas," Eli said with a grin.

I leaned in closer as he reached down with a gloved hand and pulled the mold apart. Then he pulled the piece of copper out and held it out for us to inspect. Alex brushed some bits of sand off and slid his gloved hand along the surface. In my looping script, the word "inspire" hung in the air between us. The metal was a deep reddish brown, a textured surface that caught the light like hammered steel. The looping script looked delicate, like a rope—even though it weighed several pounds.

"How'd we do?" Eli said.

"Spot on," Alex said. He was no doubt already imagining how he'd join the words into the leaves, calculating how many points would be welded. He turned to me and smiled. "What do you think?"

"I think I want to see the rest."

"Then let's get crackin'," Eli said to me, motioning toward the mallet.

Soon there were bits of sand flying all around as the three of us pounded the molds. When we'd broken them all open and removed the casts, we found that they only had some minor flaws—and certainly nothing you'd be able to see from ten feet below.

When I held out the last word for Alex to see, *Rise*, I asked him, "What do you think?"

He fixed his big green eyes on mine and stared. "Perfect," he said, and there was that electric current again, sweeping along my skin, all the way down to my toes.

# Chapter Twenty-Nine

FIONA

IT WAS NEARLY eight that evening when Alex dropped me off at Delia's. I felt like a big sweaty mess from working in the heat all day, and I had sand in plenty of places where it should not be. Spending the day making something felt good, even if it was still awkward being around Alex. He hadn't said much on the drive home, and had mercifully not mentioned anything about feelings—buried or otherwise.

When I got out of the truck, he said, "I'm going to start the welding in the morning, so come on over." He was all business, as if his lips hadn't grazed my ear just hours before.

"I promised to see this thing through to the end, right?"

This would be the last part to finish, welding the casts we made today into the leaf shapes.

He nodded, raking a hand through his hair as if he wanted to say more. "Okay," he said at last. "See you tomorrow."

As his truck rumbled down the drive, I turned toward the porch and realized that something was missing.

Eric's tent was no longer set up in the backyard.

Curious, I walked down to the edge of the woods, thinking he might have moved it. But there was no sign of it anywhere, and his

Jeep was gone, too. The ground was squishy near the tree line, where the tent had been. He'd probably just gotten rained on and splurged on another night at the inn.

Inside, I found Delia in the living room, watching a movie with Rufus perched on her lap. One look at her face told me something was wrong.

"What happened to Eric?" I said.

Rufus squinted at me with his judgy little cat face.

"He's gone, sweetie," she said.

I felt a twinge of something deep in my chest. I didn't want Eric to be gone. I didn't want the excitement to be over. "He gave up? But I just saw the articles talking about—"

She frowned. "No, honey. He caught it. And then he packed up everything and left. Took the bird with him."

"You're joking."

"He promised me it wouldn't be hurt," she said, but she looked like she didn't entirely believe that.

All the air whooshed out of my lungs as I fell back against the sofa cushions. This was not how things were supposed to go. He was supposed to record the bird, and get visual proof that his peers could corroborate. He wasn't supposed to trap it and take it away. Delia would never have agreed to let him stay here and search for it if she thought the bird would be harmed.

"Aunt D, why didn't you call me?"

"You couldn't have done anything. And I knew you were working with Alex. I didn't want to make everything worse."

"I'm so sorry," I said.

Delia nodded. "Me too."

I pulled my cell phone from my pocket and dialed Eric's number. When it went to voicemail, I stood up and took a deep breath. In the friendliest tone I could muster, I said, "Hey, it's Fiona. I heard you found the bird. Give me a call as soon as you can—I'd love to hear about it."

The words tasted bitter. What I wanted to do was grab Eric by his tousled blond hair and dunk his head into the swamp water in the darkest part of Congaree. Misleading me was one thing. Hurting Delia was something else entirely.

---

"HE DID WHAT?" Alex said. He had his welding glasses pushed up into his hair, sipping a coffee. On the worktable was one of our words that he'd been attaching to a leaf frame when I barged into the studio. It wasn't even nine a.m. yet, and I was already hopped up on coffee and fury and ready to take that blowtorch to something. I'd tossed and turned all night, fuming over Eric, and now I was mad enough to spit fire.

"I can't believe this guy," I said. "We let him stay at the house. Delia fed him casserole. And as if all that wasn't enough, I had to tell a dozen people they were trespassing this morning when I caught them roaming all over the property."

"They were in the yard?" he said, his brow furrowed.

"Aunt D saw a bunch of cars parked on the road this morning and when I went out, there were all these strangers wandering through the woods with their binoculars. Apparently, this warbler story broke the birding internet yesterday."

Alex crossed his arms over his chest and arched a brow. "Is that even a thing?"

"Apparently it is. People flooded this little town in New Jersey last year when a painted bunting showed up for the first time in five years. I googled it last night because I couldn't sleep a wink. These people fly thousands of miles when an unusual bird shows up. What if this is just the beginning?" My heart pounded in my ears. "What have I done?"

He frowned. "Is Delia okay?"

I paced by the table. "She's annoyed, and feeling hurt. And betrayed. She'd never tell me it was my fault, but it sure feels like it is."

His jaw tightened, and I figured he'd lay into me. And I probably deserved it.

"Go ahead," I said, my voice cracking. "Tell me *I told you so.* You thought he was taking advantage, and I should have listened to you. So go ahead and tell me—I know you're dying to."

He stood then, and laid his hands on my shoulders.

"Fi. Tell me how I can help." His tone was so gentle it nearly broke me in half. Alex was a lot of things, but unkind was not one of them.

"I don't know what to do. The people left, but there will be more. I called the sheriff, and he said he could send someone out if we need them. But how long will this go on? We can't have people coming out to the house like that. Delia loves her privacy, and then there are the animals getting disturbed by the ruckus. Delia shouldn't have to deal with the trouble I caused." Tears pricked my eyes. It never occurred to me what the consequences of finding a rare species might be. I'd been too trusting of Eric. I thought he would go back to his nerdy life and write a master's thesis no one would read. I didn't think he'd want notoriety. I was naive, and now Delia was going to have to deal with the fallout.

My coming back here had caused nothing but trouble.

"We can handle this," he said. "It's just a bunch of tourists that don't know any better. They're annoying but harmless."

"And what about Eric?"

The way he raised his brow indicated he had several ideas about what to do with him. "We'll figure it out," he said.

* * *

TWO HOURS LATER, we were back at his studio. We'd gone to both hardware stores in town, bought all of their "no trespassing" signs, and put them up everywhere at Delia's—along the road, at the gate by the drive, and along the tree line on the perimeter of the property. Because Delia's land bordered Congaree, a public park, folks could still be out in the swamp—but at least the signs would deter them from parking in her driveway and walking all through the yard.

Eric still hadn't returned my calls or texts.

"There's nothing else we can do," I said. "We might as well finish the sculpture."

"I understand if you don't want to," Alex said. "It's okay. I can finish up."

"But I want to help you," I said. "I don't want to wreck that, too." And I wanted to keep my word.

Every time I didn't, I now realized I became a little more like my mother.

He studied me for a moment and said, "Okay. I'd like that."

Welding the last of the leaves onto the sculpture was a two-person job. My task was to hold the giant leaves steady with a long clamp while Alex welded them into place. Now that the sun was out from the clouds, it was easy to see the shadows that the words made on the ground.

"The Arts Council is going to love this," Alex said. "They'll lose their minds."

"You're going to have a two-year wait list."

He smiled. "I may have to hire an assistant."

When we'd worked our way to the last empty spot in the tree, he said, "There's one last leaf. I think you should do the honors."

"You trust me with a blowtorch?"

He paused, staring at me like he could see straight to the bottom of my soul. "I'd trust you with anything, Fi." Then he took the last leaf from the table, the smallest one that said *thrive*. When I climbed up the ladder next to his, he met me at the top and held the leaf in position. "Just point the fire that way and go until I say stop."

The blue flame of the torch licked at the copper of the leaf frame and the metal quickly began to fuse. Alex studied the progress, gesturing for me to keep moving the flame in the slow back and forth motion he'd shown me.

"Great," he said. "Almost there."

After another few minutes, the leaf was in place. Alex took the torch and waved the flame over a couple of rough spots to smooth them out. When he was satisfied, he turned off the torch and said, "That's a wrap."

We climbed down the ladders and stood at the base of the tree.

"I can't believe we finished it," I said. "With a couple of days to spare, even."

"We work pretty well together, Fi." He pushed his protective glasses up into his hair and smiled. "Stay right there."

He jogged back into the studio, leaving me to examine the tree. He was right—it *was* amazing.

"It's nothing fancy," he said, "but we need to celebrate properly." He had a bottle of red wine in one hand, and two stemless glasses in the other. He pulled the cork out with ease and filled the two glasses. When he handed one to me, my fingers brushed over his.

"I'm lucky you came to town when you did," he said.

"Good thing Aunt D needed a bionic knee, I guess."

"Here's to Delia," he said. "And to you." He fixed me with an intense gaze as he sipped his wine.

"To Delia," I said. "And to the Inspiration Tree."

He smiled. "I couldn't have done it without you," he said, clinking his glass against mine. "And I wouldn't have wanted to do this with anyone else."

The tree towered over us, easily fifteen feet at its tallest spot. It was the most beautiful thing I'd ever helped to build, and I never would have done it without Alex and his prodding.

"I've got a crazy idea," Alex said. "Want to hear it?" Before I could answer, he turned back to me and said, "Stay in Jasmine Falls."

I took a long drink from the glass. "I can't. My job at the gallery starts next Tuesday." I didn't tell him that I still hadn't confirmed things with Janet.

He leaned against the tree, sliding his hand along the metal bark.

"You like it here. I know you do. You've got friends, you've got Delia. And you could build a career here. You've already got superfans." He took a step closer and lowered his voice. "And me."

"You can't keep doing this," I said.

"Doing what?"

"Just turning on the charm and acting like what happened didn't happen." I lost my patience—he couldn't just sweet-talk me and expect that to make everything okay. "Alex, I was over the moon for you. I trusted you more than anyone else. When Mom abandoned me, I felt so lost—but you brought me back to myself. You were my first love. My lifeline. You mattered to me like no one else. So you hurt me worse than anyone could." Once I said the words, I couldn't stop myself. All the feelings I'd buried came raging up to the surface, and all I could think of was how humiliated I'd felt on that awful night.

"You made me feel like I wasn't good enough for you, that I'd never be good enough. You tossed me right back to where I'd been before, feeling like I wasn't worth fighting for." I couldn't meet his eyes, blinking back tears. "And the worst part was that I never saw it coming—I never thought you'd hurt me like that. And then you did. And you acted like you didn't even care."

"I'm so sorry, Fi." He set the wine down and put his hand on my arm. "That night is the biggest regret of my life. I never wanted to hurt you. Not ever."

"But you did. I can't just pretend that didn't happen. And no matter what I feel for you now, I can't forget how you made me feel then."

He nodded. "I know. I want to make it up to you. More than anything, I want another chance with you."

There was no reason to avoid this anymore. "Why'd you do it?" I asked him.

He stared up at the tree as if he might find the words there. "I was a stupid kid, Fi. I didn't know what I wanted, and I didn't know how good I had it."

"Not good enough."

He sighed and looked at me with the saddest expression I'd ever seen.

"Tell me," I said.

"Fi," he said, his voice cracking. "I never wanted you to go."

"Was it Lori? Were you cheating on me?"

He shook his head. "Fiona, no. It wasn't that at all."

"Was I not good enough?"

He stepped forward then, and put his big hands on my shoulders. "No, darlin'. If anything, you've always been too good for me."

"Then what was it? What don't you want to tell me?"

He stepped aside then, and turned away from me, kicking his boot in the sand.

"You want a second chance, and you can't even be honest with me?" I said. "Are you kidding me? It was eight years ago, and you still can't tell me why?"

"Penelope," he said, his voice quiet.

One word that cut like a knife. "What do you mean?"

He turned back to me then, but refused to look me in the eye. Staring a hole in the ground, he said, "Your mother told me that I wasn't good enough for you. That I'd just drag you down."

"She didn't." But even as I said the words, I knew it wasn't such a stretch.

He looked at me then, and his eyes were glassy. "She told me you had a bright future, and it wasn't here, and it wasn't with me. She told me to break it off."

"Alex. No."

He scoffed. "At first I said no. Then she tried to pay me off."

Those words landed like a punch in the gut.

"I didn't take it, of course. I ripped her check up right in her face, even though it was a whole lot of money." He shook his head. "But then she told me that if I didn't break up with you, she'd tell you I was cheating on you. And a lot more lies. And I knew you'd believe her. She had a spell over you. She's still your mother, no matter how badly she treated you."

"So you did what she asked."

"I had to. I knew she'd make you despise me if she made up some story like that. And I just couldn't stand thinking that you'd hate me so."

"I can't believe you didn't tell me this." All of that pain came rushing back. The way he'd brushed me off so quickly, as if what we'd had together was nothing.

He sighed. "I was barely old enough to drink beer. And deep in my heart," he looked at the ground, "I believed she was right about me." He looked up. "So I let you go."

I felt like the ground had swallowed me up. Everything hurt, and nothing made sense.

"But the killer," he said, "was that I couldn't protect you from the gossip train, and you ended up hating me anyway."

"I have to go," I said, choking on the words.

"Please stay." He stepped closer and touched my arm again. "We can fix this. I know we can. We were kids. But we aren't kids anymore."

My eyes filled with tears, but this time I didn't bother holding them back.

"All this time I thought you saved me from Penelope, but I was wrong. You were her closer."

He didn't try to defend himself. So I left.

# Chapter Thirty

FIONA

THE SENTIENT BEAN WAS PACKED. When I showed up with a box of six new paintings, Gwen squealed. When I told her I'd been painting all through the night because it had been impossible to sleep after what Alex told me, she barreled over to the espresso machine and cinched her apron like she meant business.

"Step aside," she told Maggie. "Emergency."

Maggie's pencil-thin eyebrows shot up and she stepped to the side, taking the frothing pitcher with her.

"I'm just going to put these in the back," I said, and took the paintings into the tiny closet off the kitchen that served as Gwen's office. They were small studies I'd done, even better than the last batch.

A minute later, Gwen was at the office door, holding two big mugs of coffee. "Triple latte," she said, handing me one.

"You are my favorite person in the whole world," I said.

"Ditto. Now tell me what happened." We went out the back door, over to where a tiny table with two chairs was set up under a big oak tree. It was the secret spot where her employees could take breaks and escape the cafe noise.

After I gave her the rundown of the night before, she leaned back in her chair and sighed.

"But he married Lori," she said. "So what gives?"

"I don't know. But I can't believe he just walked away because my mother told him to."

"Penelope can be terrifying," she said, sipping her coffee. "She's also really good at making people feel small." She leveled her big blue eyes on mine and waggled her finger at me. "Case in point."

"That's different."

Her jaw tightened. "Honey, I love you to bits, but your mother did a number on you. She's the reason you have this ridiculous imposter syndrome that extends into every facet of your life."

She wasn't wrong. Whether she'd intended to or not, my mother had made me self-conscious about a lot of things.

Okay, about *everything*. From the jobs I took to the color I dyed my hair. But I was getting better about all of that. Wasn't I? Moving away meant I didn't hear her constant barrage of opinions. It meant I wasn't subjected to her surprise visits to check up on me and squash whatever dreams I had.

"You had to put three hundred miles between you just to breathe," Gwen said. "Not that I blame you for doing that."

"Is this supposed to be a pep talk?"

"I'm just saying, you've worked hard to get out of your mother's orbit and make a life for yourself. But hiding from her isn't going to solve the problem. It's time to stand up for yourself. You need to stop waiting around for her approval because I hate to tell you, but she's never going to give it to you."

"I know." And I realized I did know. Finally.

She leaned over and put her hand on mine. "And do you also know that you can live a long, happy, love-filled life without it? You need her approval about as much as you need a monkey with a typewriter."

"How'd you get so wise about all of this?"

"Well, you met *my* mother. If you stick around, I'll introduce you to my therapist."

I smiled, sipping my coffee. "I miss you, Gwen."

"I miss you too, babe. But I have a solution for that. Want to hear it?" She gave me a sly smile and I knew exactly what was coming.

"My job starts next week. And Delia doesn't need me anymore."

"I thought you hated that gallery job."

I shrugged. "It pays all right. And it keeps me connected in the art community around Asheville." But I still dreaded going back there, selling work that wasn't mine.

She squinted at me like she could see right through me. "You could work here if you wanted."

"Please. I can barely make my French press work. I'd be your worst barista ever."

"First, Maggie holds that title, and you'll never knock her off her pedestal. Second, you can sling coffee if you want, but you could also be my administrative assistant. I've been thinking about hiring someone part-time so I could take a dang day off once in a while. If you had something part-time, you'd have time to keep painting, right? Because obviously, that needs to be your priority."

It wasn't a terrible idea. The gallery wasn't full-time either, and there were no benefits attached. When I went back, I'd still be looking for a new apartment. I'd be right back where I was: barely getting by, paying too much for rent, and too tired to feel like doing what I loved most when I got home each day.

"Just think about it," she said. "And don't you dare factor your mother into this decision."

I snorted. But deep inside, I still worried.

"I'm dead serious." Gwen pointed her finger at me and gave me her tough-love stare. "You've made enough decisions based on your mother's influence. Try to make this one on your own."

"There's Alex, too," I said. "I'd see him everywhere."

She raised a brow. "Please don't say this town isn't big enough for both of you. I will take that latte away from you."

"It would be so weird, Gwen. I'm not sure I can handle seeing him all the time. At the grocery store, at the library, at Delia's, for Pete's sake. There'd be no way to avoid him."

"I can ban him from the cafe. Toss his cute butt right out of here."

I laughed, knowing that she absolutely would if I asked her to.

"Give it a little time," she said. "It might not be as bad as you think." She stood, straightening her apron. "Let's go get these paintings up," she said. "You have fans waiting."

"Gwen, you're a pretty good art dealer."

"See?" she said, swatting my arm. "One more reason to stay."

WHEN MY PHONE RANG, I was shocked to see that it was Eric's number. I was putting the finishing touches on my painting for the gala—a big acrylic panel full of goldfinches. Part of me was terrified it wouldn't go for much, but any amount was a help to the Arts Council.

When I saw his name, my chest tightened and blood whooshed to my head, but I answered the call anyway.

"Fiona," he said, sounding far away. "I got your messages."

When I said nothing, he went on. "Listen, I'm sorry I left in a hurry. Things just happened so fast, and I got caught up."

"We had strangers roaming through the yard, Eric. Delia's home became a tourist attraction."

"I'm sorry," he said, his voice lower.

"Were those articles your doing?" By now, they'd been spread all over social media and were in the national papers. "We were on one of the morning shows, for heaven's sake."

"That was an accident," he said. "I never intended for my discovery to get out this way. You have to believe me."

I snorted. "Oh, do I?"

"One of my colleagues called the state paper," he said. "He was trying to work an angle to get the department a grant. The deadline was a few days ago, and he wanted us to have a leg up. I had no idea he did that until it was too late. Then things just took off—I never expected that to happen."

"We trusted you, Eric. Delia invited you into her home."

"I'm so sorry. The publicity was never my goal." He sighed and sounded sad. "This could be a huge discovery, yes—but I planned to write a scholarly article, get it published, and apply for my own research grants. It would help the university too, of course, but I never dreamed it would explode and feel like a media grab."

He sounded sincere. But then, I'd always thought that about him, and look where that got us.

"What happens now?" I said. "Where's the bird?"

"Here at the lab. With me."

"You promised Delia it wouldn't be hurt. She's really upset by all this."

"It won't be," he said quickly. "And look, this discovery can be a great way to get the public interested in conservation. Having a bird like this to show people gives them a way to connect to something that often feels intangible. Like, what does 'conservation' really mean to the average person?"

My head was feeling less like it would explode. He made a good point, but I still felt like he'd yanked the rug out from under us.

"They even want to show it off at the gala," he said.

It felt like my heart stopped beating.

"They called me yesterday," he said. "It's one of the biggest fundraisers for non-profits in the state. Did you know that?"

"Of course," I said, even though I had not.

"Everybody who's anybody in the regional arts is there," he said. "Atlanta, Charlotte, Charleston. People with deep pockets and money to burn. Politicians, executives, millionaires who want to support the arts." He was talking excitedly now, the way they did when he was on a roll. "The chances that those people could also invest in conservation isn't a big stretch. And you know we need all the help we can get."

I should never have posted that photo of the warbler painting. Money for conservation was great, but did it mean this bird would die in a lab?

"Fiona, if my department could get some big donations, it could make a huge difference in local conservation efforts and outreach. This kind of chance doesn't come around that often."

"Will the warbler be banded and released?"

He paused. "It's hard to say."

"Isn't that usually what you scientists do? If you really cared about its conservation, shouldn't you release it so it can meet a little girl bird and carry on the species?"

"Ideally yes, but sometimes that doesn't happen."

"You made a promise. To me, and to Delia."

"Look, Fiona, I have to go. I have a meeting to get to." Sounding more agitated, he said, "This is a good thing. Trust me."

He hung up before I could answer.

As a general rule, I never put my faith in anyone who said, "Trust me."

# Chapter Thirty-One

FIONA

"I FEEL LIKE AN ENCASED SAUSAGE," I said.

Gwen raised a brow and pulled another dress from the pile on her bed. She was slimmer than me, which meant most of her dresses were so tight in the bust and hips that I was sure to split a few seams the moment I sat down. Public nudity wasn't the kind of legacy I wanted to leave in Jasmine Falls.

"So don't sit down. That red looks amazing on you," she said with a smile.

"I'd rather be able to breathe."

"You're so practical." She grinned and pulled a light blue silk dress from the bed. "This one's A-line."

"What if I just don't go," I said. "You can be Delia's date."

"Hard no. You don't get to miss your big night because of a couple of lunkhead boys."

"It's hardly my big night."

"That sculpture's a big deal," she said, unzipping me. "Don't act like it isn't. And don't you want to see your painting in the auction?"

"Not really."

She frowned, helping me wriggle out of the red dress of doom.

"We really need to work on the way you deal with the good kind of attention. You made a splash here. Go accept some accolades. You deserve it."

"Thanks, Gwen."

When I slipped the next dress on, she zipped it up and said, "Now that's what I'm talking about. Hello, bombshell."

***

THE GALA WAS HELD at the Arts Council, which had a huge outdoor courtyard and a botanical garden that looked like it belonged outside of a Scottish castle. Two big white tents were set up near the garden, wrapped with about a million twinkling fairy lights. One tent held the cash bar, and the other was for the art auction. When Delia and I arrived, there was already a crowd milling around with their cocktails, browsing the work in the auction.

"It's almost time for the unveiling of the tree," she said. "Do you see Alex anywhere?"

"No, but we should head over." The sculpture had been installed at the library already, just a block from here, but it would be officially unveiled in just a few minutes. After the big reveal, they'd start the auction.

By the time we got to the library, there were a few people gathered already. The staff had erected a huge curtain around the sculpture so you couldn't see any hint of what it was.

"They're going for maximum surprise here," I said.

"Smart," Delia said. "They're going to wow everyone, get them boozed up, and then they'll be excited to spend their money at the auction."

As the crowd began to gather, I saw Gwen and waved her over. Her hair was piled on her head in a loose bun, and she wore a slinky charcoal dress that showed off her muscular legs.

"Look at y'all," she said. "You need a red carpet."

"Thanks to you," I said. "Otherwise I'd have been here in jeans and a tee shirt." Gwen's blue A-line halter dress had fit me better than anything I'd ever put on. She'd insisted I keep it forever.

Delia wore black dress pants and an elegant black blouse with a big multi-colored scarf. She'd even bought a new cane for the event, black with a silver handle. "I don't need too many fancy dresses," she said, "but I never miss the gala."

As more people crowded around us, Delia started chatting with a couple of her friends from the library.

"Have you seen him?" Gwen said, scanning the crowd.

"Trying to avoid either of the *hims*."

She leaned closer and said, "You're kinda hard to miss in that dress, babe. You might make Alex's poor heart explode."

My breath hitched in my throat. I wasn't so sure she was right. He'd finally told me the truth he'd been so obviously afraid to tell me, and now I thought maybe I'd been too hard on him. I'd pushed him to tell me, and he'd done what I asked—and then I'd walked away.

Next to the sculpture was a small podium with a microphone. Maxine was standing near it with Eli and Alex.

When Alex saw me, he raised his hand but froze mid-wave. Next to him, Eli waved more emphatically, calling me over.

"You're up, slugger," Gwen said, staring over at them.

"I feel sick."

Alex was still staring at me, his eyes ablaze. I could feel their smolder from clear across the courtyard.

When Maxine put her hand on his shoulder, he finally snapped out of his trance, but I couldn't let go of the fire he lit inside me.

Gwen nudged me in the ribs and handed me her drink. "Bottoms up, babe. You got this."

I knocked back the rest of her drink, which tasted more like gin than tonic, then handed her the glass as I walked toward the podium.

Maxine beamed as I approached. She wore a deep magenta ball gown that complimented the dark tones of her skin. Her braids were arranged high on her head, threaded with gray. She wore a big necklace made of handmade glass beads—no doubt something created by a local artist.

"Fiona," she said, shaking my hand. "It's so wonderful to have you here tonight. The tree sculpture is amazing. Truly."

"Thank you," I said. "But I only helped a little."

"Alex says he couldn't have done it without you."

"Alex exaggerates."

She smiled. "He has an unusual amount of humility, that man. He also told me all about you and your paintings. I'm so excited to have you back in Jasmine Falls. We need more artists like you here."

"Oh," I said. "Thank you so much, but I'm not sure how long I'll be staying."

She smiled, squeezing my hand. "Let's talk later tonight. I have some ideas I'd like to run by you." With that, she stepped toward the podium.

"Great to see you, Fiona," Eli said, flashing me his movie-star smile. He wore a perfectly tailored tan suit with a white shirt and no tie, looking like he'd just stepped off the cover of a magazine. "Mimi's going to make some remarks and introduce y'all real quick. Then we'll head over to the auction tent."

He followed Maxine and left me with Alex.

"Hey." Alex wore a slim-cut light gray suit that fit him like a glove and made his eyes look a deep shade of green. His hair was tousled in that way that made me ache to run my fingers through it. My heart flip-flopped and my knees felt weak. This effect he had on me was never going to go away.

And I wasn't sure anymore that I wished it would.

"Nice dress," he said.

"Nice suit." And it was. It should be criminal to wear a suit that fit that well.

He slid his fingers along the lapels. "So the plan," he said, leaning in close, "is to introduce you and me, drop that curtain, and then send everyone back to the auction itching to buy some art." His tone was light, as if our last conversation had never happened.

How could he put these things behind him so easily?

I swallowed hard, not wanting to be re-introduced to Jasmine Falls quite so formally. Couldn't I just fly under the radar? Have my name put on the plaque and disappear?

"Relax," he said.

I snorted. "I'm relaxed."

He raised a brow. "You're wound so tight your hair's curlier."

"Hilarious."

"Look," he said. "About before. I need to say something."

When he put his hand on my arm, it felt like I'd been struck by a lightning bolt.

"I should have stood up for you. For us. I know that now." The crowd began to applaud and he leaned closer. "No one will come between us like that again. Not for as long as I live on this earth."

Whistles erupted from the crowd as Maxine stepped up to the podium and begin her remarks.

"Alex," I whispered. "Let's talk after." This wasn't a conversation I wanted to have in a crowd. Plus, I wanted him to have my full attention, and right now the chances of me hurling on his shoes was not exactly zero.

"But I need you to know this," he said. "I want to start over with you. I want that more than anything." He took my hand and wrapped it in his, pulling it to his lips, and my heart banged against my ribs.

"Stay here," he said, his eyes searching mine. "Give us a chance."

Maxine greeted the crowd and waved to us, smiling broadly.

Alex removed his hand and clapped slowly, but he didn't move away. There was the faint scent of cedar and spruce, and I was helpless, already leaning closer to him like I was pulled by a magnetic force. When I took a deep breath, he turned and gave me a long look that nearly cleaved my heart in two.

Alex Fox had wormed his way back into my heart. Maybe staying here wasn't a step backward after all. More than anything, I needed to move forward—was staying here the way to do it?

He stared at me from the corner of his eye as Maxine described the idea behind the sculpture. She was passionate about the library and this community, and there was no doubt that she wanted to foster a love of the arts in everyone there. This woman was dazzling, and as her words rang out, there were shouts and cheers.

My heart pounded in my chest as she introduced Alex, and then me. Someone clapped me on the shoulder as there was more applause, and then Alex was looping his arm in mine and leading me towards the podium, turning me towards the crowd.

"So I'd like to thank Alex and Fiona," Maxine said, "for creating this absolute delight."

Alex gave a humble wave, and I did the same, my head spinning because of all of the attention.

The curtain dropped, and a few well-placed spotlights came up, casting the shadows of the words on the wall of the library. It was magnificent, towering above us, with its stylized leaves reaching toward the stars, the branches and trunk a blend of two contrasting metals that complemented each other so nicely.

Just like Alex and me.

Applause and whistles filled my ears. Right in front was Gwen, grinning and jumping up and down, and next to her was Delia, beaming.

"And now I'd like to invite you to take a look in the auction tent," Maxine said. "Alex and Fiona have both donated pieces, as have dozens of other gifted artists from across the state. There's something for everyone, so go pick your favorites before the auction begins!"

There were more hoots of agreement, and as the crowd began to meander back toward the tents, Alex pulled me aside.

"What do you think?" he said. His hand drifted to the small of my back as he gently turned us away from the crowd. "Could you stay here and start over with me?"

My heart banged against my ribs. This tangle of feelings I had for Alex would never go away. I'd been fooling myself to think that it ever could.

"I feel like I'm inside a hurricane," I sputtered. "When I'm around you, I can't think straight. I just want to start over, but I don't know how, and I have all these feelings about you, and this town, and I don't know what they mean, and being back here has scrambled my brain." I felt like everything I'd kept bottled up was pouring out, and there was no way to stop it. "And you're asking me to make a big decision, and it's a huge amount of pressure. I came here wanting one thing, and now I think I want something else, and every time I'm with you, I feel like I'm going to explode."

He blinked at me, and then gave me a reassuring smile. "It's okay," he said. "You—we—don't have to figure it all out right now." He squeezed my hand and said, "We just have to take the first step. Together."

I wanted to believe him, but it didn't feel like it could be that simple.

"Do you trust me, Fi?" He slid his hand along my cheek.

"Yes," I whispered.

He gave me a tender smile. "Then take this leap with me."

How was he so calm and confident right now? I felt dizzy, but looking into his eyes steadied me, just as it had so many years ago when it felt like my whole world had turned upside down.

"Hey!" Gwen said, slipping in between us. "That thing is amazing. I can't even believe what I'm looking at right now."

"Agreed," Delia said. "You kids outdid yourselves."

"It's a good thing Fiona showed up in town," Alex said, as though he hadn't just promised me the world. "Without her, it would be a pile of scrap metal."

"Well," Gwen said, "We're off to go look at the art. Want to come?"

"You bet," I said, still reeling from Alex's words. "Delia might need something for her living room."

As Delia and Gwen turned toward the tent, Alex reached for my hand. "I'll see you over there," he said. "Just think about what I said, okay?"

I nodded, then turned to catch up with them.

THE AUCTION TENT was as busy as a beehive. There were a few select pieces on prominent display, the ones that would get the most attention and the highest bids. Glass and ceramic pieces were placed on pedestals, and one long table along the side was covered with smaller objects in the silent auction. A podium was set up at the front of the tent, along with dozens of chairs with an aisle between them. Most of the art was inside the main building—the bottom floor was a gallery space and tonight it had been filled with art for the auction. People were free to browse the gallery and get a close look at the art before each piece was brought out during the live auction.

We chose seats near the back, where we had a full view of everything.

"I've got my eye on a pair of earrings that Samantha Blake made," Gwen said. "How about you Delia?"

Delia smiled. "I might have put my name on a few things in the silent auction."

"Your painting is gorgeous," Gwen said to me. "Sadie said her chief ranger always comes to this event, too. It would look amazing in my bedroom, so Miss Ranger's gonna have to pony up big time."

"You know I'll paint you anything you want," I told her.

She grinned. "Yeah, but this is more fun."

When the auctioneer gave a five-minute warning, Delia said, "I want to go put one more bid in."

"I'll go with you," Gwen said. "I'll check mine, too."

Gwen took Delia's arm and they walked toward the table with

the silent auction items. A rumble of laughter came from two men as they sat down in the row behind me.

"Too bad it's not part of the auction," one of them said, his voice gravelly. "I wouldn't mind having that myself."

"Everything can be bought," the other one said. His voice was more nasal, his drawl more pronounced, like an old man who came from even older money. "I'll talk to that kid again afterward. He won't turn away the obscene check I'm going to write him."

I rolled my eyes. Delia had told me there'd be a few folks like them here. All money and no manners.

The first man laughed. "You'll have the most expensive critter in the world. What the hell are you going to do with a pet bird?"

Another guffaw. "Stuff it and put it in my trophy room next to the Carolina Parakeet."

I cringed. Surely I was not hearing them right.

"Don's always bragging on that stupid lion he shot on some fake safari. This'll shut him up for good."

"There's no way he'll sell it to you," the younger man said.

Eric. They had to be talking about the warbler.

"I heard the department is desperate for cash," the other said, lowering his voice. "Hemorrhaging money like all of the snooty ivory towers. I might get myself a bargain and my name on a building, too. What I'm offering is more than a dozen dinky research grants all put together."

More laughs.

My face felt like it was on fire. I wanted to think that Eric, Mr. Conservation, would tell these two where they could shove their checkbooks. But the person with cash almost always got what they wanted. In my experience, principles didn't last long when you poked at them with a long line of zeros.

"You already have your name on a building," the younger man said.

The older man snorted. "Please. That one doesn't count and you know it."

At the podium, the auctioneer welcomed the crowd just as Delia and Gwen squeezed back into their seats next to me. All around us, people were sitting shoulder to shoulder, some fanning themselves with their auction booklets.

"That Sophie Denton was hovering over my earrings like a hawk," Gwen said with a huff. "Every time someone wrote down a bid, she'd swoop in and put down another one. Where's the fun in that?"

"Cary Sheehan got my scarf," Delia said. "It'll probably look better on her, though."

"What's with you?" Gwen said to me. "You look like you swallowed a fly."

"The warbler. Eric brought it tonight."

Gwen's eyes widened. "Why?"

Before I could reply, a slim woman in a black dress walked out carrying the first painting, and the auctioneer began taking bids. It was a big abstract landscape that already had a dozen paddles waving.

"I need some air," I said, feeling like my head might explode. It was impossible to shake the vision of our mystery bird stuffed and perched on some guy's wall, hanging next to the bar with humidors and thousand-dollar bottles of scotch.

Gwen raised a brow and whispered something to Delia as I stood. I hadn't been out of the tent thirty seconds when Gwen came up behind me.

"You okay?" she said. "You look like my mom right before she blows a gasket."

As I told her what I'd overheard, Gwen chewed her lip, staring at the back row under the tent. From here, we could see the two men clearly. They both wore expensive-looking summer suits. One had white hair combed back in a ridiculous peak, like meringue. The other was stockier with close-cropped dark hair that was turning gray. They drank from lowball glasses and pointed towards the podium as they talked.

"They're just talking crap," Gwen said. "Stupid trust fund lug nuts."

"What if they're not?"

"Idiots. That one looks like Colonel Sanders."

"What if they do talk Eric into selling it? Can he even do that?"

Gwen looked like she wanted to spit fire. "Seems to me that when you have that much money, you can do whatever you want."

The auctioneer slammed down the gavel and moved to the next piece.

I sighed, fidgeting in the tight, borrowed heels. "I need to do something that might be illegal."

"Oooh," she said, her face lighting up. "Tell me more."

# Chapter Thirty-Two

## FIONA

A FEW YARDS away from the drink tent, Gwen and I were huddled behind a massive camellia bush with blossoms as big as our heads. Everyone else was focused on the auction, except for the few people milling about between the tents.

"I have to set it free," I told her.

"What about Eric?" she said. "He'll just come back and try to catch it again, won't he?"

"All I know for sure is that this bird's going to be toast if we don't do something."

"There you are." Alex stepped around the camellia and said, "I've been looking all over for you."

Gwen raised a brow.

Alex gave her a polite nod as if he knew he was on thin ice with her, and then turned back to me. "Is everything okay?"

"Not exactly. We're in crisis mode."

His eyes widened. "Is it Delia? Is she okay?"

"She's fine," I said. Having him stand so close to me was already causing an ache in my chest.

"Fiona heard two morons talking about buying the bird from

Eric," Gwen said. "Sounds like someone's determined to take it home and mount it on the wall."

Alex scowled. "What? He can't do that."

I shrugged, feeling nauseated again. "He might, for a big pile of money. All I know is this jerk wants to leave tonight with that bird. And I can't let that happen."

"Fiona has a plan," Gwen said.

"What can I do?" Alex said. He looked determined to help.

"We have to figure out where it is," I said. "They're supposed to show it off at the end of the auction, so we've got less than an hour."

"We've looked all around out here and in the gallery," Gwen said. "No luck."

Alex pulled his phone from his breast pocket and tapped the screen.

"Is Eric here?" Gwen said, peering through the big leaves.

"I saw him earlier," I said. "But haven't since the unveiling."

"Little rat," Gwen spat out.

"I don't think he meant for all this to happen," I said. "He just got swept up like the rest of us."

Gwen frowned. "You know, it's super annoying sometimes, the way you always see the good in people."

*Except Alex*, I thought, regretting how I'd spent the last two weeks only seeing the bad.

"Eli says it's in Maxine's office," Alex said. His phone buzzed again. "He wants to help, too."

"Maxine," Gwen said, her eyes widening. "Will she get in trouble for this?"

"Eli says he can go unlock the office," Alex said, still typing. "He can't be missed, so he'll have to do it fast and get back. He says not to worry about Maxine. He'll talk to her."

"We can't leave Delia," I said.

"I'll stay with her," Gwen said. "You two handle the bird." She gave me a quick nod and then smoothed her dress as she headed back to the tent.

Alex, still texting, glanced up and said, "It's time. Let's go, Fi." He shoved his phone into his pocket and gently took my arm, leading me through the garden towards the main building. To anyone else, we looked like two people just taking a stroll in the nice summer air—definitely not two people about to sneak into an office and steal an animal. He stepped out of the hedges first, and after a quick look around, took my hand and led me into the front door of the building.

Once inside, we hurried through the gallery and up the back stairs like a couple of burglars. When I tripped on a step, Alex caught my arm and frowned.

I grabbed his arm to steady myself and slipped off the high heels.

"Why on earth are you wearing those ridiculous shoes?" he said.

"Sorry, but I left my caper shoes at home. And these make my legs look amazing."

"Agreed." He opened the door to the second floor. "Okay," he said, "All clear."

By this time, I knew they were getting to the higher-priced auction pieces, so everyone would be laser-focused on the tent. No one wanted to miss the big items even if they weren't bidding.

We hurried down the hall to Maxine's office. When Alex tried the knob, it opened with a click.

Inside, Alex flipped on a lamp and we quickly scanned the room. In the corner was a pedestal with something on top, covered with a sheet.

Alex pulled out his phone and started typing.

"Everything okay?" I said.

"Yep."

I rushed over and pulled up the corner of the sheet. Inside the cage was the warbler, his bright yellow bib glowing in the dim light. He let out a surprised chirp.

"Thank you, Eli," I whispered.

Alex picked up the cage and I said, "Wait, we have to put it inside something else. Then we'll make it look like someone left the cage open and it flew out the window."

He nodded. "Good thinking." By the desk was a cardboard banker's box. He removed a handful of files from it and set them on the desk. "It's not fancy, but it'll do."

I moved the sheet and opened the door to the cage. The bird chirped and hopped away from my hand. Each time I reached for it, it hopped away, startled.

Alex muttered something, still typing on the phone.

"What's going on?" I said.

"Nothing. No worries."

"Then could you maybe save the texting for after the catch and release? I could use some backup here."

He arched a brow and stuffed the phone into his pocket, then went to Maxine's desk.

I reached for the bird again and it hopped away, flapping its wings.

"Come on," I said, in my most soothing voice. "It's okay."

"Let me try," Alex said, stepping closer.

"Is that Maxine's scarf?"

He unfurled the brightly colored fabric in the cage, and in a deft maneuver, caught the bird inside it and then carefully placed the scarf and the bird inside the banker's box and closed the lid. "It's for a good cause," he said. "She'll understand."

Inside, there was a tiny thumping sound, a few annoyed chirps.

"Sorry little guy," I said, "This will be over soon."

I left the cage door ajar, left the sheet off the top, and then opened one of the office windows just a few inches. Now it would look like a simple accident. Carelessness, and nothing more.

Nope, no evidence of shenanigans here.

Alex opened the office door while I carried the box. We were halfway to the stairwell when Alex said, "Shoot, I forgot to lock the door back. Wait for me by the stairs."

He hurried back to the office and I went around the corner and into the stairwell.

And bumped right into a woman dressed in a short black dress.

"Hey," she said. "Is that for the silent auction?" She looked down at the banker's box and reached for it. "They sent me to get the last of the jewelry pieces."

"Oh," I said. "Um, no. I think those are downstairs in the gallery."

"Nah, I checked there already." She eyed the box and I held my breath, hoping the bird would stay calm.

The door behind us opened and Alex said, "Oh, hi," as if he was surprised to find us there.

"Hi," the woman said, giving Alex a full head-to-toe assessment that made my face feel hot.

"That was some sculpture," she said to him, stepping between us. "Exquisite work." Her eyes followed the line of his suit, which was exquisite also. He shot me a look that said, *trust me.*

"Thank you," he said, and gave the woman a warm smile.

The bird chirped and the woman snapped her head towards me. "Eep," I said, placing a hand over my chest. "Hiccups."

She frowned at me, but turned back to Alex, her attention piqued. "I've admired your work for a long time," she said. "My name's Chloe Caldwell." She extended her hand and angled her hip towards him, pushing her chest out, and grinning like a cat who found the canary.

Alex smiled his mischievous smile, and as he shook her hand, he motioned at me with the other—it was the tiniest gesture but one that was unmistakable: *Go.*

"Have I seen you around here before?" he asked her. Her smile widened and I slipped out of the stairwell, holding the box tightly as I hurried out the back door and towards the parking lot.

•  •  •

ALEX'S TRUCK was parked several yards from the building, in the gravel lot that was usually reserved for employees. The bird chirped and flapped its wings inside the box as I walked over to Alex's truck, hoping it might be unlocked.

It wasn't. *Who locks their car in Jasmine Falls, Alex?*

Just as I stepped into the shelter of the trees, I heard a low whistle and turned.

"Let's roll," Alex said. He slipped from the shadows and was at the truck in three quick strides. He opened the passenger door for me and I slid inside, dropping my shoes onto the floorboard. I held the box steady as he shut my door and then jogged around to the driver's side.

Once inside, he cranked the engine and said, "That was close."

"Good use of charm," I said. "But I wasn't sure you'd make it out."

He raised a brow as he placed one hand on the seat behind my head and backed out of the lot. "Sometimes you have to take one for the team," he said. His eyes caught mine for a brief moment, and then we were on the road headed to Delia's.

My phone buzzed with a text.

**I just heard they want to show off the bird after the auction,** Gwen wrote. **Where are you?**

**Headed to the house,** I replied.

**Delia's asking about you,** she typed. **What should I say?**

**Make something up.**

**I'll tell her you're making up with Alex,** she wrote.

**Except that.**

**Making out?**

**You're a riot.**

Heart emojis. Bird emoji.

Alex's phone buzzed in his pocket. Twice, then three times.

"Do you need to get that?" I said.

The bird flapped in the box, letting out a string of annoyed chirps.

"It's fine," he said, raking his hand through his hair.

He was quiet the rest of the way, his brow furrowed. When we got to Delia's, I climbed out of the truck and grabbed the box. We started toward the woods, the grass tickling my bare feet with each step.

"You sure about this?" he said. "There's no going back."

"Positive," I said. When we got to the edge of the woods, I took the lid off the box. The bird cocked its head to the side and looked up at us, still halfway under the scarf.

"Okay, guy," I said, moving the fabric away from him. "Try to keep a low profile."

The warbler let out one short chirp and flew out of the box in a blur.

I handed Maxine's scarf to Alex and said, "We should probably get that dry-cleaned."

"Fiona McIntyre," he said, staring at me with the goofiest grin on his face. "Trespassing. B and E. Bird thievery. What am I going to do with you?"

"I can think of a few things. Can't you?"

Above us, the moon was full and bright, casting the yard in a cool, ethereal blue. He stepped closer, and his gaze dropped down to my lips. My heart thudded against my ribs, and I swallowed hard. It felt like we were alone in the world, two people sharing a secret moment that no one else would ever feel. Our past felt so far away now, meaningless. Out here in the moonlight, all of our past mistakes had been stripped away, like we might be able to start over after all. All this time, I'd thought that moving forward meant moving away—away from Alex, away from Jasmine Falls. But I'd had it all wrong.

My phone buzzed, and I fumbled to fish it out of the pocket of my dress.

**They're down to the last five pieces,** Gwen wrote. **How's it going?**

**Handled,** I texted back.

"We should go," I said, turning back towards the truck.

"Wait," he said, catching my arm.

"It'll look weird if we're not there. People might think we had something to do with it."

"I have to tell you something before you leave," he said, pulling me closer.

"Tell me when the auction's over."

His eyes were wide in the moonlight. "I've been waiting all night. It can't wait any longer."

"Alex," I said, "we have to hurry." I reached over and put my fingers to his lips and tried hard not to think about how soft and kissable they were. "Tell me on the way," I said, and hurried back to the truck.

# Chapter Thirty-Three

## ALEX

EVERY TIME I tried to tell her, she ran away. It was maddening.

Fiona raced back to the truck, barefoot and wild, gorgeous in that blue dress that drew my eyes to every curve as she moved and made me desperate to trace all the seams with my fingers. I couldn't stand thinking of how this was her last night here, that in twenty-four hours she'd be gone, and Jasmine Falls would never be the same.

And neither would I.

I couldn't bear to watch her walk away again.

She texted Gwen as I drove us back to the Arts Council, checking in on Delia. I couldn't understand why she wanted to leave here so badly—it was obvious that she loved spending time with Delia and with Gwen. She'd sold a pile of paintings at the cafe, and Maxine had already asked her to be in a group show at the Arts Council. Everybody here loved Fiona—she had to see it. It seemed like Jasmine Falls suited her down to the ground, so I couldn't figure out why she'd want to leave all that behind.

Unless it was because of me.

But no. I knew I wasn't imagining her softening toward me. What I felt was real, and she was feeling it too.

She chewed her lip while she typed. I wanted so badly to pull onto the shoulder and tell her everything I'd been too afraid to say before, but this night was important to her. First I had to get us back to the auction. I'd just have to find time to talk to her later.

Her fingers raced across the screen, her brow furrowed.

"Everything all right?" I said.

"Yeah, they're down to the last few pieces. We don't have much time."

When we pulled into the parking lot, I could see that the crowd had only thinned a little inside the auction tent. The gala tended to go well past midnight, and it was only 11:30.

Fiona took a deep breath when she got out of the truck and slipped her heels back on.

"Okay," she said. "Whatever happens next, we have to act surprised."

I nodded and offered my arm as we walked across the gravel lot and toward the crowd. When she looped her arm in mine, it felt like two puzzle pieces snapping into place.

"Actually," she said, letting me go. "Maybe it's better if we don't show up together. Just in case."

"Okay," I said. But I was definitely not okay. Time was running out.

"Hey," she said. She stepped closer and I caught the scent of lavender. "Thank you. For tonight."

My breath hitched. I wanted to fold her into my arms and never let her go. "Of course," I said. "I meant what I said. I'd do anything for you."

She placed her hand on my cheek. A silent thank-you that burned hotter than Eli's forge.

Then she was gone, making a beeline for the auction tent, no doubt looking for Delia.

• • •

WHEN I GOT to the drink tent, I ordered a whiskey because my heart felt like a jackhammer. Across the garden, Eli nodded in that way that meant success. As I made my way over to him, I heard a cheer from inside the auction tent and the smack of the gavel.

"We good?" I said to Eli, and he nodded, clinking his glass against mine.

"All set," he said. "No problem."

"I owe you one."

Eli smirked. "Definitely more than one, but we'll settle up later."

"So it was a good night, then?"

"Mimi's thrilled," he said. "Says it's a record year." He sipped his drink and said, "And she's over the moon about the sculpture. Y'all outdid yourselves."

"Fi and I make a good team."

He said something about my piece in the auction, but I was too busy watching Fiona as she left her spot by Delia and Gwen and headed back my way. It hadn't seemed possible that she could look more beautiful than she did every day, but tonight she took my breath away. She gave me the tiniest smile and time stood still like we were the only two people left on earth, and I wanted her to look at me that way for the rest of my life.

The breeze lifted her dress just above her knees, and then she stopped abruptly as Eric stepped into her path. The look on her face made all the blood rush to my head, and I strode toward them before Eli could stop me.

Fiona pulled her arm away from him. "I don't know what you mean," she said.

His voice was low, angry. "What did you do with the bird, Fiona?"

"You okay here, Fi?" I stepped next to her and Eric had the good sense to remove his hand from her arm.

Smart, because I was considering how I might twist it behind his back and have him face down in the grass in three seconds flat.

Fiona looked at me, her eyes wide. "We're fine," she said, her voice light. "Just a misunderstanding."

Eric shot me a dismissive look and then turned back to her. "Do you realize what you've done? You've ruined everything."

"Keep your voice down," Fiona said. She didn't want a scene, but Eric was getting more flustered by the second. I'd seen that look in plenty of men, right before they did something stupid.

If he did something stupid, it would end very badly for him.

"I think it's time for you to leave," I said to Eric. "You've officially worn out your welcome in this town."

"If you helped her, you're going down, too," Eric said, blood rising in his cheeks. "You've compromised a significant study. Stolen university property. I'll press charges."

"I'd think about your next words very carefully," I said.

He turned back to Fiona. "Why would you do this? You know how important the warbler discovery is. Not just for me."

When he reached for her again, Fiona jerked her arm away, stumbling in her heels. By the time I righted her, Eli was at her other elbow, staring Eric down with a look that could melt steel. And there was Maxine, right next to him.

Fiona paled when she saw Maxine. The older woman stepped forward and said, "Mr. Reiker, I'm very sorry about this, but it appears to be simply an oversight. I must have left my office window open. I take full responsibility. But I will not stand for harassment."

Fiona's eyes widened. She opened her mouth to reply, but Eli placed his hand on her arm and pursed his lips.

"We've had a very successful evening," Maxine said, "and I'm sure the council would approve of making a sizable donation to your department so it can continue its work."

Eric glanced at Fiona, then back to Maxine. By then, several other patrons had left the tent and drifted over to see what the noise was about.

Eric scoffed. He looked at me, then back at Eli in a calculating way that I didn't like one bit. "My department head will be in touch," he said to Maxine, and then trudged toward the parking lot, defeated.

Maxine said, "Fiona, can I have a minute?" and Fi swallowed hard, looking mortified.

# Chapter Thirty-Four



MAXINE TOOK my arm and led me a few steps away. Her red ball gown swished as she walked and I had to concentrate hard to keep myself upright. My thoughts of staying in Jasmine Falls were slipping away like a cool breeze. Getting on Maxine's bad side would end my career before it started, and I'd raised plenty of a ruckus tonight.

"You don't owe me one second of your time," I told her, "but I'd like to explain."

She smiled, looking over at the crowd in the auction tent. "No need," she said. "Eli told me everything."

I let out a big sigh. "I'm sorry I put you in such a difficult position."

"I thought about it," she said. "And I'd have done the same thing in your shoes. This has always been one of my favorite events because it gets people so excited about the arts, but I've been around long enough to know that some people spend their money because their hearts are big, and some people do it for their ego and a tax write-off."

She brushed a loose braid behind her ear and said, "As far as I can tell, what we had here was an unfortunate moment of carelessness. It was a busy night, and there were lots of people in and out of my office today. The air conditioning's bad in that building, and it's not uncommon for people to open the windows when it's scorching outside. Someone must have done so without thinking, you know?"

I nodded.

"It's an accident. Not a tremendous loss," she said. "That man took plenty of photos and video while he had it in his hands. And some wild things ought to stay wild. Don't you agree?"

"Yes ma'am, I do."

She fixed her big brown eyes on me. "And some secrets are best taken to the grave."

"Agreed."

She nodded. "People will be talking about your piece for a long time," she said. "That was one of the highlights of the auction. You have a tremendous amount of talent, Fiona, and I'm really happy that you're here."

With so much happening, I'd forgotten about my painting. I'd been afraid they'd have to do that thing where they go lower than the starting bid, dropping the price until some poor person finally felt sorry enough to put it out of its misery.

"Thank you so much," I said. "I'm so honored that you asked me to be a part of the gala."

"Let's talk soon about a show for you," she said, touching my arm. "Now if you'll excuse me, I'm going to say goodbye to a few guests."

She didn't so much walk as glide through the grass toward the auction tent, where a few people still stood chatting over their drinks. When I went back to the bar tent, the bartenders were cleaning up and Alex and Eli had vanished.

"Hey," Gwen said, stepping up beside me. "There you are."

Next to her, Delia grinned and said, "Way to go, kiddo."

"You told her?" I said to Gwen.

Gwen rolled her eyes. "Who can keep a secret from Delia?"

"At this rate, the whole town's going to know."

"And they would totally support you," Gwen said.

Delia nudged my ribs. "You did the right thing. I'm proud of you."

"I hope so." I still felt a little bad for Eric. Wrecking someone's career wasn't on my to-do list.

"I just hate you missed seeing your piece go on the block," Delia said. "It was quite the show." She made it sound like one of those moments like seeing a comet, or a total eclipse—something that you were lucky if you got to see just once in your life.

"Me, too."

"Good thing I recorded it," Gwen said.

"Really?" I said.

She grinned, pulling her phone from her purse. "Well, duh," she said. "I wasn't going to let you miss your big moment entirely." She tapped the screen of her phone and Delia walked us over to an empty table. When Gwen played the video, we all leaned in close.

From her vantage in the back of the tent, I could see one of the assistants carrying the painting across the tent, past the front row. As soon as the first number was called, paddles started waving in the air.

Not just a couple, either.

More like twenty.

My mouth fell open as the auctioneer ran through numbers so fast I couldn't keep track. The paddles kept waving as the number went higher, and soon it was down to three bidders, ping-ponging back and forth. Two of the bidders I didn't recognize, but the third was sitting not far from Gwen, wearing an impeccable tan suit.

Eli.

The auctioneer continued and Eli looked at his phone. I heard "going once," and Eli's arm shot in the air again.

*Going twice.*

The other paddles stayed down, and the gavel slammed against the block. Cheers erupted all around, and someone patted Eli on the back. Eli flashed his megawatt smile as he gave someone a thumbs-up. Then he turned back to his phone.

"Holy cow," I said. "Eli?"

Gwen and Delia exchanged a look.

"He was a proxy," Delia said. "You can't be in two places at once, you big goof."

I turned back to the bar, but it was empty, the bartenders clearing up the last of the trash.

"I'll take Delia home," Gwen said, giving me a wink. "You have someplace you need to be."

IT WAS NEARLY one in the morning, but I didn't care. Something told me he wouldn't either.

Alex's house still had a couple of lights on. First I knocked on the door, and then pounded harder when there was no answer. "Alex," I yelled up toward the window. "Alex, open this door!" I looked around for a tiny rock, but there wasn't a single one on this lush green lawn. I pulled off my shoe and chucked it at the window, but my aim was awful. It bounced off the siding with a thump and landed in the hedges below. When I tossed the other one, it clattered against the glass and I cringed, thinking I'd surely broken the window pane.

Alex came to the window and looked down for a moment, then disappeared from view.

A minute later, he was standing in the doorway, barefoot, wearing jeans and a tee shirt.

"Fiona," he said. "What's the matter? Why are you throwing shoes at my window?"

"Why did you buy my painting? That was a ridiculous amount of money."

He arched a brow. "Um, because I wanted it." He said this as if it was nothing unusual for him to drop thousands of dollars on a piece of art.

"But why?"

He leaned against the door frame, fixing his big green eyes on mine. With a smile, he said, "You know why."

Before he could say anything else, I did what I'd been wanting to do for days. I draped my arms over his big shoulders, stood up on my toes, and kissed him like I'd die if I didn't.

It was tender at first, and then I felt his big hands on my back and I kissed him harder, so he'd have no more doubt about how I felt. I kissed him with all of the love I'd been holding back for weeks, the love I'd been too afraid to admit that was real—the love that made me create those words for the tree: *rise, inspire, thrive.* Words that Alex Fox made me believe in again.

I kissed him with forgiveness, for him and for me.

He stepped backward into the house, winding his arms around my waist and pulling me against his chest. My heart banged against my ribs as I raked my hands through his hair. I could never get enough of him. Not ever.

But eventually, I'd need to breathe again.

When I finally pulled away, he said, "You're here," his voice gravelly. "But something tells me this is not about a painting."

"You asked me something earlier. And then we didn't get a chance to talk again."

"Yeah," he said. "We didn't." He stared into my eyes, his hands still gripping my waist "What did you want to tell me?"

"I don't want to leave. I told Janet I'm not going back." I didn't need to tamp down my feelings for him anymore. He was my home, and there was no other place I wanted to be.

His eyes were fixed on mine, wide and green and full of longing. "You already know that I want you to stay."

"Tell me why," I said. "I need to hear you say it."

He slid his hands along my back and smiled his rakish smile. "When you came back here, I fell in love with you all over again. Or maybe I never stopped. It's always been you, Fi. I don't ever want to be without you again." He slid his hand along my cheek and said, "I want to spend the rest of my life with you. If you'll let me."

I tightened my arms around his neck, and my heart flip-flopped in that way that I knew it would never stop doing around him. "You're the only one I want to collaborate with," he said, making *collaborate* sound oh so naughty.

"Good," I said, tightening my arms around him.

"And you're the only person I want to steal birds with," he said.

"Liberate," I said. "In the name of conservation."

He grinned, and there were his delightful dimples again.

"We make a pretty good team," I said.

"That we do. It would be a crime not to keep working together."

"Agreed."

Alex pulled me inside and brought my hand to his lips. He was staring at me like he was deciding where to kiss me next, and I couldn't get inside that house fast enough.

"Does Delia know you're here?" he said, kissing my palm. His stubbly beard rubbed against the inside of my forearm and I could hardly see straight.

"She won't wait up."

He gave me a devilish smile, and I was lost. "Good," he said. "We have some catching up to do."

# Chapter Thirty-Five

## FIONA

*Six Weeks Later*

"YOU CAN'T SELL THAT ONE," Alex said. "I like that one."

"You say that about all of them," I said, laughing.

He wrapped his big arms around me and kissed me on the cheek. When he stood behind me like that, folding me in his arms, I didn't want to be anywhere else. Right now, we were standing in the gallery at the Arts Council, so we had to behave ourselves.

Alex made it very hard to behave. He could melt me with a stare from across the room, and when he was next to me, I felt like I'd surely catch fire.

When I heard footsteps approaching, he quickly released me and stepped to my side, placing his hand on the small of my back. But not before placing a kiss on my neck that promised we'd pick this up later.

Maybe we could leave a little early.

This was my first group show in Jasmine Falls—Maxine had added me in at the last minute when one of her other artists dropped out a couple of weeks before the show. Thanks to Gwen and her one-hour rule, I'd kept doing quick studies and used them as practice compositions for my larger paintings. Five of my most recent ones were in this show, and it felt pretty amazing to see them up on the walls here. Ever since the gala, I'd been selling my work consistently in the cafe—even after the hubbub about the warbler had died down. That had taken a couple of weeks to blow over, and some people still asked about it. But by now the next big story had come along, and the warbler was old news.

It had disappeared into the local folklore, just like the Lizard Man of Lee County.

And that was just fine with me.

"These look stunning, kid," Delia said. She'd already strolled through the gallery to get a sneak peek at the other artists' work. "I'm so proud of you." She was still favoring her knee a little and was still going to therapy, but she signed up for next week's bird walk at Congaree.

"I have you to thank," I told her. "You gave me the perfect place to work."

She smiled. "You can have it as long as you like, sweetie. You know that."

I'd been staying with Delia for the last six weeks. She'd insisted I didn't need to hurry to find my own place, even though I'd offered to. Part of me thought she still needed a little help now and then, and part of me figured she just liked not being all by herself. I'd thought about renting some place close to her, but she seemed so sad when I started looking in the ads that I quickly gave up on that idea. I'd been working for Gwen and spending more time with Alex anyway, so it wasn't like we were in each other's way. It was fun being there with her—she was teaching me how to cook and grow vegetables in a raised garden, and it felt like we were making up for lost time.

Watching Delia, I realized that I had always had a mother who believed in me, I just was too stubborn to see it. Past Me had been too preoccupied with what she felt she was losing to see all the love she'd gained.

I wouldn't make that mistake again, either.

So far, I was finding all the things I wanted in Jasmine Falls. I might never have come back if it hadn't been for Delia—I was starting to think her woo-woo universe talk might have some truth to it.

Alex and I had decided to take things slow—even though we could barely keep our hands off each other. He wanted to date "for real," he'd said, with his preferred dates being the ones where he cooked me dinner and then snuggled up on his big sofa to watch movies. He was totally showing off with his fancy cooking, but I wasn't complaining because a man who knows his way around a kitchen is almost as hot as a guy who shapes metal with fire.

As it turned out, we needed to make up for some lost time, too.

My phone buzzed and I fished it out of the pocket of my dress— it was the blue silk one that I'd worn to the gala. When I'd slipped it on this evening, Alex had nuzzled my ear and said, "When I first saw you in this dress, I had a heart attack. Wear it forever."

Noted.

Tonight he wore pale gray trousers and a navy shirt that made his eyes look a deep shade of green. I was going to enjoy staring into those eyes for a long, long, time.

My phone buzzed with another text.

**On my way!** Gwen wrote. **Running a little late. Ranger Chris stopped in to say hi.**

Heart emojis.

**I had to tear myself away,** she wrote. **But I did, because I love you.**

**Bring him with you,** I typed. **I need proof he exists.**

**Gotta play it cool,** she wrote. **Maybe next time.**

When my phone buzzed again, I grinned, thinking about Gwen and how suddenly she was all shy around Ranger Chris. Usually, Gwen didn't have a shy bone in her body, but something about this guy had her overthinking every move she made.

The text wasn't from Gwen, though, and I had to read it twice.

**This is weeks overdue,** Eric wrote. **But I wanted to say I'm sorry. I got carried away. I was a jerk. I never meant for things to blow up the way they did.**

"Everything okay?" Alex said.

"Sure." I stared at the screen, wondering if I should respond. What could I even say? No problem? Forget about it? Go take a long walk off a short pier?

"I'm going to find the wine and snacks," he said, "before the crowd gets here."

**I know I'm the last person you want to hear from,** Eric wrote. **But I just wanted to say that I feel terrible about what happened, and I understand why you did what you did. I'm so sorry.**

After the gala, there had been more birdwatchers who came in search of the warbler—and a few ornithologists, too. For a week or so there was a flurry of activity online, where it seemed everyone wanted to study Eric's videos and weigh in on whether the bird we'd seen was really Bachman's warbler. Soon there were blog posts everywhere from both amateurs and prominent biologists—and people who just wanted to troll for fun. Who knew that birders were so easy to get riled up? You'd think they'd claimed to have found Nessie out here based on the endless comments and views.

One of the premier ornithologists in the country had written a scathing piece that called the whole thing a hoax—a way for an unknown grad student to make a name for himself, and a way for a wilting university program to raise their enrollment and move to the head of the line for research grants.

Turns out video isn't quite as convincing as it used to be.

Eric's videos had been shared about a bazillion times, but then people started manipulating it and making their own deep fake videos with different birds in its place—someone even made one with a pterodactyl, and that pretty much made him a meme.

I felt a little bit bad about that one. But just a little.

That was probably the best outcome for everyone, though: the folks here in town were happy to have a new wave of tourists coming through, but we didn't have the unwieldy crowd we would have had if the bird had been verified as the mystery warbler. I felt a little sorry for Eric, though—despite everything, he'd just been an overzealous guy looking for a small wonder. He'd find a new wonder to study, though—I was certain of that. This likely wasn't a career-ending move for him. It was a gaffe that would be forgotten soon enough when the internet found someone else to turn into a joke. Guys like him—who could charm people with good spin and a big smile—usually came out of fiascos like this just fine. It was like their superpower.

I still sat outside sometimes though, listening for the buzzing call like a cicada, and watching for the bright yellow face in the leaves. I liked to think our bird found a home deep in the swamp, back in one of the dark corners, high up in the canopy where it couldn't be spotted so easily. I hoped he found a little girl warbler and was just as happy as I was. Content with a fresh start in a place that felt new, but not too unfamiliar.

When Alex came back into the gallery, he was carrying two glasses of wine. "Quite the crowd out there," he said. "Everyone's grabbing snacks on the way in."

The first folks started to wander inside, and Delia went over to talk to one of her friends from the Arts Council. Before I knew it, there was a steady stream of people coming up to talk to me— congratulating me, asking me how long I was staying, and telling me how nice it was to see me again.

While I was chatting with one of the other artists, a weaver named Melinda, Alex squeezed in next to me and whispered in my ear. "Come outside for a minute?" he said.

I looped my arm in his and he led me out the back door, into the garden. The parking lot was filled with cars, and even more were parked on the street. It was a huge turnout, and I hadn't even had a chance to talk to Maxine yet. She'd been drifting through the crowd all night, and had flashed me a big grin and a thumbs-up—but I still wanted to talk with her long enough to thank her.

Alex pulled me into the garden, where the rose bushes were heavy with blooms. The hedges were taller, making it feel almost like a maze. "I just wanted to steal you away for a minute," he said, squeezing my hand.

"You can have me for more than a minute," I said. "Like, every single day."

He smiled, stepping closer. "I certainly hope so." White fairy lights twinkled in the hedges, giving us just enough light to see by. "I thought you might want a little air," he said. "Also, I've been dying to do something that I can't do in there."

Before I could answer, he pulled me close and kissed me, gently at first, sliding his hands down to my waist. I wrapped my arms around his neck and then he was kissing me like the whole world was on fire and these were our last few seconds in it.

When he finally pulled away, I felt my knees wobble, and not because of the high heels.

"Hi," he said.

"Hi, yourself."

"I'm so proud of you," he said. "You're like a rock star in there."

"Hardly."

"You're right," he said. "Better than a rock star. Gorgeous, charming, brilliant."

"Yeah, okay," I said, giving him a playful shove. "I love these people, and being part of the gallery is all incredibly flattering," I said. "But my little introvert self is completely exhausted after all that talking. Everybody means well, but I don't think I can answer one more question about myself, or my process, or my plans for the future. It's like the world's most pleasant interrogation—but still utterly exhausting."

He laughed. "What if I have a question, though?"

"Ugh. How about you choose the restaurant, and surprise me. I skipped dinner and I'm starving. And I missed out on the hors d'oeuvre because stuffing my face between all of those questions seemed rude, and everybody scarfed them down before I could sneak away and grab any."

"Fair enough," he said, taking my hand. "But that wasn't my question. It's more of a proposition, really. Another collaboration."

"You're not tired of working with me yet, huh?" I nudged his shoulder and he arched a brow.

"Not exactly."

And then he dropped down on his knee and pulled something from his pocket, and the world froze right then and there. Alex Fox, kneeling in the grass, his eyes all wide and hopeful, was enough to knock the breath right out of me. If someone had told me two weeks ago that this would be happening, I'd have told them they were bananas.

"Fiona," he said, pulling my hand to his lips again. "I know we're going slow here and I'm not rushing, but I can't wait another minute to ask you." He pulled a ring from his pocket, and the elegant stone flashed in the moonlight as he held it towards me. "Will you marry me, Fi? We can wait as long as you want, but I want to spend the rest of my life with you. I can't promise we won't have hard days, but there's no one else I want to spend them all with."

My heart hammered in my chest. "Alex Fox, don't you dare make me cry. My mascara will run and I have to go back in there and schmooze."

He grinned, and there were those adorable dimples again. The ones I wanted to see every day that I was left on this earth. "What do you say? Can I spend the rest of my life making you the happiest woman alive?"

"I like the sound of that. Does that house of yours have room for one more studio?"

"Obviously," he said, giving me a mischievous smile. "You can have anything you want, darlin'."

"Okay, then," I said, teasing him with a shrug. "Deal."

He smiled as he slid the ring onto my finger and pulled me close.

He kissed me gently, his lips moving down to my neck as he squeezed me tight. "Now let's go finish saying hello to these lovely people," he said, his lips moving against my skin. "And then we're going to sneak out and celebrate by ourselves for a long, long time."

He took my hand and led me out of the garden, back towards the gallery. The moon was high now, and a breeze had come along—one of those that only comes in summer, on the nights when the air smells sweeter, and the sky's clear enough to see beyond the stars, and you know you're exactly where you're supposed to be.

---

THANKS FOR READING! If you enjoyed this book, please take a moment to leave a review—they mean the world to an indie author like me!

WOULD YOU LIKE A FREE BOOK? Join my author newsletter and get a free copy of the short novella **You Got This, Maggie Monroe.** It's a standalone story in the Jasmine Falls Love Stories series, and is not for sale anywhere—just available as a thank you to my newsletter subscribers.

## Acknowledgments

First, thank you to my dear friend Katie Pryal. You are always my first and best reader, and I wouldn't have it any other way.

Thank you to my friends and family, who always encourage me to keep writing new stories and going off on new adventures. Your support means the world to me.

To my readers, thank you for spending a little of your time with me. You make me excited to keep thinking of new ways to write about love, and I'm so happy and humbled that you come on these journeys with me.

Finally, to Andrew: you inspire all the love stories. Here's to the next one, and all the ones after.

# About the Author

Born and raised in South Carolina, Lucy Day loves sweet tea, summer nights, and big-hearted love stories. She started writing in college and wrote her first novel after leaving her job at a web comic in St. Louis. Lucy is a bird nerd who can't live without strong coffee and wide open spaces. She's married to her best friend and when she isn't writing a new love story, she's out walking in the woods, looking for adventure.

To learn more, visit lucydayauthor.com. Subscribe to Lucy's newsletter and be the first to learn about new releases and special offers.

9 781947 834446